MW00526842

Dear Nan,

WHO SHE LEFT BEHIND

Tell their stories + pray for peace!

VICTORIA ATAMIAN WATERMAN

Victoria

HISTORIUM BOOKS

This is a work of fiction. All characters, locations and events in the narrative - other than those based on family history - are products of the author's imagination and are used fictitiously. Any resemblance to real persons, living or dead, is entirely coincidental and not intended by the author. Where real historical figures, locations and events appear, these have been depicted in a fictional context.

First Edition published by Historium Press

Images by Shutterstock, Imagine, & Public Domain
Cover designed by White Rabbit Arts

Visit Victoria Atamian Waterman's website at
www.victoriawaterman.net

Library of Congress Cataloging-in-Publication Data on file

Hardcover ISBN: 978-1-962465-00-7
Paperback ISBN: 978-1-962465-01-4
E-Book ISBN: 978-1-962465-02-1

Historium Press, a subsidiary of
The Historical Fiction Company
New York, NY
2023

THIS BOOK IS DEDICATED IN LOVING MEMORY OF

The Karadelian Matriarchy:
Vartouhy, Victoria, Yeghsabet, Mariam, Lucine

and their Pesas (grooms):
Hovsep, Kachadoor, Levon, Bedros, Ardashes

I am grateful to God for granting me the ability to channel their voices, ensuring that they are not only heard but will also echo endlessly within the pages of this creation.

CONTENTS

WHO SHE LEFT BEHIND

PROLOGUE

North Burial Ground, Providence, Rhode Island
September 1991

Tory Churmartian squinted against the hazy sky overhead as she took a pot of red geraniums from her husband Jim.

Jim stopped when she did. "What is it?"

"Do you see that?" she asked.

All around her were the stones and markers of the women who'd come before her. Her grandmother, her great-grandmother, and her great-aunts were laid to rest beside the men they'd rebuilt their war-shattered lives with.

She and her husband came every week to lay fresh flowers, and every week it was the same routine. Collect the wilted pots of mums or geraniums, depending on the season, and replace them with fresh.

Tory laid a hand on her great-grandmother's stone and stretched up on her toes to see better.

Two rows over, a small, colorful bundle was laid across her Great Aunt Vicky's granite marker.

It wasn't the remnant of the pink geraniums they'd brought the week before. From her vantage point Tory could see the fading blooms in their plastic pot at the base of the stone, exactly as they ought to have been. Her twin brother, Michael, hadn't been down to Providence recently, nor had any of her many cousins–second cousins really–on her mother's side of the family.

Tory wove her way between the stones, pausing occasionally to touch a marker. As they had in life, her grandmother's sisters rested together, surrounded by friends, children, and partners.

As she drew closer to her great aunt and uncle's stone, the colorful bundle revealed itself to be a woven scarf, which she untied gently, laying aside the needle-lace borders. Her great aunt was famous in the family for her handmade lace. Tory wondered what Vicky would make of this.

Inside, a pair of dolls nestled together, their dark hair and almond eyes very like Tory's own. She recognized one doll's traditional Armenian costume, and the other was similar, but not exactly the same. Perhaps Turkish, but she couldn't be sure.

The weather was mild for September in New England, warm and overcast, but a chill rose over her arms nonetheless.

The dolls were beautiful, obviously lovingly hand-crafted. Tory had a similar doll tucked away in her closet, too beautiful to play with, a precious gift from her grandmother.

These dolls were a beautiful tribute, and an elaborate gesture for a woman who'd died nearly thirty years before. Tory wondered who would go to the trouble and then leave them there, exposed to the elements.

Though she'd never met Aunt Vicky, Tory felt as though she'd known her grandmother's oldest sister from the stories her mother and grandparents talked about Gram's family. Her favorite had always been the story of how her great aunts Vicky and Yessa buried a treasure under a tree near their home on the night before they were forced out of their village by Turkish soldiers.

Speculation among the cousins ran high. Gold? Jewelry? So the story went, the two oldest sisters also buried their favorite dolls with the treasure. Her grandmother hadn't remembered anything about the village in the former Ottoman Empire where she was born, so the secondhand stories were most of what remained of Tory's connection to that part of the world.

Two dolls...

Tory picked up the Armenian doll, and a small stationery envelope tumbled out of the bundle. Jim, who'd caught up with her, picked it up and gave it to Tory.

Tory turned it over and gasped. Her mother's name was written across the front in formal script.

She looked at Jim, who reached out to touch his mother-in-law's name. "*Do you think it could be*?"

1

Gürin, Western Armenia, Ottoman Empire
May 1915

The village slept uneasily if it slept at all. Even the dogs were quiet, tails and ears low as they slunk along the sidewalks, hoping for scraps from the Turkish soldiers.

Further from the village center, the Karadelian house stood pale in the moonlight.

The night was mild, the scent of light rain in the air, but Victoria's palms were clammy where they lay flat against her sheets. Her next-youngest sister Yegsabet had crawled into bed with her an hour before, but Victoria was sure she wasn't sleeping, either.

She heard nine-year-old Mariam crying, her middle sister likely woken by baby Shenorig wailing in the night, and their mother's steps in the hallway to comfort her. Mariam had already cried herself to sleep once that night. Two-year-old Lucine would sleep through it all, as she always did. She was too little even to be frightened.

Earlier that day, when the soldiers came to draft the men and boys for a special project, they'd pushed their way inside to scour the house for anything the family might have used to defend themselves. Victoria heard warnings from the soldiers of insurgents and enemies of the state, but she didn't understand how it applied to a prosperous cloth merchant whose shawls were the envy of every nearby village. She couldn't understand why her family would need to defend themselves.

Bitter bile rose at her own naïveté and she reached for Yegsabet's hand beneath the coverlet.

The search was frightening. Their father followed the soldiers outside, stopping only long enough to whisper to his wife to pack what they could carry. Trouble was coming, he had heard from connections in other villages, though he hadn't expected it so quickly. Victoria heard him say he was afraid they would have to leave as well.

"Where are you going, *Hayrig,* father? And why must we pack?" As the eldest of the girls, Victoria asked the questions reflected silently in her sisters' eyes.

Her mother shushed her, but *Hayrig* only stroked her cheek. His eyes shimmered with tears, and Victoria's belly cramped. "The soldiers need our help, *anoushig,* my sweet. Listen to your *Mayrig,* your mother, and take care of your sisters while we're away."

Their home was on a road which led out of the village, and the rest of the men and boys from the village were clustered together on the road under heavy guard.

Victoria's two older brothers watched the house with anxious eyes. They stood with the other boys from school, including her friend Hasmik's older brother. The soldiers must have collected them from the village center. She and Hasmik had left them playing football in the field behind the church.

She was afraid to wave to them, but her brother Simone caught her gaze and tried to smile. When she stepped toward them, Simone shook his head slowly to warn her away.

"Why Yenov and Simone as well?"

Yenov was the oldest of them all at eighteen, and Simone was just behind him. Both boys were learning the family's weaving business. Victoria couldn't picture them, properly, but mussed from their game, in their shirt sleeves and trousers like their father's, being useful to the army.

"Because," their father said, "we must all go quietly so they don't make trouble for you girls. You must promise to be strong and help your mother. Do you promise?"

Victoria could only swallow her remaining questions and nod.

Her mother's knuckles were white where she clenched them as their father and two brothers, along with every other man and boy, walked out of the village in a loose formation under heavy guard.

What kind of special project required them to drop everything and leave without so much as a change of clothes?

The women of the village followed, propelled by fear, to watch the men being marched away. Victoria ran down the lane after them, *Mayrig* calling for her to come back, but a menacing young soldier waved a gun at her, and she fell back, startled by fear.

All the while overhead, the heat of the May afternoon sun beat down on them all as if the world weren't crumbling under her feet. The foothills and cliffs beyond the village bore witness to the train of men and boys walking down the road that led out of the town. Victoria watched the last of them, followed by the soldiers on horseback, disappear around a curve in the road.

They heard a volley of rifle fire not long after, and cries cut short, but the soldiers and their guns kept the women and children from following. *Mayrig* crumpled to the ground, her eyes filling. Her ragged, anguished cry seemed to Victoria to belong to a *Mayrig* she didn't know. Around them, Victoria heard sobs and cries of "*Amman,*" my God. Hasmik's mother knelt, crying, and wrapped her arms around *Mayrig*. The girls glanced uneasily around, lips trembling, tears sliding down their cheeks.

Victoria's heart pounded and her hands shook.

Another rifle crack split the air, this one aimed over their heads. The women's weeping silenced as they faced the soldiers.

"Go back to your homes!" The soldier in charge, or maybe the one with the loudest voice, called out to the assembled group of weeping women that they should be prepared to leave the village in the morning. He didn't answer when some of them asked where they were going or why, only that this was for their own safety.

Their mother's expression hardened. Victoria recognized it as a no-more-arguing face. This was the *Mayrig* that Victoria knew. "You heard *Hayrig*. We must prepare. The soldiers say we must leave in the morning. For our own protection."

Victoria heard the bitterness in her mother's voice and shuddered. What protection? These soldiers were the terror, not the protection, and she and her family were defenseless.

Mother handed Shenorig to Mariam, told her to watch Lucine, and sent Victoria and Yegsabet to gather what she deemed necessary and portable. Almost as soon as Mother's list was complete, Victoria ran to find Hasmik.

Hasmik's family, the Choulijians, lived not far from the end of the lane that led down from the Karadelian's sprawling Arabic-style house. Hasmik's father was an importer of fine silks and jewelry, and the two men prospered by their acquaintance.

Both families lived on the outskirts of the village, but nowhere in Gurin was so far you couldn't walk the distance.

The two houses faced one another across an open piece of land through which a small stream flowed. Where it turned, the Karadelian's house was built right over it, so it flowed through the central courtyard.

The village cemetery was across the road from the two houses, a safe distance from the center of town, but not so far from the church. When she was younger, Victoria was afraid of the dead resting so close, but now, on the verge of young womanhood, the cemetery no longer frightened her.

It was a beautiful place, quiet and peaceful.

Hasmik's face was blotchy with weeping, but neither girl could give voice to the great black chasm of fear and grief that opened ahead of them. Hasmik said they were burying her mother's jewelry in the garden so the soldiers wouldn't steal it while they were gone.

Lying in the dark, the idea consumed her; she stood in the road helpless while her father and brothers were stolen from them, but she could save some of their precious things from the soldiers. She could do something. Victoria rolled on her side to face her sister. "Are you awake?"

"I don't want to leave." Yegsabet sounded far younger than her thirteen years. She stroked her doll's long, dark hair, so like their own. "Can I take *Nuri*?"

Victoria reached behind her for the sister doll that sat on her nightstand. At fifteen and not quite thirteen, they were both too old to cuddle their dolls, but Victoria touched the hem of her own doll's dress where *Mayrig* sewed in the blue bead to ward off the evil.

Victoria hadn't said a word when her sister carried her doll into the bedroom.

"I don't think so. *Hayrig* said nothing that wasn't essential."

Yegsabet made a small, sad sound.

"Hasmik's mother buried her jewelry in their garden."

Yegsabet's sigh was resigned. "We don't have much jewelry."

"We have our dolls," Victoria said. "And the *lira* in our jewelry boxes. We could bury them somewhere safe."

Yegsabet's eyes widened. "And *Nuri* will be there when we can come home?"

"Exactly." Victoria thought of their kitchen garden behind the house, and of the meadows that fanned out beyond their house and Hasmik's. No good place for a buried treasure, but there was a perfect spot in the cemetery.

A plan bloomed in Victoria's chest, shoving some of the heavy feelings aside for a moment. They could bury their dolls to save them. Their dolls and the small, matching wooden jewelry boxes that held their treasures–two golden Turkish lira, hair pins, their Armenian crosses on delicate gold chains.

"Let's do it. Under the big tree on the road to the village. We can sneak out now and be back before *Mayrig* knows we're gone."

Now, under the sickly, waning moon, surrounded by the watchful headstones of their ancestors, Victoria carried the hastily packed bundle as she and Yegsabet crept through the shadows to the old olive tree; she held her sister's hand as well, as much to comfort herself as her sister. Yegsabet carried the garden spade.

Hasmik's brother said the tree was planted by Noah after the flood, but Victoria didn't believe him. Thinking of him made her feel a little sick. He'd walked out of the village with all the other men and boys, handsome and tall. Her heart shied away from what her deepest, most frightened instincts already knew.

That rifle fire wasn't a warning. It was death. They'd promised *Hayrig* they'd stay strong, so Victoria pushed the thought away and kept walking.

The olive tree was vast, if not Biblical, gnarled and ancient beyond memory. Thrown into stark relief by the night sky and flickering with the reflections of the sentry's campfires, the tree's canopy beckoned to her.

They scurried into the deeper shadows where the roots rose from and plunged again into the soil like serpents. Victoria stared hard into the darkness to where the cypress- and scrub-dotted cliffs and hills smudged the horizon beyond the city.

"Where?"

Her whisper struck the silence like gunfire; Victoria winced, searching the ground near the tree for a good spot. "Shush. There."

Neither girl had experience digging holes in hard-packed, root-addled soil. The morning's soft rain hadn't softened the soil much. For what seemed like hours, they traded the spade until the hole was nearly big enough for their bundle. Victoria's stomach clenched when she pushed the bundle into the misshapen hole. The dolls didn't know what was happening, but she couldn't bear to think of their unseeing eyes, like dead girls in a grave.

Yegsabet's eyes were huge and wet with unshed tears.

Victoria took the spade. "Tell *Nuri* to be a good girl, and we'll be back when she wakes up."

The mound of disturbed soil was obvious when they were done. "Let's find some rocks and cover it up."

The rocks didn't make a lot of difference; the disturbed ground was obvious, but they were out of time. The light was shifting.

Sweating and chilled, they slipped through the house, stashing their dirty clothes under the bed and washing hastily. *Mayrig* would be furious with them for sneaking out if she found out.

The next morning, the soldiers came again, this time to escort them out of their home, and out of the village that comprised their entire world. They were to leave right away, on foot, but they might bring a mule if they had one.

Victoria wiped the dust of a sleepless night from her eyes and helped Mariam and Lucine onto their mule. What little they were taking was slung over the mule's back in bundles. *Mayrig's* eyes were empty and hard as she helped Yegsabet put on her rucksack, but she crooned softly to tiny Shenorig as they started to walk.

Victoria sneaked a last look at their house, its whitewashed walls bright in the morning sunlight. Wherever the soldiers were taking them, they said it was only for a little while, and their treasure would wait under the olive tree for their return.

2

Providence, Rhode Island
Spring 1963

Rose parked her car down the block from the Frank Street triple-decker where her parents and her Aunt Vicky lived and smoothed her skirt over her still flat belly.

It was always a pleasure to see her favorite aunt, but today was special. Today she had news to share, and a favor to ask.

Her parents were likely still at the jewelry store, but Aunt Vicky would be home. Lately, when the weather was fine, she was to be found on the front porch reading her newspapers, playing *tavloo,* and backgammon, with Rose's dad and the other men when they got home from work.

Those lively games, full of teasing and spirited competition, brought color back to Vicky's increasingly faded features.

It was early yet, and Rose found Vicky tucked into a rocker on the porch, swaddled in a crocheted afghan, but the newspaper lay at her feet, the corners of the pages fluttering helplessly in the spring breeze.

"Aunt Vicky?" On closer inspection, her aunt wasn't at all well. Her eyes were bloodshot, her cheeks damp with her tears, and a faraway expression–so sad it took Rose's breath away–clouded her eyes.

At first, Rose wasn't sure Aunt Vicky had even heard her. She took her aunt's hand. "What's the matter?"

Her aunt blinked, returning from somewhere dark and private. "Rose, *aghchigus*, my sweet girl, what are you doing here in the middle of the day*?"* Her voice trembled slightly.

When Vicky leaned over to reach for the newspaper, Rose swooped down and plucked it from the porch floor. The paper was folded to the Local section, where the headline announced *Local Artist Finds Inspiration in Turkish Bazaar.*

It wasn't the headline that stopped Rose's gaze. It was the photo., set against a bazaar stall with shelves lined with exquisite dolls of every size. On the left, a pale-skinned, light-haired woman in a proper suit, gloves, and hat held a beautiful doll dressed in traditional Ottoman costume. At her side was another woman whose dark hair was streaked with what was likely gray. Her shockingly familiar dark, almond-shaped eyes crinkled with pleasure as they gazed at the camera.

The date on the masthead was today. The clothing was in fashion, but Rose would have sworn the Turkish woman in the photo was her Aunt Vicky, but twenty years younger. The caption was no help; it named the Providence woman but referred to the other woman only as a Turkish doll maker.

"Who is this?" Rose said without looking up from the image.

When her aunt didn't reply, Rose dragged her gaze from the two women on the page. Tears tracked down Aunt Vicky's careworn face. Almost of its own volition, her hand stretched towards the folded pages.

Rose crouched by her side. "Auntie, what's going on? Please. Let me help."

Aunt Vicky's voice, pinched with pain, barely rose above a whisper. "I don't know if I can."

"Is my mother home?" Rose glanced over her shoulder towards the front doors, the second of which led to the more spacious upstairs apartment where her parents lived. "Maybe she…"

"They're still at the store," Aunt Vicky said in a strained breath. For a long moment, she stared into a place Rose suspected was far from the homey, triple-decker-crowded residential street in Providence. "Come inside, *aghchigus,* my girl. I have a story to tell you if I can."

Rose helped her aunt inside, shocked by how frail her dear aunt's bones felt beneath her housedress and cardigan. She settled Aunt Vicky in the Barcalounger the cousins collectively bought her the Christmas before and put on a pot of strong coffee.

Rose had a feeling they would both need it.

***

When Aunt Vicky finished her story, the sun was low in the afternoon sky, and Rose was late to get home to put dinner together, but that would have to wait. She dabbed at her damp eyes with her handkerchief.

Her mother and aunts were as reliable as the seasons, the solid foundation of the family Rose had always known–practical, full of laughter, and benevolently ruling the neighborhood. They never dwelt in the ugly past they shared, never invited the children into those terrible times.

Now Rose knew why. And she knew she had to help Aunt Vicky find the woman in the picture if she could.

She swallowed her tears. "We'll find her, Auntie. Together. I can start right away with this article if I can take the paper?"

"I don't know, sweet girl. It's been so long, and what if I'm wrong? What if I'm mistaken?"

Rose's heart squeezed. Vicky's usual vibrancy, even dimmed slightly by her recent health decline, was never dull like this. "Auntie, what if she *is*? We have to try."

"Thank you, dear Rose." Vicky squeezed her hand, her bloodshot eyes once again glimmering with hope, and considered Rose for a moment. Rose wondered if she imagined Vicky's gaze slipping to her tummy, but the sight curves at the corners of Vicky's lips were unmistakable. "But you didn't come here today for this. Do you have something to tell me?"

Not for the first time, Rose wondered if her mother, sisters, and her maternal grandmother possessed a second sight.

Her hands fluttered to her belly, where the baby was barely a suggestion of the little boy or girl and she smiled. "I'm expecting, Auntie. In October. I came here today to ask if you would make the Christening gown."

Vicky's tears overflowed again, this time pooling in the brackets around her mouth, drawn wide by a joyful smile.

3

Gürin, Western Armenia, Ottoman Empire
May 1913

Victoria and Yegsabet frequently walked home from school with a large group of children from the village. Mariam was just old enough to go to the village school this year, so it was up to the two older sisters to see that she got home safely. By the time they reached the outer edge of the village proper, the group had dwindled to Victoria, her sisters, and her friend Hasmik who lived down the same lane. Hasmik's older brother, Davit, was apprenticed to the apothecary in the village, and no longer walked home with the girls after school.

Victoria would never admit it to her friend, but she missed Davit. His teasing smile was a little shy around her lately, and her cheeks blushed hotly when she caught him looking.

On this particular afternoon, the older girls lingered along the road from the village, speculating about the Feast of Ascension, and what they might learn from the fortune-telling and wish-granting.

Victoria hoped to catch a glimpse of Davit, but he was nowhere to be seen.

Hasmik was pensive; Victoria was painfully aware that her friend was worried over something.

"What's bothering you?"

Hasmik pinched the folds of her skirt but said nothing.

"Come on, I tell you all the silly things I worry about," Victoria said. *Almost all of them, anyway.*

Hasmik glanced at Victoria, hesitating. "I heard *Mayrig* talking with the ladies who visited. She was reading the coffee grounds, going on about terrible trouble coming…"

Victoria snorted. "There's always terrible trouble coming…it's usually rain on a feast day or some cousin won't be able to travel for a wedding."

"Oh I know," Hasmik said. The older women and their superstitions seemed very old-fashioned. "It was something *Mayrig* said after that."

"Something about me?" Victoria couldn't think of a reason why the mothers would be discussing her. Unless…*Hayrig* wasn't interested in arranging an early marriage for any of his children, but maybe someone had brought up the idea of her marrying. *Maybe even Davit? That wouldn't be so bad…*

"I heard them talking about *Hayrig's* trip to Constantinople last month. Your mother was saying your father knew about it as well. Someone killed a high-ranking official, and the Grand Vizier resigned." Hasmik turned to Victoria. "I don't even know who those men are or what that means, but *Mayrig* sounded worried, and she said some of *Hayrig's* business contacts won't meet with him anymore because he is Armenian."

Their families sometimes spoke of terrors a generation before, usually when the fathers and grandfathers were deep in storytelling, but such grim tales seemed impossible and far away to Victoria.

Under the bright May sunshine, she couldn't imagine why anyone would turn away from Hasmik's father simply for being an Armenian. Everyone knew Hasmik's family supplied the village with the best fabrics.

"I'm sure they were overreacting," Hasmik said, backpedaling. "You know how mothers are."

Victoria did know how mothers were. When the ladies got together to sew or make lace, they shared coffee, reading fortunes in the grounds and laughing over the strangest things. Victoria often wondered if that was part of becoming a woman–learning to understand the language of women's humor.

"You're probably right."

Having unburdened her worries, Hasmik was curious.

"What if it were true though? Do they hate us in Constantinople?"

Victoria felt a sharp tug at her braid. "Why would someone hate you two all the way in Constantinople, unless it's for being the silliest girls in Gürin?"

She spun around to find Hasmik's brother Davit doubled over laughing at them.

"*Babam*, come on, go away." Hasmik screeched at her brother to go away and leave them be. "Why aren't you at the apothecary's?"

"I am delivering a tincture to a customer," Davit said loftily, patting the bag slung across his chest.

Victoria did her best to look down her nose at him–a good trick when he stood several inches taller than her. "Better go on your way then."

Davit blinked at Victoria's coolness; her heart pounded. He really was very handsome, though she'd never say so to Hasmik. Then he reached out and pulled her other braid before racing away down the lane, crowing with laughter.

Victoria and Hasmik dawdled, enjoying the fine weather and freedom. Both girls had chores and lessons waiting at home. Davit must have cut behind the houses to return to the village, for they didn't see him again as they walked.

They found Victoria's sister Mariam by the retaining wall that marked the Karadelian's property. Hasmik skipped up the path to her family's home, waving goodnight to Victoria.

Victoria found her sister Mariam in the courtyard. Her sister was cooling her feet in the spring-fed stream that bubbled up and flowed out of their house. That stream was the envy of many, and Victoria was proud of it somehow, as though she had anything to do with the placement of the spring.

Mariam sat with her elbows on her knees with a *Nuri* doll on either side of her.

Victoria recognized hers immediately. The doll sat on her bed, or the chest beside it, but Victoria didn't play with it anymore. "What are you doing with my doll?"

Her sister swung her feet out of the stream and dusted off her skirt. Mariam was only nine, which seemed babyish from Victoria's thirteen-year-old perspective. "Mine needed a friend."

Victoria snatched the doll back. “Take Lucine’s. She’s too little to notice.”

“You’re so mean. I wish *Nuri* was my sister.” Mariam’s eyes glittered with anger.

Just then, their mother breezed into the courtyard from the direction of the kitchen. "Victoria, Mariam, there you are. The music teacher will be here in a few minutes. Go wash up. And no more sniping.”

Just as quickly, their mother breezed out of the courtyard, presumably to check that the instruments were prepared for the music lesson.

"You heard *Mayrig*,” Victoria said to Mariam. "Let's go wash before the music master arrives."

Victoria was preoccupied throughout the music lesson, to the point where their instructor grew frustrated and made her repeat scales. Her mind wandered to the moment she’d stuck up her chin at Davit, and the little flash of wounded sadness in his eyes, as if she’d actually hurt his feelings.

Her skin was hot at the thought that he might care if she was unkind to him. He’d teased her like a sister since they were all small.

After the music lesson, there were chores to be done and an evening meal to eat. *Hayrig* told a funny story about one of the weavers at the shawl factory, which reminded Victoria of Hasmik’s worries.

The coffee cups were a fun superstition. Tradition, not true harbingers of danger, and anyway, why would it matter to them that someone in Constantinople didn’t like them? That was hundreds of miles away.

By the time she washed and climbed into her night dress to go to bed, Victoria had turned the puzzle over in her head enough that she was almost certain Hasmik had heard something out of context.

She and Yegsabet shared a bedroom on the third story. The older boys, Yenov and Simone, shared a bedroom down the hall, and Mariam shared with their little sister Lucine, who was only two.

Shenorig was fussing and even from down the hall, Victoria could hear Mariam talking in her sleep in response. Lucine slept like a little stone, but Mariam frequently talked in her sleep.

"Go to sleep." Yegsabet rolled over and patted Victoria's pillow. "You're thinking too loud."

Victoria turned to her sister. They shared a large bed; there was plenty of space under the snug blankets.

"Hasmik said her father had business trouble in Constantinople."

Yegsabet yawned. "That's none of our business. Go to sleep. Tomorrow, we start preparing for the Ascension Day feast, and we all know what you're wishing for…"

***

A year passed quietly in Gürin, and once again the Feast of Ascension approached. This year, Victoria and Hasmik would be permitted to take part in the ritual of *Vichak*, filling special clay jars with seven handfuls of water from seven springs, seven petals from seven flowers, and seven stones from seven flowing streams. The older girls and young women would weave flower crowns and make *Vichaki Arus* dolls to wait atop the jars in the moonlight until the next day when they would grant wishes and predict fortunes.

Victoria knew her wish.

She wished *Hayrig* would arrange a betrothal for her with Hasmik's brother Davit, so they might marry when she was done with school and had joined his father's business.

She knew she was too young still for such a thing, but wasn't that the beauty of wishes?

A few days before the feast, Victoria and Hasmik lingered in the village admiring her father's shop window while the younger children walked on.

Hasmik turned to Victoria. "Your father was visiting mine yesterday. I heard them discussing your father's plans to renovate the other side of the house next year."

The Karadelian's home was an old house, grand and sprawling, and one whole wing was closed off and musty with disuse.

Hasmik continued. "Your father said because of the spring, the one that feeds the stream in the courtyard, the ground was not so solid under the other half of the house, but things were going well with the shawl business, and he wanted to bring in builders to shore it all up."

Victoria was astonished. She'd heard nothing of this. Then again, she was a girl and still a child in the eyes of her parents. Unless, of course, you counted her courses which had come on in recent months. *Mayrig* said that made her a woman.

"Well, that's good news," Victoria said brightly. "I wonder if we will all get our own bedrooms?"

Hasmik giggled. "Your father said to my father that he wants enough space for when Yenov gets married and moves his future wife in to start a family."

That was less exciting than the idea of having her own room, but it made sense. Yenov and Simone would take over the business when *Hayrig* retired. If the oldest brother were already living in the house with his family–the idea of her older brother married with children made her giggle–her parents would be taken care of in their old age.

The thought of Yenov's marriage made her think of her own eventual marriage. She blushed hotly and pressed her palms to her cheeks to hide it.

Davit had carried her books twice in the last month, and her wish was her most private secret.

Her second most private secret was that Victoria wondered what it might be like to kiss him.

"I wonder who *Hayrig* wants him to marry," Victoria said, hoping Hasmik didn't notice her flaming cheeks.

It was Hasmik's turn to blush, and Victoria forgot her preoccupation with Davit. "You like my stupid older brother?"

"I hardly know!" Hasmik turned away. "I heard my mother tell my father he would be a good prospect in a few years when your father retires. I don't want to think about being a married lady yet."

Victoria was usually able to tease her friend out of a bad mood. She gave Hasmik a teasing smile. "No one should be home this afternoon. Let's go see your future home."

Without waiting for Hasmik to reply, she danced away down the lane, but she could hear her friend laughing behind her.

As Victoria hoped, the Karadelian's house was empty. Yenov and Simone were at the looms with their father. Yegsabet and Mariam were playing with friends in the village. *Mayrig* and Lucine were visiting, and the housekeeper was doing the weekly washing.

The coast was clear. Victoria and Hasmik dashed across the courtyard and up the stairs to the second-floor gallery. They tested the doors, fully intending them to be locked, but the second bedroom's door was unlocked–or loose enough in its housing to open anyway.

Victoria took hold of the knob and pushed the door open. It swung wide to reveal a room just like the family gathering room on the other side. The shutters were closed, casting the room into deep shadow. The air was musty with neglect, and spiders had colonized the corners of the space.

Hasmik blew out a breath. "I think your father was telling the truth about the need for repairs."

They stepped into the empty room, displacing clouds of dust that settled on their shoes.

Victoria tried to imagine her brother, with a wife and babies, living there. "It's going to need a lot of work," she said, dismayed.

"Yes, it is, *anoushig*, my sweet," her father said from the doorway.

Both girls shrieked and whirled around. Hovsep Karadelian's eyes were laughing, but he fixed as stern a look as he could on his daughter and her friend. "What have I told you about staying out of this part of the house? The foundation is not sound."

"I'm sorry, *Baron*, Mr., Karadelian." Hasmik was quick to apologize.

Victoria adopted her most contrite posture. "Me, too, *Hayrig*."

"Out, both of you. Silly girls," her father said. "What possessed you to come in here today?"

Victoria lifted her gaze to meet her father's. She was tired of feeling like a child, left out of the loop about her brother, about the house, about everything. "I wanted to see where Yenov will live when he's married.

She braced herself for a scolding, but her father only stroked her hair gently.

"Where did you ever hear a thing like that?"

"I heard you speaking with my father, sir," Hasmik offered.

"You two needn't worry about anyone getting married any time soon." He laughed lightly. "And you needn't eavesdrop on your father's conversations."

Victoria's and Hasmik's replies tumbled out together.

"Yes, sir."

"Yes, *Hayrig*."

"Go on, girls. I'm going to lock this door."

Victoria and Hasmik scurried out ahead of *Hayrig*, headed for the kitchen. Perhaps the housekeeper would have something for them to soothe the sting of embarrassment.

The sound of Victoria's father laughing and muttering under his breath followed them.

4

The Armenian Deportation Route
June 1915

Victoria kept her eyes down and her hand on the bony mule's lead–Lucine and Mariam rode with what remained of the saddlebags–but her ears were always listening for news. Yegsabet walked with their mother, clinging to *Mayrig's* hand like a lifeline. Vicky supposed this was a good thing; there was a faraway, untethered kind of look in Vartouhy Karadelian's eyes that scared Victoria almost as much as the soldiers.

Tiny Shenorig died of a fever twelve days outside of Gürin. The soldiers didn't let them stop to bury her, so their mother, dry-eyed and white-lipped, carried her dead child, for half a day. There was no water for tears, and if Victoria's sadness threatened to tear her apart, she couldn't imagine her mother's pain.

That night the women who still had the strength dug a shallow pit in the dry ground and covered her shawl-wrapped body with stones. Victoria watched from the pitiful fire they were allowed as her mother curled her body around that tiny pile of stones as if she could shield her small daughter's body in death as she hadn't been able to in life.

Two days later they entered the desert. All around them, sand drifted in an endless, undulating sea as the scrub-dotted foothills fell away beyond the horizon. Their footprints were erased as the wind tossed the sand, and Victoria began to fear they were going to disappear, just like the trail their dragging feet made as they walked.

One night, the sky overhead as vast and cold as the desert around them, Victoria overheard her mother whisper a prayer of thanksgiving that Shenorig's body at least lay in the ground of her homeland, and not the merciless sand.

No one dared to cry. The soldiers barked at those who wept to cease their caterwauling. One old woman was shot for falling to her knees over the body of her daughter, who'd collapsed and died by the side of the trail.

There was almost nothing left of the few, hastily packed possessions they'd carried out of Gürin. When they encountered nomadic tribes, Victoria and Yegsabet traded what they could for food and water as the days dragged into weeks with no word of where or why they were walking, only that to stop or disrupt the march was asking to be shot.

Every day more women, children, and the occasional grandfather joined the march. Every day more bodies were left in the dust of the trek. Fear walked with them, hand-in-hand with death. Whispered rumors clung to the convoy like flies as they walked. The days blurred together, leaving Victoria and her family adrift in a sea of confusion and grief.

The Turkish soldiers who'd been wordlessly cruel when the march began, grew more familiar as they marched. Victoria would have preferred their cold silence to the insults and slurs the youngest among them hurled at the women as they walked. Emboldened by their own authority and the fear of their victims, they kept up a litany of accusations. Armenians were traitors, Christian filth. A threat to the glorious Turkish homeland they were building, a threat to Allah and their faith.

The Armenians must be expelled from Turkey, they said, and so what if some of the vermin died on the forced march. Their captain would silence them if he heard them, but not because he cared for the fates of his starving, terrorized charges. He believed it to be beneath their dignity, but he could not be everywhere along their grim procession.

Hasmik fell into step with her. Silently, Victoria offered her free hand to her friend. Like Victoria, Hasmik knew to keep her eyes down. The day before, the soldiers shot her mother for begging to rest. Hasmik had no sisters, so the other mothers gathered her close and moved her along the road as silent tears streamed down, leaving streaks on her grimy cheeks.

That night, the mothers tucked the smallest children under their skirts to sleep, making a circle like a walled city for the rest of the girls. Overhead the stars wheeled across the sky, but Victoria refused to name them.

Her father loved the night sky and told his children the Greek stories written in the constellations. Their names–like their stories–belonged to her father's memory now, too painful to contemplate.

"We will be your family now," she'd promised Hasmik. The two girls slept close that night, keeping Yegsabet, Mariam, and Lucine between them and *Mayrig*.

When the day came, they walked again, shawls over their heads and necks to keep the sun and dust at bay as best they could. Hasmik's hand rested limply in her own, but her feet trudged on.

They came to the outskirts of a Bedouin encampment around twilight. Their leaders rode out to speak with the soldiers, and trades were made. Several girls of marriageable age were offered. Victoria and Hasmik watched wide-eyed and silent from the protective circle of the mothers and grandmothers.

Men and women alike wore long robes, and the women were veiled, their veils secured by a piece of cloth tied around their heads. They wore long coats over their robes, not so different from the ceremonial Armenian dress they wore for holidays and weddings back home.

After dark, two women brought a bucket of goat milk to their huddle, ladling it out first to the babies and smallest children whose eyes were dull with hunger and thirst.

One stopped near Victoria's mother, perusing the clutch of young women like scarves at a stall.

She pointed to Hasmik, then addressed *Mayrig* in Arabic. "Are you her mother?"

Victoria rarely heard her mother speak any Arabic. What little she had was reserved for traveling tinkers and their father's business associates.

Mayrig narrowed her gaze and lied. "Yes."

"I can't take more than one. I have five children and she looks like a capable nursemaid."

Despite the stranger's cool tone, Victoria glanced up in time to see a slight softening around the woman's calculating expression, even as a sick feeling rose in her belly.

"*Mayrig*, no," she whispered, tugging her mother's sleeve.

The woman wrapped her shawl around her shoulders. "She will have food and shelter and when she is old enough, a husband."

Victoria watched as her mother turned sad eyes on Hasmik.

"*Mayrig.*" Victoria grabbed Hasmik's arm.

Mayrig looked at her own daughters, then at Hasmik, whose sturdy frame was honed from walking hungry, but not so wasted as their own. She touched Hasmik's cheek. "We will not forget you."

Victoria's tears blurred Hasmik's silent departure in the shadow of the robed woman and her companions; her friend already carried the bucket for her new mistress. There was no time to say goodbye. The Bedouin women had already lingered longer than was prudent. The soldiers might turn a blind eye to the goat milk, but they wouldn't tolerate being left out of a trade.

Hasmik never looked back, but Victoria understood. There was no point. The only way was forward.

5

Aleppo, Syria
August 1915

Victoria lost track of the passage of time and distance. There was only fear, hunger, and the pain and weariness that trailed them like dogs. While so many others were lost–a few like Hasmik, to opportunistic moments, some in trade for the benefit of the gendarmes who forced them ever farther from their homes, but most to the crack of rifle fire shattering the shuffling silence of the dusty track–her mother and her sisters walked into the ragged edges of a city at the end of a nameless day, and were herded into a refugee camp someone said the missionaries had organized.

The mule died on the march, but there was nothing left to carry. Victoria and Yegsabet took turns carrying Lucine on their backs. They arrived naked, the shreds of their clothes lost to the desert, their bundles reduced to what they could drag behind them as they walked.

At first, Victoria wasn't aware they'd arrived anywhere. It was only when the missionaries surrounded them, wrapping them in blankets and loose robes, and began gathering their ragged numbers into smaller groups to follow harried-but-kind-looking people away from the dust of the road that she realized they were there–wherever there was.

A maze of impromptu streets made of lean-tos and haphazard shelters made up a shantytown of hollow-eyed women and children. Here and there, priests and volunteers guided new arrivals to places where they could rest. When a man in clerical clothing led them into a canvas-walled shed off the main path, Mariam burst into tears.

While Mama comforted Mariam and Yegsabet settled Lucine on a cot in the corner, it was Victoria who learned from a priest called *Der* Mikael where to find water, food, and clothing, and that there would be someone to help them find work if they could, but not until they'd had a chance to rest.

A woman peered inside their new makeshift door. "You must be exhausted. Rest. I am *Yeretzgin* Susana, *Der* Mikael's wife." She looked at Victoria. "Come, *aghcheegus,* my dear girl. I will walk with you to the well."

"*Mayrig*, may I go?"

Her mother only nodded, as Mariam hiccupped into her bosom, too parched to cry for long.

Refugees streamed into the camp. Theirs was not the only column of terrified people pouring into this place. Victoria sidestepped goat droppings and fetid puddles to find her way to the place where the food was.

It was as if a village sprang up out of the dry ground, made of the wreckage of a real town. A broad main street of sorts formed the center of the camp. Already, Victoria sensed the energy of the place. There was desperation and sadness, yes, but it was busy and teeming with life.

Yeretzgin Susana sent her back in the direction they'd come and was off on an errand of her own.

Carrying water and a loaf of bread back in the direction she'd come, Victoria saw a girl about her own age sweeping in front of a slightly more solid version of their own camp dwelling. A flash of dark hair under a scarf, a strong arm peeking out from a rolled-up sleeve…She called out Hasmik's name.

The girl who turned wasn't her friend. Her eyes, unlike Hasmik's, were hard and wary.

Victoria forced back tears and smiled at the girl. "I'm sorry, I thought you were someone I knew."

The girl's eyes softened. Victoria thought she might be the older of them, despite her smaller stature.

"It happens a lot," she said. "With so many…missing."

Victoria set the water jug down at her feet and ripped the end off the loaf. She offered the bread to her new acquaintance. “We have only just arrived, my sisters and me. I’m Victoria. Victoria Karadelian.”

The offering bolstered the girl. “Eva. Poladian. I’m here with my aunts and cousins, but I have a brother called Peter, in America. Peter will find a way to help us.” Eva took the bread and bit into it, her expression hardening again. “You have anyone in America?”

The desert threatened to rise up around them and swallow her whole. She didn’t have anyone anywhere but here, wherever here was.

Victoria shook her head. “Where is this place? The soldiers said Syria, but they could have taken us anywhere.”

“Hamidieh Camp. Syria. Aleppo, or at least the edge of it.” Eva appraised Victoria’s filthy clothes and grimy skin. “You’re pretty under all the dirt. Pretty girls get work as maids, they say.”

Everything this girl said only sprouted more questions in Victoria’s mind, but her mother and sisters needed the bread and water she carried.

“Thank you,” Victoria said, reaching down for the jug. “I’m sure I will see you again.”

“I hope not,” Eva sighed. “The best thing for any of us is we get out of this place as fast as we can.”

With that warning in her ears, Victoria left the girl and her broom and sought out her family’s new home.

6

Hamidieh Camp, Aleppo, Syria
1918

Over the years which followed, Victoria crossed paths occasionally with Eva Poladian, but the girl and her cousins must have moved on at some point, because one afternoon, on her way back from getting water, she found a new family occupying the space where Eva and her family had been.

That was how it was. People moved on, or they were moved along. They disappeared, and either news of them circulated or they simply disappeared. When you heard good news, you thanked God. When they vanished, you prayed for their souls and cared for those they left behind as best you could.

Victoria tidied up the breakfast dishes before cleaning up, then she gathered Yegsabet and Mariam for school. It wasn't precisely like the education they'd had in Gürin–riding and literature, the Bible, sums and Greek, needlework and managing a household–but it was something.

Life, like the other migrants they lived with, moved on or moved you along. Their one-room dwelling, with its salvaged canvas and drafty roof, had sleeping space for all five of them, with the little girls tucked snugly together in one pallet. They still went to church on Sundays and celebrated the refugee community as often as their diminished circumstances allowed.

The missionaries were teaching weaving and carpet repair to many of the women and girls in hopes of finding them employment in Aleppo. As the wife of the owner of a prominent shawl-making business, their mother had some understanding of the looms and the traditional patterns. Before too long, Vartouhy Karadelian was assisting the missionaries in teaching the younger women and girls, her daughters included.

Almost three years passed like that, living in the refugee camp, working as best they could. Surviving. Then in 1918, the Turkish forces withdrew from Aleppo.

Victoria was nearly eighteen, old enough that she might have been considering marriage back home. The only men she knew in Aleppo were the missionaries and aid workers; they might as well have been grandfathers, they seemed so old. Some of them probably were.

Soldiers, she stayed far away from. A young man in uniform only turned her stomach with memories best left in the past.

With the army gone, they were able to find a place to live. It wasn't much, a cellar really, but it had a door with a bolt, a cookstove, and a privy. Mother wept bittersweet tears the first night they slept in their own room.

They fell into a kind of routine. Mariam, still too young for the looms, cared for Lucine. She and some of the other girls her age managed a pack of smaller children, escorting them to the missionary school. Victoria and Yegsabet accompanied their mother to the looms, and in the evenings, the little family gathered for their evening meal.

On Sundays, the missionaries taught Sunday School. Mariam was nearly twelve, but already she was the little mother in their neighborhood, determined to learn her lessons so she might find a husband and make a good wife and mother. *Der* Mikael took notice, and Mariam was helping to teach the Sunday lessons.

Mayrig became adept at trading. Among the refugees, a kind of market grew, in which families traded goods and food, and Vartouhy had a good eye for a bargain. One evening, she arrived home with a skein of fine ivory thread for Victoria.

"You always liked needle lace," she said, laying the fine woolen thread on their worn table. "I even found a needle."

Victoria fingered the soft thread. At home, she'd had a basket with balls and skeins of thread for making lace. In another life, she'd already have started working on a bridal veil. She looked up at her mother. "What use is lace here, *Mayrig*?"

"We trade it. We sell it. You make your dresses prettier. It's something. It's our history. We'll keep it." Her mother pulled the needle she'd acquired from her cuff where she'd secured it.

Victoria's cheeks burned; she hadn't thought of any of that. She took the needle and jabbed it into the skein, but after their meal, by the light of their one lamp, she tied the first knots of a simple pattern and threaded her needle.

It took a few thwarted efforts for her fingers to remember the knots, but eventually, she had a doily worth trading. One of the Danish missionaries had a collection of hair combs and gave Victoria a pair of tortoiseshell combs for her doily.

When *Mayrig's* birthday came a few weeks later, Mariam had scraped together enough to make a bigger meal. They invited as many of the other families they knew, and there was food and music and laughter–almost like the old days. Victoria presented her mother with the combs, and Yegsabet, who was the best with hair, put up their mother's hair with the new ornaments.

Vartouhy gathered her daughters close and whispered prayers of thanksgiving as the singing enveloped them.

After that, Victoria took thread and needles in exchange for the lace she would make from it, and the trades gave them a few precious luxuries–coffee and fabric for dresses, another lamp, treats like dates or sugar for their modest pantry–and the cellar rooms began to feel like a proper home.

The same American missionary was the one who found Victoria a job as a maid. Vartouhy was relieved. The missionaries said she would be paid in real money, and that she would be working for a prominent businessman's household.

If Victoria balked at the idea of working as a domestic servant, she kept it to herself. In addition to her wages, she would live with the family, which meant one fewer mouths for her mother and sisters to feed. Instead, she continued to work on her lace, leaving her mother and sisters with as many pieces of needlework as she could.

On the night before she was to join the Yavuz's household, they had a big gathering. The little girls sang songs for her before Mariam led them off to play in the street outside. The women laughed and talked, and there was food for everyone.

As the evening wound down, Victoria settled into their threadbare blanket with sleepy Lucine in her lap. Yegsabet was cleaning up. Mariam flopped down between Victoria and their mother.

Victoria took a moment to look–really look–at her mother and sisters.

Three years had aged Vartouhy Karadelian. Her hair was streaked with ivory, and deep lines marred her face. Lucine barely looked older than she had at not-quite-four, save that her baby nose had come unsnubbed. Victoria realized Lucine was big enough to go to the grammar school at home, to have riding lessons. So much time had passed, and she was still so small.

Vartouhy smoothed Victoria's hair. "I hope they feed you well. You're too skinny."

Victoria laughed. "We're all too skinny. Even Yegsabet."

Yegsabet looked like a young copy of their mother, right down to the way she narrowed her eyes at Victoria as though she'd misbehaved. "What's that supposed to mean?"

"It means we're all too skinny," Victoria said. "Even you."

"Don't argue," their mother said to Yegsabet. "Your sister won't be around as much, and you'll miss her."

Yegsabet snorted, and Victoria was reminded of her brothers, teasing her when they were all closer to Mariam's age. Simone had a snorty laugh, just like Yegsabet's.

They hadn't picked on Mariam as much, but Mariam hadn't picked on them.

Victoria shoved Simone back into the locked box of memories from *Before*, along with *Hayrig* and Yenov, the dolls, and Hasmik, their lane stretching toward home, sunlit and winding…and Davit with his handsome face and kind eyes.

Lucine tugged on a lock of Victoria's hair. Looking down, Victoria saw that her sister's eyes were opened wide, enthralled but fearful. She tracked Lucine's gaze to where, across the room, a snake was making its way along the seam where the floor met the wall.

Victoria sensed rather than heard her baby sister's distress. Lucine still didn't cry; Victoria wondered if the dusty, endless miles of the march had swallowed Lucine's tears forever, leaving her preternaturally quiet as well as small for her age.

Now, Lucine began to shake, small whimpers rising in her throat as the snake turned in their direction, likely drawn by the heat of the stove.

"Hush, *kooyregus*, sister, it won't hurt you." Victoria wasn't sure she was telling the truth. Stroking her baby sister's hair, she crooned a lullaby over the top of her sister's head. With her eyes, she begged Mariam–the most practical of them–to dispense with their slithering intruder.

Mariam crossed the room to the stove. Her hand closed around a panhandle. Victoria cringed; the last thing little Lucine needed was snake brains smashed on the grimy floor, but Mariam stopped.

Victoria's eyes slid back to the snake.

Long ago, before Mariam and Lucine were born, *Hayrig* saw an Indian man who could make a cobra dance to a musical pipe. When he told the story, Yegsabet giggled in disbelief. Victoria begged for a pipe and snake of her own.

She liked to imagine the man as her father described him, turbaned in front of his basket of snakes, and puzzle out how the trick was managed. She'd asked at school, but snakes and foreign men weren't deemed an appropriate topic for young ladies of a good family, so her imagination had to suffice.

Now, with memories of school so far behind her as to be ghosts, her heart thumped thickly in her chest. The snake's long body rose up from the floor, undulating in place like a living vapor, its narrow pupils fixed on Victoria herself as she sang.

"Victoria," Mariam breathed the words. "It likes your song."

Out of the corner of her eye, Victoria saw Mariam set the pot back on the stove and reach for her shawl–a ragged, second-best one she wore every day.

"Keep singing," Mariam hissed, creeping closer to the snake.

Slowly, Victoria shifted Lucine's weight to Yegsabet's lap and edged off the divan, creeping backward towards the stairs that led to the street above. The lullaby had run out of verses; she started again to hold the snake in this strange spell.

And spell it must be, for the snake's attention stayed on her as she moved. Its sinuous body curved and glided to keep Victoria in its sight while Mariam closed in on it from behind.

With a triumphant yowl, Mariam dropped the shawl over the snake, snatching it up in a writhing bundle. Shrieking, she dashed past Victoria and up the stairs.

The muffled sounds of Mariam flinging insults at the serpent drifted down the stairs as Victoria sagged against the wall, her heart kicking over and reaching away.

Mayrig and Yegsabet stared at her, open-mouthed. All Victoria could do was stare back and hope her sister wouldn't make signs against evil when her back was turned.

The long silent moment was broken by Mariam's breathless return. She stopped at the bottom of the stairs, shook out the shawl, and flung it dramatically around her head, eyes brimming with laughter.

"You should tell your new employers how you can charm snakes, *Kooyr,* sister! Maybe they will pay you extra," Mariam sniped.

"Maybe you should be quiet, Mariam," Victoria said. Fear and wonder still were coursing through her, along with the fresh sorrow of missing her father.

Mariam's laughter dried up.

Mayrig reached out her arms, gathering Mariam and Victoria to her and hugging them close. "Come here, Yegsabet, Lucine. I want all my girls in my arms before we go to bed."

Safe in the haven of her mother's embrace, Victoria reached behind to squeeze Mariam's hand and her sister squeezed back. She snuggled her head into her mother's shoulder and memorized the feeling of them all, together and sheltered from the city outside.

7

The Yavuz Residence, Aleppo, Syria
1919

The missionary led her on foot through the streets of Aleppo. Yegsabet was right, she was still too skinny. Her plain dress hung on her frame, but at least her clothing fit. The missionaries taught them how to sew, and how to make the best of secondhand clothes. Victoria had always enjoyed fine needlework; mending holes in old dresses and putting in new pleats and hems wasn't the same at all, but she had a knack for it.

Eva Poladian had been right, years before when she'd predicted Victoria could be a maid. Victoria had been singled out, along with some of the other older girls, for placement in wealthy homes in the city. The volunteers at the camp promised she would be well-treated, and her family needed the income.

Still, her hands were fisted tight in the fabric of her dress as they approached the home of Ibrahim Yavuz and his wife. Yavuz, she was told, was a prosperous and respected businessman, desiring a lady's maid for his wife.

The name was Turkish; the family was Muslim. Once, she'd have thought nothing of being in the home of Muslim Turks. They'd been her neighbors in Gürin; their children had been her friends and schoolmates. But that was before.

Victoria had her suspicions as to why they'd chosen the girls like her. It wasn't just that she was pretty. The more time passed in Aleppo, the more she saw how different her life in Gürin had been from many of the other's lives.

She would know how to be a lady's maid because she'd been

raised with fine manners. She could read and do sums, she understood not only her native Armenian and the Turkish spoken in her village, but she'd been taught some Arabic and French, as well as needlework, riding, dancing, and music.

She'd have been a lady herself, had she continued to live that life.

Never mind, it was a job. A year's wages paid in advance. Her mother's frugality would make it last. With any luck, the extra income would mean a better home for them, maybe even someday passage out of Aleppo.

The Old City was far removed from the refugee's neighborhood. Victoria heard the voices of the Muezzins calling the Muslims to prayer as they walked. The streets were crowded, and the air was heavy, but after months of the same faces, the same sounds, and smells, Victoria was ready for something more.

They stopped at a door set into a plain, windowless stone façade. The windows and a small parapet were on the upper floors. She could just make out the minaret-like silhouettes at the top of the walls, and the scrollwork in the window shutters.

They were received by a stern older woman in a simple dress and an apron. Her expression hardened as she took in Victoria's worn clothing and threadbare shawl. "Is this the new maid?"

"Yes," the missionary said. "Victoria."

"Sounds European. The mistress will like that," the stern woman said to Victoria's chaperone. "Thank you for bringing her."

The missionary took her leave, kissing Victoria once on each cheek and whispering, "God be with you, child."

Taking a deep breath and forcing her fingers to uncurl from the folds of her skirt, Victoria followed the stern woman inside.

Once inside, the house was achingly familiar to the one her family had left behind. Victoria gaped at the central courtyard. Where a stream flowed through their courtyard at home, this one boasted a fountain and lush potted greenery.

The stern woman caught her staring. "You were not brought here to stare. I am the cook and housekeeper; you may call me Sidika *bayan*."

Sidika took Victoria by the upper arms, looking her over. "You will get two dresses, an apron to keep them clean, and a pair of shoes in addition to the wages Ibrahim *bay* is paying the missionaries. You will wait on Ayşe *bayan* and her guests as well as assisting myself and the kitchen maid. You will address your mistress as *Hanımefendi*. You will not address the master unless spoken to. If you must, you will address him as *Efendim*, and you will strive to stay away from the male servants."

Victoria could only nod, turning the Turkish forms of address over on her tongue. She spoke enough Turkish to know these words, but the forceful nature of Sidika's speech startled her into muteness.

"Come. I will show you your room." Sidika didn't look back; she merely glided away over the tiled courtyard. "Can you sew?" Sidika continued briskly when Victoria nodded. "You will mend your own things, and Ayşe *bayan's* as well."

The servants had rooms in a separate part of the house, away from the family. Hers was no better than a broom closet, but there was a low sleeping pallet, and it was clean. The dresses, apron, and shoes were laid over a single chair with a sewing basket nearby. There was a high slit of a window that faced the narrow street below. Victoria had no possessions but the second or third-hand clothes from the missionaries she wore. There was nothing to do but sit as close to the window as possible and make use of the sewing supplies until she was called for.

The two dresses were modest and serviceable, but too long in the skirt and far too big around her shoulders and waist. She wondered who had worn them before.

After some time, the light faded, and the Muezzins called the city at sunset for the Maghrib prayer. Victoria marveled at the cacophony of voices. So many, all calling at once. The sound was dissonant and strange, unlike the singular, melodic call from the mosque in Gürin.

Homesick tears pricked the bridge of her nose. She hadn't given a thought to the *adhan,* the Islamic call to public prayers, at home. It was simply part of the day, like the bells at their family's church.

Sidika appeared in her doorway shortly thereafter. "You are not a Muslim?"

"I am not," Vicky said.

Sidika frowned. “Tomorrow you will cover your hair and wash before prayers.”

When Victoria opened her mouth to argue, Sidika quelled her with a squint-eyed glance. “You will do it.”

***

Sidika woke Victoria before dawn. Victoria’s eyes were grainy with fatigue, but her clothing was altered to the best of her ability, and she was suitably dressed, if Sidika’s critical gaze was any indicator. The cook showed her where the female servants prayed. Sidika had a kitchen maid, whose liquid brown eyes pleaded silently with Victoria, but the skittish, fragile creature never spoke a word.

When the Muezzins called the city to the *Fajr* prayer, first of the day at dawn, Victoria washed her hands and face and knelt on the prayer rug between Sidika and the kitchen maid, listening hard to the Arabic words. The consonants and vowels that flowed along the prayers, like the *adman*, were familiar to her ears, but the actual prayers were foreign.

When they finished, Sidika led her to her new mistress’s room, instructing Victoria in her duties all the while. Ayşe Yavuz, having woken for her prayers, now lounged on a divan with her eyes closed against the dimmed sunlight. She did not acknowledge Sidika or Victoria as they moved around her.

“Ayşe *bayan* will call for you if you are needed, outside of your regular duties,” Sidika said, showing her around the house. Several doors remained closed to her. These, Sidika explained, were the master’s apartments, and forbidden to women.

Hours later, after washing, kneeling, praying, mending, laundering, and fetching, Victoria collapsed in the kitchen, where she learned the servant girl slept by the fire.

“The master bought me for a handful of *kuruş* in the market. I was taken from my aunt in the desert.” the girl whispered to her.

“What is your name?” Images of her friend Hasmik, bartered

away in the night, flickered in Victoria's memory.

"I have no name," she said. "Nor should you, if you know what's good for you. Go to bed."

She was gone three days later.

Three days after that, Sidika had another kitchen maid, this one more timid than the last.

***

Ayşe was irritable and aloof, but not cruel, which suited Victoria fine. She kept her head down and her heart closed to the prayers she was made to recite five times a day. For weeks she performed the duties Sidika outlined, as well as hundreds of small tasks. Fetch tea, fetch slippers, fetch a headscarf, clean this, mend that, attend Ayşe's friends and the wives of Ibrahim's business associates.

Her thoughts were the only freedom she had anymore. She was forbidden from leaving the household walls. She missed her mother and sisters fiercely and longed for the small community they'd managed to build in the years they'd spent in the camp and living in the cellar apartment.

The steady routine of her new existence had its effects on her, however. In the third month, Victoria's menstrual courses started again. After three years, it came as a shock. Hunger, strain, and upheaval had dried up her womb for so long. When her belly cramped in the night, she woke with dark circles under her eyes and blood between her thighs.

Sidika told her to stay in her rooms during prayer time until her courses were complete.

When she brought Ayşe tea one afternoon a few weeks later, she noticed dark circles under the older woman's eyes and wondered if it was monthly bleeding that caused her fatigue and irritability.

Victoria lingered outside *Ayşe bayan's apartment,* wishing she might spend a blissful afternoon lounging with tea and sweets while her monthly cramps plagued her, but when *Ayşe bayan* didn't need her, Sidika always had a list. And besides, her sleeping pallet, while not uncomfortable, was no plush divan.

Sidika caught her idle loitering; Victoria was so surprised she nearly blurted out an impertinent question about the mistress's courses.

Instead of a reprimand, however, Sidika gave her a treat.

"There you are. Ayşe *bayan* requested that I make *lokum* to give to the wives of the master's guests tomorrow evening. I need more dates and orange blossom water and Ibrahim *Bay*'s manservant is busy. You must go to the market."

Victoria sensed Sidika's reluctance to entrust her with a task outside the house and stilled her expression. It wouldn't do to let the cook know how badly she wanted to venture beyond the Yavuz's walls.

"Yes, Sidika *bayan*," she said meekly. Sidika repeated her instructions, which stalls to buy from and how much to buy, what she should pay, especially how much change she expected back, while Victoria's feet itched to walk free on the streets, to search the faces of passersby for her sisters and her mother.

"Don't dawdle," was Sidika's last advice.

The market was crowded and noisy, its dusty body perfumed with spice and sweetness under the heavy weight of midday heat. She whispered Sidika's directions to herself until she found the stall. A fine sweat broke out along her hairline.

Her Turkish was better after living with the Yavuz family, but to haggle in the marketplace?

She squared her shoulders. She was no longer a child, and the market represented a kind of freedom if she proved useful to Sidika.

As Victoria walked, she peered out from under her headscarf at the sea of eyes around her. Her mother and sisters might be among this crowd. Or someone who knew them and where they were. Surely, after all these months, they had found somewhere better to live. At the very least, they would wonder how she was. Victoria had no way of knowing if the Yavuz's reported on her wellbeing, or even if they were paying the missionaries as promised.

She was, in many ways, little more than an indentured servant, one with no idea how long her indenture would last.

"Do you want them or not?" The fruit merchant was holding out her purchase in expectation of payment. Proud that she'd managed the purchase with coins to spare, she shook off her daydreams and added the dates to the bottle of orange blossom water in her basket.

At the edge of the market, the crowd was larger, rowdier, with a miasma of fear hanging low over the air. She caught a glimpse of a scrawny, naked girl with a lifeless expression and the men who inspected her like livestock before she was jostled into the custody of a man she recognized as her master's manservant.

Her heart leaped into her throat. She'd only just escaped notice.

Now she knew where her master acquired his nameless servant girls.

***

It was weeks before Victoria left the Yavuz's house again, this time to fetch spices and vegetables for Sidika.

Victoria absorbed the city around her, desperate to understand her surroundings. Another long stretch of time confined inside the courtyard and the cool rooms of the house set her teeth on edge. Ayşe barely left her rooms and had grown increasingly irritable over the first month after the wives had come and the *lokum* gifted.

Underneath her mistress's fretful mood, however, Victoria sensed a fluttering hopefulness, so foreign to her heart she almost missed it. When, in the fifth week, the bleeding came—stronger, darker, muskier than monthly courses, Sidika told her the mistress had lost a baby.

Victoria learned that the Yavuz's had been trying for years to have a child.

Before, she would have pitied Ayşe's sorrow. Children were the greatest blessing a family could receive. There was no room in Victoria's heart for pity now; she was too full of longing for her family, for freedom, for information. Anything that might connect her to the life she'd left behind.

Sometimes it was too much to think about–how much she'd lost. Twice now. Her home, her father and brothers, her community, her church, and teachers. Now her position in this foreign household had robbed her of what family remained. She might as well have been adrift on a wide ocean.

She walked to the market with purpose, memorizing the buildings to make a kind of map for herself. *Here is the house, here is the market, here are the midday sun and the shadows on the street.*

Sidika preferred one spice merchant over all the others, and it was to that stall Victoria walked, lingering for a moment over a finely woven shawl, swamped by memories of visits to her father's shawl factory to see the great looms and the men who operated them.

"You." A hushed whisper from beneath a modest head scarf shattered the memory. Victoria startled, ready to defend herself, but the young woman next to her with a market basket was peering into her face. "You work as a maid for the Yavuz's."

Victoria looked closely at the young woman. There was nothing truly familiar about her; still, Victoria couldn't look away.

"I know you." The girl put a hand on Victoria's arm. "I was a kitchen maid there for a few weeks. Months ago."

Recognition came slowly, but Victoria began to see it. The girl was no longer a walking ghost with haunted eyes. She was wiry now, fed and clean and clothed, but wary.

"I only lasted a few weeks. I was sold again when I didn't fall pregnant."

"By whom?" Victoria was shocked. She was aware of the male servants, the valet, the gardener, and the boys who kept Ibrahim's horse and the goats and chickens…none of them even came to the kitchens when Sidika and the maids were working. It was forbidden; the punishment for offenders was brutal.

The girl's laugh was grim. "Ibrahim, you fool. He doesn't rape you? He will. Unless you get out."

"Get out how?" Victoria's heart was racing. "With what? I have no money. No friends. My wages went to the missionaries for my family. Besides, Ibrahim doesn't notice me."

The girl barked a bitter laugh. "I doubt that. He will notice you eventually. Unless the women can rescue you…"

"What women? What do you mean?"

"You two! You buy or you make room for those who will!" The shawl merchant was shooing them away.

The girl melted into the crowd with pity in her eyes, leaving Victoria to slink away to the spice stall.

***

Twice more, Ayşe's courses stopped, and the hushed expectancy settled over the household. Twice more, the blood of loss came, and Victoria scrubbed it from her mistress's clothing and sheets. She spent hours scouring the linen in icy water to draw out the stains, only to find Ayşe had later burned the clothes in her misery.

This was how Ibrahim Yavuz found her.

He'd never looked at her or spoken to her in all the months she moved silently through the rooms, hurried across the courtyard on mincing feet, or left tea for Ayşe and her husband, but now she feared he'd been watching.

With the servant girl's whispered warnings in her ears, Victoria kept to her chores and tasks. She did what she could to warn the next girl to come to Sidika's kitchen, but no amount of keeping herself small and quiet could hide the inevitable.

The better part of a year of enough to eat and work to tone her muscles told a story of bodily health, though her soul still starved and raged. Her hair had grown back where it had fallen out in great hanks in the desert. The sunken pockets of her eyes were once again full and supple. Her breasts and hips were those of a slim young woman, not a skeleton.

"What is your name?" He said, his shadow falling long over the washtub.

She kept her eyes on her work. "Victoria, *Efendim.*"

The honorific tasted ashy on her tongue, but he left, and Victoria shuddered.

***

Perhaps if things had gone as they should have, if she still lived in a fine house outside Gürin with a circle of aunts, cousins, and friends around her, by now Victoria would have heard from the older girls about the marriage bed and its secrets. She might have stolen a kiss or two.

She might even be married, she thought, then pushed away memories of Hasmik's handsome brother.

Victoria had a woman's body, but she had no experience of how it was between a man and a woman. They'd kept horses, and she had seen–though her father never knew–a stud covering a mare for breeding. She thought sex must be something like that.

She knew rape was the man taking sex when the woman wasn't willing. It was a sin, the act of a beast. She had seen and heard it on the deportation route through the desert.

She had not imagined it would hurt so badly. She hadn't understood the violation. Or the strange mundaneness of the violence.

He came in the early hours of deepest night, when Sidika was gone home, and his wife retired to her bed. There was no lock, no bar on her door. He simply walked in.

Victoria woke to the rasp of his trousers coming down over his haunches as he knelt over her. She picked her head up in alarm, only to have her face shoved down into the bedclothes.

When he was done, she lay there, shivering and weeping into the sheets while the door closed after his retreating steps.

There were no more trips to the market after that, only the nights when he returned to force himself on her again and again.

Sometimes Victoria wondered if he'd known, seen her talking to the girl in the market, or heard her thoughts when she dreamed of escape, of finding *Mayrig* and her sisters and running far from the Turks and her lost homeland.

It was foolish to wonder. In her most rational moments, she knew he simply took because he could, because his wife's womb couldn't hold a baby, because she was there.

He came night after night, until her courses came and she was unclean in his eyes, but he returned. Victoria had learned to hide herself from his mindless invasions and the knowing expression in Sidika's eyes. The woman was not a fool.

He might push into her body and leave her filthy and sore and full of rage, but he could not push his way into her soul or poison her heart, for she had closed it off. It was as dead as the past she lost, as lost to her as the mother and sisters she dreamed were free, somewhere far from Aleppo.

Victoria was the last to realize she was with child.

She realized it when Ayşe slapped her and cursed her for a whore and no better than a breeding sow.

The slap was followed by an apology. Ayşe helped her to her feet. "Go lie down. The kitchen girl will see to me for the afternoon."

Things moved both quickly and slowly after that. Within days Sidika was given two more maids and Victoria was confined to her room. She was taken on daily walks around the courtyard and fed hearty food, like a prize bitch carrying a litter.

Sidika became her only conduit to the world beyond her room. The only work Victoria was given was mending and sewing, and her thoughts turned inward. She cursed the brute who'd put the baby inside her against her will. She raged at the invisible life she could not even feel, save for when she was retching before her breakfast.

When the morning sickness abated, she found she couldn't resist speaking to the child in her thoughts, as though it might hear her and know her voice despite her silence, and by the time she could see the bump of her pregnancy nudging the waistlines of the dresses she let out to accommodate it, she was singing remembered snippets of old lullabies while the needle flashed in her fingers.

After that, the days passed in a dull but not unpleasant cadence, but the nights dragged. In the darkness, she would shiver and sweat when nightmares of Ibrahim's body over hers woke her. She would lie for hours wondering what would become of the two of them when the baby was born while the child fluttered hopefully under her skin.

Time sped up once again as the mound of a child in her belly grew and dropped low like ripe fruit. She felt, rather than saw the mood of the household shift around her, and all the while terror warred with anticipation while the small knobs of her child's form pushed toward the light of the world.

***

The birth was hard. Her body, though stronger after so long in the house in the Old City, still bore the invisible scars of the endless march through the desert. She was still frail, beneath the earthy glow of motherhood, though there was no midwife to tell her so, not until it was too late and the baby was tearing itself through her to escape into the world.

For what felt like days, she bore down against the weight of the baby, panting and sweating and screaming while Sidika and Ayşe bathed her forehead in cool water and watched her, secrets passing between them in the spaces between Victoria's pain.

She was too tired, too focused, to care what the older women who held her destiny in their hands whispered about with their eyes.

Her daughter slipped into the world on a tide of musky fluid and blood, wailing at the injustice of air on her skin, and Victoria's arms reached out to comfort the cries. Her hair was soaked through with sweat, but the pain was already receding into the murky gray depths of forgetfulness that nature gives mothers so they would want to try again.

Instead, Sidika, who'd caught her child and cleaned the baby before wrapping her flailing limbs, handed the child into Ayşe's waiting arms.

The lady of the house shed tears of joy as she whispered, "*Welcome, my child.*"

Without looking back at Victoria, Ayşe took the baby away, calling to Sidika as she went. "Clean her up and bring her to nurse the child in an hour."

There was a flash of pity in Sidika's eyes, but no more. "Let's get you bathed."

"Sidika *bayan*, please," Victoria whispered. "What is happening?"

Sidika squeezed Victoria's arms hard enough to pinch and held her in a hard gaze, daring her to say otherwise. "Ibrahim *bay*'s child was born today. His wife will need to rest after such an ordeal, and the wet nurse should be ready to perform her duties."

8

Istanbul, Turkey
Late spring 1963

The letter from America was addressed to Gül Yavuz, her maiden name, care of the address where she'd grown up. The battered international mail envelope was marked for forwarding to her married address. The unfamiliar postage and incorrect address printed out carefully in English were from a place so far away; Gül's husband Ahmet looked it up in the atlas: Providence, Rhode Island, USA

She was in the midst of stitching miniature *yelekler,* long Ottoman-style jackets, for a pair of dolls, and her table was covered in remnants of wool and silk, leftover from previous clothing made for the fine dolls she sold in the Grand Bazaar.

"Who is it from, my love?" They knew no one in America, but there was no censure in Ahmet's question. Gül would have married him solely because her grandparents arranged it, but she'd grown over the years to love him for his kindness and curiosity.

Still, such a missive was unexpected and worrisome. Gül hid her nerves in teasing. "I'll have to open it, won't I?"

Slitting the envelope with her stitch ripper, Gül slid out a single sheet of onionskin paper, covered in tidy script.

Dear Miss Yavuz, the letter began. Dated almost three weeks before, the letter was written entirely in English. She'd learned the language in school, but her opportunities to use it were reserved almost exclusively for interacting with English-speaking tourists in the bazaar. To see the foreign words flowing across the page was overwhelming. She folded it again, flattening her palm over the page as if she could somehow transform it.

My name is Rose. I am writing on behalf of my aunt, Mrs. Victoria Minassian, née Karadelian. We saw your picture in The Providence Journal several weeks ago, alongside an American doll maker traveling in Turkey.

Gül remembered the American woman. She'd stopped at Gül's stall to see–and ultimately purchase some of–her work. Americans were rare customers, and this one had haggled respectfully, asking questions about her craft and sharing some of her own history in the same trade. She'd asked the man she was traveling with–Gül had assumed him to be her husband–to take a picture of the two of them in front of her stall with the doll she'd purchased.

"For the story in the paper," he'd said, but Gül hadn't been paying attention, too intent on conversing with the woman.

Gül returned to the letter.

My aunt believes you to be her lost daughter, born October 26, 1919 in Aleppo, Syria. I am using the name my aunt believes you were given at birth because we have no way of knowing what name you may go by now, or truthfully, if this letter will find you at all.

My aunt is not well, and it would mean a great deal to her to know you received this. If you are who she believes you to be, knowing you are alive and aware of her would begin healing a lifetime of grief and loss...

Gül's blood seemed to thicken in her veins, thudding painfully against her temple.

"What is it, *Gülüm*?" Ahmet's endearment, also a play on her given name, usually brought a smile, but now it startled her.

She snapped the folded sheet closed and slid it between the split sides of the envelope. Her hands were shaky.

She took a deep breath and looked into the face of her beloved husband. "Nothing, my love. A woman in the United States searching for someone else entirely."

9

The Yavuz Residence, Aleppo, Syria
1919

In the early weeks, it was easy enough to pretend that all was well, that her baby was hers and Sidika and Ayşe merely aunts who hovered nearby. Victoria drifted through her days in a weary haze. Ibrahim slept in his apartment, while Ayşe kept the baby's cradle near her bed, and for a fortnight, Victoria slept on a pallet on the floor.

Ayşe called the baby Gül, which meant *Rose,* just as Victoria's mother's name did. In the quiet moments when Vicky nursed her daughter, she whispered a secret Armenian name over the baby's heart like a blessing: *Nevart*, a pet name for Vartouhy.

She sang a song she remembered *Mayrig* singing to Lucine and Shenorig when they were little, the tune like a ghost in her memory until she'd gotten through a few lines. The meaning pushed the heaviness from her chest–*rise, my child, and bring your light to your parents…*

As Victoria sang, she imagined her mother and sisters safe somewhere, snug together and loved. When the song ended, she wasn't sure who she'd soothed more, her daughter or herself.

Gül certainly did that. The entire household was in love with the baby. *Ayşe bayan* was happier than Victoria had ever seen her, floating through the house, humming to herself or to Gül.

The forced intimacy of caring for an infant, of feeding the baby from her body while her employer kept watch, dissolved some of the established distance between mistress and servant. Victoria worked hard not to overstep, fearing Ayşe might resent any familiarity and separate her from her daughter.

Gradually, as Gül's incessant needs fell into a kind of pattern, Sidika returned Victoria to some of her maid duties, though Victoria still slept on the floor in Ayşe's room to attend to the baby's hunger.

Months passed, and Victoria felt like a nursemaid to both Ayşe and Gül. She was up before first light to lay out *Ayşe bayan*'s clothes and prepare her breakfast and coffee, wash the baby's clothing, and nurse the little one before her mistress was awake. She started making soft foods as the baby's teeth cut through.

She was the first awake and the last to sleep; her nights were punctuated by the baby's cries.

Gül grew plump and rosy, bright-eyed and curious, and Victoria fell deeper in love with her child.

As her love grew, so too did her illusions, until the evening she found her pallet gone.

Ayşe was tucked into the bed with Gül in her arms, humming tunelessly.

"She is old enough to sleep through the night now," Ayşe said dismissively. "You can return to your room."

Ibrahim sat beside them, one of his thick fingers clutched in Gül's chubby hand. Victoria barely made it back to the servants' privy before vomiting, the memory of Ibrahim's body violating hers roiling in her belly.

She wept herself dry that night, understanding truly taking root. They would not let her stay near her daughter forever, never mind keep her. As abruptly as she was dismissed from Ayşe's rooms, she could be dismissed from service, and wherever she ended up, she would never hold her precious Nevart again.

Echos of her aborted conversation in the market plagued her when her daughter cried that first night. *Unless the women can rescue you...*

What women, and what kind of rescue? A thousand times a day, she dreamed up scenarios in which she fled the Old City, Nevart bound tightly to her chest, seeking the safety of her mother and sisters, but those were foolish fantasies. She was a prisoner in all but title, and she had no way of knowing if Ibrahim had paid her family for another year's work.

They would not expect to see her again until she was released from service, if at all. She knew that now. Life moved on, or it moved you along.

In the morning, dry-eyed and stone-faced, she entered *Ayşe bayan*'s room and fed her daughter without once meeting the other woman's eyes. There was no telling how much time she had left. She cloaked herself in a mask of meekness and let the idea of rescue–both for herself and her daughter–consume her.

"Victoria." Sidika interrupted Gül's late morning feeding a few days later. "When the baby is sleeping, you must go to the market. Ayşe *bayan*'s family will arrive in a few days to meet her child, and I am too busy to do the marketing."

And I am not busy? And they come to meet her *child?* The extra maids had disappeared as quickly as they'd come; Victoria didn't dare dwell on where or how. She would be required to prepare rooms for any visiting women, to clean, to assist Sidika with serving, and there would be the extraordinary torture of hearing them coo over *Ayşe's* child all the while.

In their eyes, she was, she understood, an infidel, a servant, and her position was only safe because *Ayşe bayan* could not nurse the baby herself. No one cared how hard she worked.

Nevart was asleep at her breast. Victoria released the little rosy mouth from her nipple under the draped headscarf she wore for modesty and handed the baby to the housekeeper while she adjusted her dress.

"Of course, Sidika *bayan*. I will go now."

The luster of the market was dimmed for her now. Every step through Aleppo's narrow streets, with their dry breath swirling around her ankles, took her farther from Nevart's light, the beating heart that had replaced Victoria's own. Still, she kept her eyes open. Once, she had touched the hem of freedom's skirts in the bazaar, and she would find a way to do it again, this time, with her baby in her arms.

She lingered as much as she dared, peeking out of her headscarf as much as she dared, seeking a pair of familiar eyes or a friendly glance, but she found none. She returned to the Yavuz's house with coins and a basket of food for Sidika but had no idea how to find *the women* the servant girl had mentioned.

No idea if they'd ever existed at all.

***

Victoria had dreaded the arrival of Ayşe's family, but the chaos of an extra household gave her the gifts of anonymity and invisibility. The Yavuz's were too busy to wonder where the nursemaid was, that her market trips were more frequent, or that she was gone for far longer than she should have been.

Sidika lost track of her in the endless meals and refreshments, the entertainment that came with important visitors, and Victoria embraced this pale imitation of freedom, venturing deeper into the market, farther from the Old City and the walls of the Yavuz's house.

One afternoon, when she was meant to be securing the apricots, yogurt, lamb, and vegetables for the evening meal, she found herself on the far side of the bazaar, and from a knot of older women, the faintest whisper of her own language.

Edging closer with a racing heart, she stilled her breath to listen. They were younger than her mother, these women, but their eyes were ancient. Like her, Victoria supposed, they had come through the desert to this foreign city.

She listened, but the words didn't make sense.

Raised voices followed, and they broke apart suddenly and melted into the crowd, leaving Victoria anxiously hopeful and completely bewildered. What did the words mean, and how much of their message had she missed?

The shawl maker, the fountain in Al-Jdayde, Rescuer Jeppe, darkness, the riders…

The call to afternoon prayers startled her out of her thoughts, and she returned to the task at hand, but as she walked, she repeated the words she'd heard until they became like a prayer.

When the household was asleep, she took them out one by one to untangle their meanings.

The shawl maker, like *Hayrig*...her heart quickened, but she squashed the hope that threatened to burst out of her. Her father and brothers were dead. She'd heard the shots and the stories from others on the march and here in Aleppo. The men were killed or taken to work camps where they died or were disposed of when the work was complete.

She thought of the former maid and her warnings. She'd met the girl near a shawl stall in the market. Could it have been intentional?

She knew *Al-Jdayde*. She liked to walk that way sometimes when she was sent to the market. That was the name of a neighborhood not far from the Yavuz's, full of large *beit*–fine walled houses like the Yavuz's's, with a *souq*, *hammam*, churches and mosques, and a small Muslim school, but also a Christian Armenian quarter.

There was a beautiful fountain in the Armenian quarter, but what did it mean?

Rescuer Jeppe was another mystery on her tongue. Jeppe wasn't an Armenian name, she didn't know any Miss Jeppe from her years in the camp or the refugee housing, and *riders in the darkness*?

The puzzling only left her sleepless and frustrated, pulse pounding with the one word she held onto more tightly than any other.

Escape.

Somehow, her belly told her, the whispered words she'd heard in the bazaar meant escape if she only knew how to connect them.

***

Ayşe's family stayed a month, and Victoria was no closer to answers. She was, however, closer to her immediate fears. Gül's feedings were decreasing in frequency as she ate more soft foods and drank goat's milk and watered tea with honey.

Any day now, Gül would not need her for sustenance, and the

Yavuz's would be at liberty to release her into service to someone else. Like the kitchen maids, she would vanish from her own daughter's life and memory, with no way to find her again.

In the quiet after his wife's family's visit, Ibrahim was often away from home on whatever business concerns he had. Even after almost two years in their service, she didn't really know what he did for work. Only that now, more than ever, he entertained often and was gone for days at a time.

Without her husband in the house, Ayşe let the household run itself, under Sidika's guidance. Beyond the demands of prayer, Gül–her feedings, naps, and whims–determined the rhythms of Ayşe's days.

Ayşe stopped dismissing Victoria when the baby's feedings were done, instead allowing her to stay with them. As weeks passed and the little girl's birthday approached, the hypnotic false intimacy of sharing Gül's care wrapped around them once more. During those hours, Ayşe sometimes forgot Victoria was there, murmuring to the baby. It didn't take long for Victoria to realize her mistress missed her mother and sisters.

Isolated in her home as she was, Ayşe missed the company of women, and Victoria was the only one to fill some part of that void in Ayşe's life.

Victoria knew that the Muslim family wouldn't observe Gül's birthday as a celebration, which struck her as sad. Armenians were a people of celebrations, and a birthday was one of the best reasons for a celebration.

Her own birthday, and all of her siblings, had been celebrated with huge parties. Birthday celebrations in Gürin always included her grandparents and the aunts who lived nearby, Hasmik's family, and most of the families from their church and the village.

The addition of a new generation would have gathered them all to share food, music, and so much laughter. They'd have sung all the old songs until their throats were dry, and *Hayrig* would have blessed everyone there in place of the baby's father.

Or would he? It was easy to forget the truth of her baby's conception when she was alone inside the walls of this house, alone inside her own mind. She was soiled by every measure she knew. No longer a virgin, with a child outside of marriage, and a half-Turkish child at that.

"Victoria?" Ayşe was speaking to her. Gül had fallen asleep in Ayşe's arms, limbs soft, joints loose where her chubby knees draped over Ayşe's arm.

Victoria shook off the cobwebs. "Yes, *Hanımefendi*?"

"My husband has returned from his trip. I must dress to entertain his partners' wives." Ayşe rose and tipped the bundle of sleeping child into Victoria's arms. "See that she has her bath, and some time in the courtyard beforehand. And you may oversee her bedtime, as well. I suspect this will be a long evening."

This was more unstructured time with her daughter than Victoria was accustomed to. She tucked Nevart against her breast and carried her out of the room.

"Victoria?" Ayşe didn't bother turning to Victoria; she was already inspecting her wardrobe choices. "I find I quite like the idea of having a governess. For as long as it pleases me, you'll stay."

"Yes, *Hanımefendi.*"

Victoria inhaled the damp, sleepy smell of Nevart's hair. *Until we can steal away together,* she thought, *I will stay.*

10

Providence, Rhode Island
June 1963

Rose took to visiting Aunt Vicky every week to check for letters from Istanbul, often on Thursday afternoons when she knew her parents would be at the store, and her aunties Yessa and Mariam were out playing cards with some of their friends.

It had been weeks since she'd mailed that one fraught page of airmail paper, the international postage paid for from the grocery money to keep it a secret from prying family eyes. Privately, Rose didn't have much hope that the letter would even find Gül Yavuz, but to keep the spark kindled in Vicky's eyes, she never let on.

On this afternoon, despite the gentle warmth of the air, fragrant with the roses and hydrangeas Auntie Yessa planted in front of the porch, Vicky wasn't outside. Rose found her aunt inside, sitting at the kitchen table with a handwritten page spread out in front of her.

"You had a letter from the doll-maker," Vicky said softly, not looking up at Rose as she let herself in.

Rose cradled the slight rounding of her bell, eyes wide with anticipation. "What did she say?"

"She resented the intrusion and said it's not possible."

Rose reached for the page. "May I?"

She read the terse message and looked back at Vicky. "She also says her birth name was Gül Yavuz, and wonders how we got her grandparents' former address in Istanbul to write to her." Rose took a breath. It hardly seemed possible. "So she might really be your Nevart, no matter what she thinks."

"Oh, Rose, it's what she believes that matters. Don't you see?"

Rose hated the resignation threatening to crush her dear aunt's spirit.

"Then we change her mind. We will write again."

"Just like that?" Vicky whispered. "Even though she said…"

Rose sat next to her aunt and took her hand. "Just like that, Auntie Vicky. This is important. I'll make some coffee, and we'll figure out what to say. Together."

Vicky pushed the letter from Gül Yavuz Nacar to the side while Rose set out cups and boiled water.

"We will write it together," Rose said, measuring out coffee grounds and setting out the sugar. "And will copy it out onto the international mail paper and take it to the post office."

"There's something else I'd like you to see before we write again," Vicky said. "Letters, in a shoebox in my bedroom closet."

Rose brought the box to the kitchen, and together they read the letters her aunt had saved inside.

Rose couldn't help her tears. The letters were raw and emotional, nothing like the frail, old-fashioned woman across the table or the unflappable aunt who'd helped to raise her.

The story Aunt Vicky told her sounded like something from a film full of danger and heartbreak, bravery, and hard-won wisdom. When Rose reached out to touch Aunt Vicky's hand, she felt a new kind of connection with a woman who had carried a precious life in her womb, *just like herself.* Her chest tightened with grief for her aunt and the daughter who was stolen from her.

They sat holding hands for a few moments until she broke the moment and insisted that Rose bring the coffee tray and a few roasted nuts.

"I think we should send her one of the letters," Rose said when they'd finished their coffee. "My neighbor is a teacher, and I think she might be willing to make mimeograph copies of them if I ask nicely."

"If you think so, Rose," Vicky said, but once more, the light in her eyes was dimmed.

"I do think so. I'll ask for copies of them all, but I'll just send the first one." Rose stood up and gently folded the letters to tuck them into her purse. "While I'm here, can I see the Christening gown?"

Vicky pushed herself to her feet, her movements slow and deliberate, and Rose chewed her lip. Her aunt was fading away, illness walked with her like a companion. "Come, *aghchigus*, my sweet girl. I've done all the lacework and laid out the pattern."

***

It turned out Rose's neighbor was willing to make the copies, and a few days later, Rose hand-copied her aunt's letter and sent them off to Istanbul.

Dear Mrs. Nacar,

Thank you for your reply. I know you didn't need to have responded at all, and I'm grateful. Please forgive my hope that you will give me another chance to explain.

My aunt, Victoria Karadelian, was a refugee from Western Armenia, living in Aleppo between 1915 and 1921. She had a place as a maid in the Yavuz home and as I wrote before, gave birth to a daughter on October 26, 1919. Her child was taken from her to be raised by Mr. Yavuz's wife, who could not bear children of her own. Though my aunt has not said so explicitly, I believe Mr. Yavuz was the child's father, a fact with which the Yavuz family used to justify their keeping the baby.

Rose paused, fingers shaking as she set down the pen. This letter was antiseptic, stripped of the pain and anguish of Vicky's story, but she didn't dare alienate Gül further. She couldn't help thinking of her own baby, growing safely inside her, and how it might feel to lose her to people who all but held her captive.

She flexed her fingers and took up the pen again.

As I wrote previously, we saw you in a photograph in the Providence Journal. You bear a striking resemblance to my aunt when she was younger, and you and I might be cousins. I am enclosing a photograph from my wedding, so you can see the women in the family all together and consider for yourself.

Vicky was a beautiful woman, and you are very like her, right down to your striking eyes.

I am deeply concerned about her declining health and cannot ignore the possibility that you are her daughter.

I think I understand why you do not welcome hearing what I have to say, but the sheer improbability of you being in that photo in the paper is such a large coincidence, such a miraculous accident...how can I not try?

I am enclosing a copy of a letter Vicky wrote to her daughter. She wrote letters on her daughter's birthday every year from the time her child was five, addressing them to places she wishes you might have been, or perhaps places that brought her daughter closer to the life she led. She's kept every letter all these years.

If you are that daughter–and I believe you are, this letter and all the others are yours, and there are people here in Providence who are your family.

Yours sincerely,
Rose

To Miss Gül Yavuz
Aleppo, Syria

Sireli aghcheegus,

My dear daughter. Today you are five years old. I have never forgotten your birthday. Every year my heart breaks, so today, I have decided to write to you. I cannot send these letters, but I pretend that somehow, they will reach you. I will address them to Gül, the name Ayşe gave you, but in my heart, always, you are Nevart, after my own mother.

You won't remember that I whispered the Armenian word for Mother in your ear. *Mayrig.*

Just before the soldiers marched us away from our home, my sister Yegsabet and I buried our dolls under a very old olive tree just outside the city, in the cemetery across from our home. Some believe the tree was planted by Noah when the ark finally came to rest atop Mount Ararat after the flood.

Our gold crosses and a few gold coins were in the bundle with them. Our treasure. Sometimes I wish I knew someone to look for them there, but everyone I knew is gone or here in America with our family.

I am married now. His name is Kachadoor Minassian, but everyone calls him Pesa. I will tell you why the nickname stuck when you're older.

You were still so small when Ayşe took you away. Too small to be without your mother. I hope you were not too hungry on your journey.

Ayşe's family was from there. I remember their address from the letters exchanged while I lived in the house in Aleppo. I always assumed she sought refuge with them. When I think of you growing up with Ayşe's family in Turkey, I imagine you in Constantinople as my father used to speak of it. The soaring churches and mosques, the palaces, and the narrow mazes of streets. He said you could hear every language from all over the world in Constantinople. He spoke of markets full of cloth and spices, fruits and trinkets from all over the world, beautiful dolls and toys for loving fathers to give to their little girls. He would have loved you; I am sure.

I wonder if Ayşe remarried, if you have a loving father.

I have no other children yet, *tsakis*, honey, but I am expecting a child in the coming months. I will tell them about you when the time is right. My sister Yegsabet wants to have a baby, too. She and her husband have not been blessed yet, but I hope they will. I will watch our babies grow up together and wish you were here with them. You would play together with dolls, just like I did with my sisters.

I will see you in their faces for the rest of my life. I love you so.

Always, your Mayrig,

Victoria Karadelian Minassian

11

Istanbul, Turkey
Summer 1963

Gül walked with Ahmet to the mosque under the late afternoon sky. All that day and part of the one before, she'd been troubled by a second unwelcome letter from Rose, and the copied page from Victoria Minassian, her spidery handwriting slanting on the page.

Rose insisted Gül was her cousin, Victoria's daughter, stolen from her by the people she considered her parents. Her mind rejected that possibility even as Gül itched to read the letter through one more time. Though it left her confused and angry, there were too many things in Rose's letter story that rang true.

She would pray on it and if she were fortunate, Allah would grant her clarity.

When she completed the *Asr* prayer at sunset, Gül made her way home. Her prayers were always the same, as outlined by her faith, but she'd stayed on in the women's area of the mosque, looking inward, searching herself for the strength to examine her past, for the strength to share her concerns with her husband.

Rose sent color photographs with names and dates printed in careful letters on the back, but Gül knew without those names which one was Victoria. She stood to one side of the bride–presumably Rose–with pride in her wide, almond eyes, and her dark hair, streaked with ivory piled into an updo.

Gül knew those dark coffee colored, lushly lashed almond-shaped eyes. They stared back at her from every mirror she looked into. They'd always stood out among her mother's family, none of whom shared them. She grew up assuming they came from her father's side.

Rose and Victoria both knew things about her. Her birthplace and family name. The names of her parents.

Her birth date.

A hundred times on the walk between the mosque and her home, she decided to burn the letter, forget the old Armenian woman and her niece, and let things stay the same.

A hundred times she knew she couldn't do it. She had to know the truth, and she had to tell Ahmet about the letters.

Pandora's box was open, and she would never be able to gather its miseries back together.

***

She fretted, moving the letters from her writing desk to her workshop to the kitchen without re-reading them. She made coffee, sketched a few ideas for new dolls, anything to distract her from their contents.

Finally, there was no more avoiding it. She took up the copied sheet and began to read, consuming the words slowly and deliberately.

The letter was addressed to Gül Yavuz at the address in Constantinople where she lived with her grandparents when she was very small. By the time Victoria had written this anguished missive, her mother had remarried, and her stepfather had joined her grandparents' household.

He was a family friend, older and widowed. He'd been a kind, if aloof, figure in her life, but her mother had blossomed as his wife. She'd been an admired hostess in their circles, her guests often included her new husband's family as well as their new friends.

Gül's childhood was a happy one, full of cousins and a close, loving family.

It felt strange to read the birthday wishes from this foreign pen, echoing across the years. Her faith did not celebrate birthdays in the Western sense. For her own part, she often used the day to reflect on her life and whether she was living it according to Allah's will. The reflection allowed her to take stock of herself and the effects of the years on her body.

She rolled the name *Nevart* around on her tongue, wondering what it meant, if anything. Perhaps she would go to the library and look it up.

Ahmet's steps in the next room brought her back to the present.

Surely this was all a terrible coincidence. She knew who she was. Wife and mother. A dollmaker, an artist. Turkish and Muslim, a child of the ancient heart of this city with so many names.

Leaving the letter on her worktable, Gül walked to the window, taking in the city outside it and her own reflection in the glass.

Wouldn't she know in her deepest heart, if she were secretly the stolen daughter of an Armenian refugee?

There was no one left to ask. Her mother had passed away years before; her stepfather and grandparents had been gone longer.

Ahmet knocked on the door, asking her if she wanted to walk with him for a bit.

In a panic, Gül tidied the letters from Rose and Victoria away, hiding them in a drawer. She might be curious enough to question her own origins, but she could never do the same to her husband and their daughter.

She would forget the Armenian women, and all would be well.

***

It was not so easy to forget.

Gül went to the bazaar and found herself drawn to the Armenian scarves. She walked around the city and noticed the Armenian churches.

She left the letters in their drawer and went about her business, making her dolls, praying at the mosque on Fridays, shopping with her friends, and hosting her grown daughter and her husband for weekly dinners.

In the end, it was her work that forced her hand. A collector from New Delhi visited her stall at the Grand Bazaar. During that conversation, the man asked her about Turkey's ethnic minorities, and did she know anyone who made dolls in those traditions.

Were there specific Armenian dolls? She'd never given it much thought. She'd learned the Anatolian tradition of tragacanth dolls from one of her mother's sisters, who'd learned it from her grandmother.

She had a natural affinity for sewing as well as the actual work of making the dolls, but no formal education in it. Curiosity got the better of her, and she found herself at the library, looking for what she could find about the art of Armenian dolls.

She had no idea how long she worked her way through the reference stacks, surrounding herself with information. When she'd exhausted what little existed there, she turned to the Armenian section of the city. The churches yielded a little more. One priest, a transplant from Greece, remembered ritual dolls from the Ottoman village where he'd spent his youngest childhood.

On Ascension Day, he told her, the *Vichaki Arus* dolls were laid over jugs which contained seven handfuls of water from seven springs, seven petals from seven flowers, seven stones from seven running waters, and personal trinkets of girls who wanted a fortune told.

It sounded very pagan to Gül.

A clerk in another church recalled a doll commonly called Nuri, made to resemble an Armenian girl with dark hair and almond-shaped eyes. "Just like yours," he'd said kindly.

Gül found that while Rose and Victoria's stories still sent skitters of revulsion and unease down her spine, she felt an undeniable connection to the Armenians' doll-making traditions. Weeks passed while she sketched and researched and attempted to make her own *Nuri*, a doll who, among other miraculous attributes, carried prayers for rain in her tears.

While attempting to get the correct wide, almond-shaped eyes for the doll, she recalled the lines from Rose's letter. *Vicky was a beautiful woman, and you are very like her, right down to your striking eyes.*

The next afternoon, with a heavy sigh, Gül removed Rose and Victoria's letters from the drawer in her workroom and called her husband to her side.

12

The Yavuz Residence, Aleppo, Syria
December 1920

Gül learned to walk in the sweet air of the courtyard. Victoria clapped for her daughter's awkward steps, then, hearing the mistress's voice approaching, sat her down so that she might take her first steps again for Ayşe.

Victoria was careful to use Turkish words for familiar people and common objects as the baby started babbling more and was rewarded when Ayşe cried tears of joy over Gül's first word "*Anne.*" Mother.

If Victoria choreographed the moment so Sidika handed Nevart to Ayşe, while Victoria stood behind her mistress, prompting the little girl to use the Turkish word for Mama while her plump arms pedaled her toward her nurse, no one was the wiser.

Victoria took longer and more frequent shopping trips, scouring the marketplace for news, for spoken Armenian, for glimpses of the family she'd lost, for more of the elusive whispers of freedom she'd once heard.

Before long, she learned where the refugees were getting their water, at a place where the Quwayq River flowed through the northern part of the city. This would be where the news was. It would take planning to get there, though. The farthest depths of the market were as far as she'd dared go, even under Ayşe's more relaxed domestic regime.

Opportunity came in the form of illness. All three of Sidika's kitchen maids came down with a complaint of the bowels, and

Victoria, who slept separately, was sent out in the early morning to the herbalist for Myrtle leaves and berries Sidika required to make teas and juices to restore their health.

Sidika urged Victoria to procure as much as possible, in the event that they or Allah forbid it, Ayşe fell ill.

Sidika had her hands full, preparing the evening meal without help, so Victoria knew she had time. She slipped out of the house and set out for the marketplace. As swiftly as possible without drawing attention to herself, she changed course for the neighborhood she'd lived in before going to the Yavuz's. She barely remembered how to find the basement apartment without familiar landmarks, and hadn't time to spend seeking it out, but she slowed her steps as she walked, keeping an eye out for a young woman or a girl who might be one of her sisters.

It didn't take long to find the stream of women carrying jars and buckets. Victoria joined the line and walked alongside a pair of older women for a while before speaking.

Her own language tasted rusty in her mouth. She only spoke Armenian in hushed songs to her daughter. Using it now was like turning on a disused tap–the words bubbled and broke before she found the flow of it again.

"Good morning, Where's your jar?" one woman asked.

"You won't get much water in that basket!" the other teased.

The two old women laughed, and the gentle teasing brought back memories of her own sisters. Victoria smiled to shoo away the sting of tears.

"I'm looking for my *Mayrig*," she said. "Vartouhy Karadalian. She has three daughters, my sisters: Yegsabet, Mariam, and Lucine."

"I know Mariam Karadelian," the second woman said. "She comes here with the little girls in the morning to carry water."

Victoria's heart squeezed. "That's my sister."

"What's your name, child? We will tell her you came looking if we see her."

"*Shnorhagal em.* Thank you." Victoria reached out and took the first woman's hand. "My name is Victoria. Bless you both."

She didn't dare tempt fate by speaking the word rescue, not when she'd had word that her sister was alive and apparently still playing nursemaid to the smaller children. She left the pair and made her way along the line, feeling like a fisherman casting into murky depths.

When she reached the river, she found a group of young women her own age.

It would be simple, she thought, to disappear into the knot of women, to carry a water jug back into the camp or the refugee quarter, just one more displaced girl among thousands, if it weren't for her daughter or the fear that Ibrahim Yavuz might use his influence to harm her mother and sisters in retaliation.

Among the women by the water, she heard that her mother supervised the making of fine cloth, and that the Near East Relief was working with the missionaries to find husbands for marriageable girls. Someone thought maybe Yegsabet was going, another thought no, Yegsabet wouldn't leave her mother.

The news of her family soothed her worst fears, but as she returned to the bazaar, Victoria itched to see her sisters, to fall into her mother's embrace again. She wanted to be free to go to America, or France, or Greece, anywhere but Aleppo, where Ibrahim Yavuz's reach was long, his gaze wide, his word law. She wasn't fit to be anyone's wife, but she could help one of her sisters keep house and take care of *Mayrig*. She could tell people her little Nevart was an orphan she'd adopted.

She spun the fantasy out as she made her way through the market, stopping at several stalls to buy the blue-gray myrtle berries and leaves.

At the herbalist's, she bought the myrtle, and mint and ginger root to soothe the maids' bellies. Ibrahim's coins filled her basket with remedies, and she hurried back to the house. She'd been out most of the morning. Ayşe would be ready for her midday prayers, a meal, and some rest, which meant precious hours to dream away with her daughter.

***

On her next trip into the market, Victoria stuck to her errands, not daring to go to the river again, lest she be noticed. She used a few spare pennies to buy rosewater *lokum* for Ayşe and Gül. She presented the treats to her mistress with a respectful air, relishing little Gül's smile as she toddled over to take small bits of the candy from Victoria's hand.

The time after that, she found a lovely piece of fabric to make into a scarf for Ayşe. As weeks passed, she fell into the habit of acquiring small treasures to bring home, which served not only to ingratiate herself to her mistress but to cover her tracks when she stole time to venture as far as the river.

Many long weeks passed before she had more word of her mother and sisters.

She found the woman who knew her sister Mariam and greeted her warmly, trading some of the treats in her basket for stories of her sisters. They were still living in the basement apartment, and Yegsabet was writing courtship letters to a young man named Levon who lived in a place called Lawrence.

Victoria liked the shape of the very English-sounding places the women spoke of: Lawrence, Watertown, Providence, Worcester. That name surfaced again and again, like a fish rising in a river. One woman at the river said Worcester was a grand city, with thriving Armenian émigré to spare. They said the streets in America are paved in gold; another *tsk'd* audibly. The chatter ended in laughter.

The women, faces and hands wrinkled and hardened with the hard work of surviving, hefted their burdens and turned back to the careworn places they called home. It pained Victoria to return to the quiet of the house in the Old City. Her circumstances afforded her considerably more creature comforts, but loneliness and servitude were carving away at her sanity.

***

In the end, she was nearly trampled in the wake of *the women*–as the servant girl had called them, or at least that's who Victoria imagined them to be.

She'd come to the river while she was meant to be procuring lamb from the butcher when a group of women arrived by the desert road. Unlike the refugees of Aleppo, whose dress ranged from European to more traditional Armenian clothes, these women were swathed in fabric from crown to toe. Only their eyes peered out, downcast and dull, from their robes.

Victoria recognized their Bedouin dress.

While these women walked, they were accompanied by men, similarly dressed, on horseback, who retreated away from the women's work by the river but were still visible nearby.

Out of nowhere, a motor car rumbled into the gathering of women, accompanied by two figures on horseback. There was a frantic knot of motion by the water, then the car was driving away, with three of the robed women piled inside, the riders clearing the way for the car to make its escape.

The men gave chase, but they couldn't follow the riders and the car, and in the chaos, Victoria realized they'd escaped. Those women had been carried out of servitude in the desert by a woman in a scarf and goggles, driving a car.

It was the most glorious thing she'd ever seen.

In the aftermath, the water carriers scattered. No one wanted to be caught up in the stampede, or worse, by the angry men on horseback who'd lost their servants, but Victoria knew she would come back and find out who these angels were, and how to disappear like them with her mother, her sisters, and her baby.

It took her the entire walk back across the city to contain her excitement, but she was able to blandly report that the price of lamb was up, but she'd brought home dried apricots as well as figs for Sidika to serve with the meal.

That night, while Ibrahim and Ayşe entertained, Victoria whispered the name Nevart into Gül's sleeping ear, singing her plans to her daughter to the tune of the wedding song the older women would sing to brides as they walked toward their marriages. Toward the future.

In the darkness next to her daughter's cradle, Victoria began to plan.

***

It began with questions to the women at the river. *Who were the men from the desert? How did those women come to be their servants?*

Tribal men from villages and camps outside the cities, she was told, traded with the gendarmes in the desert, taking young women and girls in exchange for what goods the nomads carried. The desert girls were tattooed, marked by their keepers as wives and concubines. You couldn't always see the markings, because of their dress, but they were there.

Victoria hadn't forgotten losing Hasmik in the village near the border; she prayed her friend hadn't ended up as a tattooed concubine.

In her bravest moments, she imagined if she had a car, she would drive to that village and rescue her friend. Then she would smell Ibrahim's coffee-and-smoke scent in the courtyard, and it all came crashing down, and she would go back to asking questions.

Who were *these women on horseback, driving cars, and risking their necks for girls like that?*

This proved to be a more difficult question. No one knew exactly, and the rumors said everything from an American film star to an Armenian survivor who'd married a rich Frenchman. She could almost hear her mother scoff at that. *Where was a refugee going to find a rich French-Armenian boy? In the marketplace?*

From the women at the river, she learned of other women who passed messages in the marketplaces. *This!* This was what she had heard all those months ago, like a cipher. Those words she'd known for what they were, though she couldn't break the code.

Victoria grew restless–and reckless–often disappearing for hours at a time when Ibrahim was away from home, and she thought Ayşe wouldn't take notice. She was always present for Gül's meals and bedtime stories, but she dawdled on her errands, looking for the messengers or returning to the river in search of her family and *the women*.

What she found at first were nothing but whispers, rumors, stories, and dead ends, but the idea of becoming part of something like those rescues burned brightly in her chest–almost as brightly as the love for her daughter that fueled the fire.

***

Rumors eventually coalesced into the framework of a story.

A Danish woman, known as Miss Jeppe–another clue revealed–had arrived and established rescue homes somewhere outside the city of Aleppo. She–a woman and a European–negotiated to rent some arable land from a desert sheikh whose position offered him the authority to protect Miss Jeppe's settlements. Victoria supposed not every sheikh was interested solely in trading for servant girls, especially since she heard Miss Jeppe paid a fair rent and ran a tight ship, as it were.

Victoria's heart soared at the thought of the dashing women driving cars through the sands, and riding horses along the rivers, lifting the tattooed women and girls out of servitude and taking them somewhere safe.

As the Catholic missionaries had done for Victoria and her family when she first got to Aleppo, rumor had it these girls were also taught skills they could take with them into new safer lives. Victoria sifted through tall tales to find the bits that were consistent from story to story, all the while sowing the seeds of her own flight.

One ear at a time, Victoria let it be known that there were girls in the city, perhaps not marked by their keepers, but in need of rescuing as well. Word of mouth and whispers created a fine chain of information between the women who came for water at the river until, after months of searching, Victoria discovered a young woman not unlike herself whose rescue from servitude in a Muslim household was imminent.

After a while, Victoria was given a plumper purse with the expectation she would bring home sweets for Ayşe and Gül. While Ayşe had lost touch with the cost of things, Victoria was acutely aware of how far her purse could stretch. Instead of a water jar, Victoria's tools were the extra *kuruş* she used to buy bread and dried fruits which she traded for information with the girls and women at the river.

That day, as she knelt there distributing what she could, a young woman her own age approached, dropping to her knees in the silt and filling her jug.

"You work in the Old City." It wasn't a question.

Victoria didn't look directly at the young woman kneeling. She only shook out the crumbs and tucked the cloth away in her basket. "I do. Ibrahim Yavuz's house."

"I know that house. It won't be easy."

Victoria's pulse skipped and danced. "What do you mean?"

"The rescuers, they watch the movements of the tribal men." The girl kept her tone even. "That's how they know when to come to the river to take the tattooed girls away." She rinsed her hands in the river water and pressed them briefly to her face and neck to cool off. "It is more difficult in the city. Harder to watch the houses and the men, but it can be done. They are set to come for me three nights from now after the evening prayers."

Three nights from now. Victoria thought of the night sky over the courtyard. There would be no moon that night.

The young woman filled a second jar. "Do you know the fountain near the gates of the Christian quarter in Al-Jdayde?"

Victoria nodded mutely. The words she'd overheard months ago in the market began to coalesce.

"You must be there. They won't be able to wait."

Her hands shook. She gripped her basket harder to stop the shaking. "I'll be there."

***

When she arrived back at the Yavuz's home, the household was in chaos. Sidika met her in the courtyard.

"Where have you been?" Sidika's chest heaved with effort; her narrowed eyes took in Vicky's dusty skirts. "You've been gone a long time for a trip into the *souq*."

Victoria opened her mouth to make an excuse, but Sidika was already bustling away.

"The master took ill today. He was brought home in a litter. His manservant is with him." Sidika lowered her voice. "They are saying it was an apoplexy, but I don't know if that's true."

Victoria's step faltered. "Who is saying?"

"The men who brought him home." Sidika headed for the kitchen. "I have to make the evening meal. I need you to supervise the maids and see to tea and broth for Ibrahim *bay*."

There was no point in arguing that she had no idea how to see to tea or broth for an ailing man.

Still carrying her market basket, she trailed Sidika toward the kitchen wondering what this turn of events would mean.

Answers were few as the hours ticked by. Ayşe stayed by her husband's bedside, and once sufficient quantities of broth and tea were provided, Victoria was free to play with her daughter. When no one came for Gül at the late afternoon prayer, as was Ayşe's custom, Victoria went to the kitchen for a picnic of bread, cold lamb, and dates.

Victoria slept on a pallet by Gül's cradle, lulling herself to sleep with thoughts of freedom, whispering her little girl's Armenian name–*Nevart*–like a prayer.

***

Ibrahim Yavuz died the next day.

Victoria had witnessed death among the Muslim families in Gürin. She knew there would be a flurry of activity. The body would be washed and shrouded in preparation for burial and laid to rest as soon as possible.

There were dark hours in the months before the baby was born–and after–when she might have wished an early death upon the man, but there was no room in her heart now to care that he was gone. His life had meant nothing to her, she would not allow his death to mean more than an opportunity.

If she were very lucky, she could slip away with her daughter in the noise of the funeral rites the next day and hide until it was time to meet the unnamed girl by the fountain.

The men who came to the door were unexpected. Ayşe received them in the presence of her brother-in-law, who arrived within hours of the master's illness. There were debts, they insisted, that must be paid to them before Ibrahim's soul would rest. Paradise, they said, was denied him until his debts were clear.

Victoria loitered as close as possible. This was not good news. The more eyes on the household, the more uncertainty inside it, the less likely it was that she could leave easily. She couldn't follow the entire conversation, only enough to understand that the debts were substantial. More than the household had to give them without time to acquire it.

The men left, out of respect for the widow, but their promises to return after the funeral were anything but respectful. In their wake, Victoria overheard a hushed argument between Ayşe and Ibrahim's brother.

"I could offer you in marriage, after the four months of mourning, and the house would go to whoever marries you."

"I'll do no such thing." Ayşe's voice rose, thin with grief and exhaustion, edged with a note Victoria recognized as fear. "Just pay them and they'll go."

"Ayşe." Ibrahim's brother's voice was hard. "There is no money. Perhaps there might have been, but my brother put everything he had into bad business. These men he owed, they will take the house anyway, and everything I have. What will the family do in that case? You were his wife."

"Of course there's money. We eat, we keep this house, the

servants, clothes. What pays for that?"

"Credit." The brother's voice was unrelenting. "From these men who will take everything unless I can convince them that the widow and the house are valuable enough. As it is, it will drain my resources to pay all the smaller debts. Would you have the family cast into poverty?"

Victoria had heard enough. She and her daughter would be gone the next night. Ayşe would do what she must, but Nevart would not be part of some settlement of debt. As she turned to leave the place where she concealed herself, she heard Ayşe's acquiescence.

"As you say." The woman's voice was small now. Already turning inward in anticipation of personal sacrifice.

***

That night, Ayşe had Victoria bring Gül to her. Her grief was too much; she would keep the child by her side.

Victoria dawdled over washing and dressing her little girl, loathe to let the baby out of her sight, but there was a limit to how long she could delay leaving without arousing suspicion. Alone in her room, she inventoried her few possessions.

They would leave with the clothes on their backs, with her daughter and their spare clothes wrapped in the threadbare shawl that was her only tie to Gürin and her family. For a long time, she lay sleepless, listening to the uneasy silence around her in the house. The other servants would know by now what the situation was.

Victoria's stomach turned at the thought of the kitchen maid, a girl younger than her and poorer, with no prospects, no one to protect her, and no education like Victoria's to give her any kind of position. Acquired like property, worked, and used, discarded. Perhaps not tattooed like the girls in the desert, but no less marked by their experiences.

How could she leave another to this fate?

She would; she knew that. Her daughter was the only one who

mattered now. When she was free, she promised herself she would come back for the wretched girl and all the others like her she could find.

When she finally slept, Victoria dreamed of the desert in a disjointed jumble of images. Gendarmes and sand, Hasmik's tears. The women by the river, and the motor car's engine.

***

Victoria woke to shouting.

Ibrahim's brother was arguing with another man. There were running footsteps in the halls. Sidika burst through her door, panting.

"Get up. If you value your life, you'll go now."

Victoria sat up so fast her head spun. "What?"

"The master's creditors have come, and *Ayşe bayan* is gone. The men are furious. They are seizing everything and will occupy the house. If you don't disappear before they know you're here, you'll belong to them too."

Her stomach dropped and her gorge rose. "What are you talking about, *Ayşe bayan* is gone? Gone where?"

The woman rarely left the house, save when she accompanied her husband to be entertained by friends.

"Where is my–Where is Gül?"

A whisper of pity flitted across Sidika's face before her expression hardened. "Gone with her *mother*, you fool."

The room swam around her, Sidika crossed the room in three strides and shook her. "They haven't come for the women yet. You must go. We all must. Now."

Numb with shock, Victoria changed into one of her dresses and wrapped her shawl around her head and shoulders. On soft feet, she followed Sidika to the kitchens. The two women crept past the kitchen to the servant's entrance. Shouting and door slamming punctuated their flight, but none of it was louder than the pounding in Victoria's ears.

Her daughter was gone.

Safely outside and out of sight of the house, Sidika and Victoria paused to catch their breath.

"This is where we part," Sidika said. "Allah protect you."

The older woman ducked down a narrow street and was gone. Victoria began to shake. She had no friends. Nowhere to go. Her daughter was gone.

She started walking toward the market. At least she could melt into the crowd and chaos and gather her thoughts.

She did have somewhere to go. She could go to her family, but what good would that do? They didn't need another mouth to feed or the possibility that someone from the Yavuz household would think to look for her. They might not know she was the child's mother, but they might wonder if she knew where Ayşe had flown to.

Victoria shuddered. No, she would seek out her family when she wasn't a burden or a danger to them. She stared across the jagged chasm of grief in her heart. She would make her way to the Christian quarter of Al-Jdayde by the end of the evening prayer, and she would ride to freedom.

And when she had her freedom, she would ride to find her daughter.

13

Karen Jeppe's Rescue Home outside Aleppo, Syria
Spring 1921

Victoria slept more than a day, waking only when hunger drove her from the bed.

"You're awake, child." A soberly dressed woman with faded blond hair led her to the dining table. "Eat first, then we will sit down and write an intake entry for you in our book."

"Intake entry?" Victoria said, alarmed by the formality.

"We write down your information, dear, your name, family, where you come from, and how you came to us. If anyone should look for you, we will help them to find you using the entries. We'll take your photograph as well."

The scent of food made her stomach rumble.

The blond woman smiled in a way that reminded Victoria of her mother and cocked her head like a curious bird. "I am Marta. What is your name, child?"

"Victoria," she said. "Victoria Karadelian."

"Oh!" Marta's smile widened. "Your sister came here looking for you. Not more than three weeks ago. I remember thinking how lovely it was that you were named for a great queen."

Victoria felt a shiver of tentative joy along her arms. Marta showed her to the food and introduced her to some of the girls who were helping in the kitchen. Victoria recognized the young woman from the river who introduced herself as Astrig.

When she finished her meal, she went with Marta to tell her story. Victoria gave her information–her mother, sisters, and father's name and where they'd come from, but grew wary when she was asked if she had children.

"Did you leave a child behind in the Muslim household?" Marta's voice was gentle, and her hand over Victoria's was kind. "It's more common than we imagined."

Victoria nodded, eyes stinging. "She was raised as the master's daughter by his wife, but she is mine."

"We never know God's plan. Should she ever come here looking for information, we can tell her who her mother is," Marta said. "Let me put her name down here."

Victoria's days at the rescue home were no less exhausting than they had been working for the Yavuz's. Here at least, her work had a purpose that left her far more content.

Miss Jeppe was an extraordinary woman, with a warrior's heart and a merchant's soul. Victoria studied their leader intently as she worked closely with outsiders to secure funding for the rescue home, boldly negotiated with a Sheikh, and insisted not only that they all contribute to the running of the home, but that they all learn a trade or skill they could use to support themselves.

When it came to meals, cooking had never been her strong suit, so she helped with washing and cleaning, welcoming the sting of her cracked skin in the hot dishwater after they all shared a meal. The work was hard, but this community fed more than bellies.

She could, of course, sew, and immediately volunteered to mend and alter clothing for the young women in the home.

When it became clear Victoria had a gift for needlework, Miss Jeppe suggested she study every type of fine needlework the women in the rescue home could teach her.

For hours every day, as long as there was light to stitch by, Victoria learned not only how to make the stitches, but how to teach them when the women who held the skills moved on. She learned a little *Aintab kordz* and perfected the needlelace she'd learned as a girl and helped to teach the weaving methods she'd grown up surrounded by.

The pride Victoria felt when her teachers complimented her work was a balm on her battered soul. Their rescuer had high standards. Miss Jeppe wanted them to be able to fetch high prices and critical acclaim for their work; she felt that was the way Armenian women would restore their place in the world and rebuild their culture in the storm of relocation.

Despite her growing contentment and pride in her work, Victoria was restless. In addition to learning their trades and skills, some of the volunteers and residents helped to locate and liberate more Armenian girls and women throughout the region surrounding Aleppo.

These were the women driving cars and riding horses through the desert. This was the work Victoria longed to do, but she was not permitted to take part right away.

"You're newly come, child," Marta said. "It is dangerous work, and you have valuable skills to pass on here. We would rather reunite you with your family, and see you suitably employed. Perhaps even married."

Victoria tried to hide her dismay. Marriage would never be an option. She was soiled. No longer a virgin, mother to a bastard child. No decent Armenian man would have her when there were so many unspoiled young women in need of security. But she was desperate to reunite with her mother and sisters.

Miss Jeppe and her staff worked closely with aid societies and missionaries to reunite as many residents as possible with the families they'd lost, or what remained of them. Marriages were frequently arranged with Armenian men in America and elsewhere who had the means to support a bride and bring her out of Syria and Turkey.

"I have no wish to be married when there's so much work to do," she said to Marta.

"Not now, perhaps," Marta said, eyes twinkling, "but there will come a time when you want those things. Let's find your mother and sisters, shall we?"

A few weeks later, Marta escorted her through the city to the basement apartment where her mother and sisters still lived.

"Your sister told us there had been word of you in the bazaar and by the river," Marta explained as they walked. "If I remember correctly, she said she was to be married soon. The missionaries had found a husband for her in America, and the courtship letters had been written. All that remained was to arrange passage."

A sister in America…Yegsabet had always been pretty and charming, less intense than Victoria, who'd spoken her mind more than *Mayrig* would have liked. The march through the desert had only temporarily quelled her sister's vivacious nature; Victoria couldn't imagine Yegsabet was much changed. She would make a good wife, if a feisty one.

Victoria both hoped and feared that her sister would still be in Aleppo. On the one hand, memories of her family helped her survive the years she had spent with the Yavuz's, so to see her mother and all of her sisters again would be a blessing and a balm on her raw and broken heart, which still wept for her lost daughter.

On the other hand, Yegsabet's new life was waiting across the ocean, and who was she to wish for it to be delayed?

It was a shabby street, but not a sad one. It warmed Victoria's heart to see lights in windows, to hear the women haggling and gossiping, but when they came to the basement apartment, she knocked on the door with nervous hands, suddenly unsure of her welcome.

Would her mother sense her ruin? Would she turn away a soiled daughter to avoid contaminating the younger girl?

She was suddenly glad Yegsabet was going to America to be married. Eventually, her sister would be able to bring *Mayrig* to live there in safety and comfort. Their mother would have a good daughter to care for her.

Her worries were for nothing. The door cracked open, and *Mayrig's* eyes widened in shock. A huge smile spread across her face.

Her mother's embrace was softer than Victoria remembered. She'd put on some weight while Victoria was away, but her face was deeply lined, creases bracketing her mouth, and a web of fine lines surrounded her eyes. Her hair, once thick, dark, and lustrous, was thinner and streaked with ivory.

Her mother had gotten old.

Victoria supposed she must look different as well. There was neither time nor space for vanity at the rescue home. She'd had no looking glass at the Yavuz's house, only her reflection when the water in the fountain was still, or a watery image of herself when she passed a window. Did her body betray her secret?

"Girls, come!" *Mayrig* took her hands and squeezed hard. "It's your sister. It's Victoria."

Yegsabet was the first across the room, wrapping Victoria in a warm hug. Mariam followed, with Lucine boosted on her hip.

Their mother bustled Victoria and Marta inside the apartment; Yegsabet couldn't contain herself.

"When I found out about the rescue home, I went to see if you were there. Someone at the market said you'd been there, and our neighbor heard about someone called Victoria while she was washing clothes at the river, but none of the women knew what happened to you, I thought perhaps we would never see you again."

Mayrig smoothed Victoria's hair, touched her cheek, and held her hand while Yegsabet talked about her impending wedding.

"I'm traveling with some missionaries to Constantinople in a week's time to meet my husband, Levon."

"Then I arrived just in time to see you before you go," Victoria said. "How was it arranged?"

"The churches in America and the missionaries here," Yegsabet said. She grinned. "They call us picture brides."

Victoria couldn't help smiling back. Her sister's happiness was infectious.

"Will you go as a picture bride, too, Victoria?" Mariam asked quietly. Lucine, tiny for her almost ten years, clung to her older sister like a monkey. Her eyes were wide, and she clutched a dolly to her side.

"Probably not. Not now, anyway." The words were stilted, but Mariam didn't seem bothered. Victoria touched her sister's dark hair, overwhelmed with joy at the reunion.

The only thing missing was her daughter.

To hide the sharp stab of grief, Victoria reached for her baby sister. "Do you remember me, Lucine?"

The smallest Karadelian sister shook her head and snuggled closer to Mariam.

"I'm Victoria. Your biggest sister." Victoria reached out to pat Lucine's dolly's head. "Is she called *Nuri*?"

A shy smile appeared on Lucine's face, and the little girl nodded.

"Yegsabet and I had dollies called *Nuri* once," Victoria said. "Someday maybe we will tell you about their adventures." Victoria gave Yegsabet a sideways glance; Yegsabet smiled back.

Yegsabet would keep that secret for her, she knew, but Nevart's light stayed dammed up behind the shame of her conception. A soiled sister tarnished all the girls. Even if she could find the words to tell Yegsabet about her daughter, there was nothing to be gained by it, and so very much to lose.

Her mother made coffee, after which Marta excused herself. "I have an errand to do for Miss Jeppe. Misak will come for you with the car, Victoria. It's too far to walk back alone."

"The car?" Yegsabet teased. "Aren't you the fine lady?"

Victoria snorted and dropped into a mock curtsy. Her sisters had no way of knowing Misak was Miss Jeppe's adopted son, and a crucial part of the Rescue Home, not a chauffeur.

After Marta's departure, Victoria's mother and sisters were less guarded. She was overwhelmed by questions about her time with the Yavuz's, many of which she glossed over or avoided answering outright. There was no sense in terrifying or saddening her sisters further. They had all been through so much. Instead, Victoria focused on how she escaped.

She told them of her trips to the river. She told them of Ibrahim Yavuz's death and how she slipped out during the chaos and squeezed her hands until her knuckles went white when she thought of Ayşe's flight.

"What about all of you?" Victoria asked. "You are all well?"

"We are alive," said her mother, reaching for her hands again, and squeezing them tight. "And for a little while at least, we are together."

"I want to hear more about the American Yegsabet is marrying," Victoria said. "What do his letters tell you?"

There were two letters, both short and to the point, but not unpleasant. Yegsabet's Levon lived in a place called Lawrence. Silently, Vicky tried the long word *Massachusetts* out on her tongue, but without a reference, she was certain it sounded wrong.

"He works in a textile factory, and shares his home with two other men who also work there."

Victoria wondered at that. '*Shares his home*' sounded lovely and familiar; multi-generational families all living together were commonplace, but the missionaries warned that American cities were very different from Aleppo. Vicky had heard some of Miss Jeppe's volunteers say that new brides should expect to work hard, that American life meant safety and the preservation of their culture, but it would not feel at all like the homes they had known. Not all streets in America were paved in gold.

It was a good bargain, no matter how you looked at it, but she didn't want her sister's expectations to exceed reality.

"They won't know what hit them," Victoria said, giving her sister a sly look. Like Victoria, Yegsabet wasn't the strongest homemaker of them–that, it turned out, was Mariam, who was great with children, and a wonderful cook–but what she lacked in domestic skills, she made up for in a strong personality. There was no need to worry about her sister's ability to take care of herself.

The afternoon passed too quickly.

When it was time to go, Victoria leaned over to kiss her littlest sister on the cheek. "I'll see you again soon, *buzdig koorigus,* little sister. Maybe we can play with *Nuri* together?"

Lucine nodded with a little smile. When she spoke, it surprised everyone; she had been nearly silent all afternoon.

"You can sing the snake song," Lucine said.

Victoria glanced at Yegsabet and Mariam, astonished that Lucine remembered. Yegsabet was grinning; Mariam nodded.

"You remember the snake song, Lucine?"

Lucine nodded, but it was Mariam who answered. "We tell her stories about you, so she doesn't forget. She likes the snakes…now." Mariam shrugged. "We see them so often, she's not afraid anymore, but she likes to hear how she was so scared until her big sister sang to the snake."

Victoria whispered in Mariam's ear. "I hope you don't tell her how you wanted to smash the snake with a pan at the end of the song."

"No." Mariam laughed softly. "Now we just invite the snakes for coffee. They're our neighbors."

"Will you come to stay with us?" *Mayrig* asked. "Now that you found us?"

Victoria looked around the small apartment. She had already made up her mind not to be a burden to her mother and sisters. "No, *Mayrig*. I'll stay at the rescue home. There's work for me to do there. Important work. Helping other girls build new lives like Yegsabet is."

"But you will come and see us, I hope? Maybe for church on Sunday?" *Mayrig*'s eyes sparkled with hope and unshed tears.

Victoria hugged her mother hard. "Of course, I'll come this Sunday."

She understood the unspoken reason for the invitation. It might be the last time she saw her sister Yegsabet.

Victoria spent the walk to the rescue home reliving every precious moment with her mother and sisters. Their old life might be gone, and the future uncertain, but there was much to be thankful for.

14

Aleppo, Syria
1921

It was a month after her sister left for Constantinople in the care of the missionaries, to meet her prospective husband, that Victoria first sat down with Miss Jeppe. It was an honor not all the girls received. Victoria found herself straightening her clothes and smoothing her hair on her way to Miss Jeppe's office.

The older woman did not cut a dashing figure. She did, however, have a steady, compassionate energy. Karen Jeppe radiated conviction and determination.

"Marta tells me your needlelace is very lovely, and you're a good teacher."

"Thank you, Miss Jeppe," Victoria said.

"It's important to me that my girls leave here with dignity, knowing their value and confident in their abilities."

Victoria nodded.

"It's not enough to churn out girls who can work a loom or stitch a hem, you see. Your people, your culture, they must be preserved even as you scatter into the world. We send girls back to their families when we can. We find them marriages, but most of all we give them the gift of self-sufficiency."

"It's a great gift," Vicky said. "It's a terrible thing to feel powerless."

Miss Jeppe dipped her chin in acknowledgment.

"Authenticity and quality," Miss Jeppe continued. "These make your products desirable, they command the best prices in the market.

Fine lace and beautiful weavings bring your beautiful history to the eyes of the world and ensure your people aren't forgotten."

Victoria nodded again, unsure why she was singled out for this conversation. It was a speech Miss Jeppe and her volunteers made often.

"Marta tells me you want to help us with our work."

"Yes, I do." Victoria's pulse skipped. *This was why.*

"Marta also tells me you have family here in Aleppo, and yet you wish to remain at the reception house."

"That is also true. My mother and two of my sisters are here in Aleppo. They have work and school, and a safe place to live. I do not wish to be a burden on them, and I feel called to do what I can for others like me. I wish to stay here with you." Once her wish had been voiced aloud, her thoughts tumbled out in a rush. "I'm not brawny, but I'm strong enough. I can ride, I will learn to drive, I know my way around the bazaar. I know where the women go for water and washing. They know me at the river. I can help."

"Marta has also told me all of this." The older woman's smile was placid, but there was an energetic twinkle in her eyes that Victoria appreciated.

Miss Jeppe folded her hands on the worn desk behind which she sat. "You have much to learn, dear, but we will teach you. After the meal, I want you to find Misak. He will begin teaching you to drive. At first, you may find this work less exciting than you were expecting. If you are patient and willing to learn, I suspect you will be a great help to us."

Beyond Miss Jeppe's small office, the girls were assembling for the midday meal. The scent of cooking reached her, and Victoria's stomach rumbled.

"Go and eat, child. We will see each other again."

Miss Jeppe was correct. While thrilling in a way, the driving lessons were also frustrating. Misak was a good teacher, but Victoria was cowed at first by the noisy engine and the great rumbling vehicle beneath her.

A joy she had not considered was the horses. She and Yegsabet each had docile ponies back in Gürin. In addition to proper riding lessons, where they learned to ride side-saddle, both girls had often ridden astride, taking the ponies through the rocky foothills outside the village.

Then, of course, the girls were accompanied by a trusted groom. With a shock, Victoria realized their groom had probably been dead for years. Another young man's life stolen by violence.

Victoria took great pleasure in caring for the horses and tack. She enjoyed the company of the other young women who cared for the horses and other animals that helped to keep the girls fed.

While it was worlds away from the home she'd left–worlds away from her childhood home–the routines at the reception house were familiar and homey. As the weeks stretched into months, Victoria realized this was not an accident. The shared work of caring for one another and maintaining the household gave the residents back some measure of the peace and normalcy they had lost after losing their homes, families, and freedoms.

In addition to driving lessons and helping with the horses, Victoria studied maps of Aleppo, especially the roads, rail lines, and riverbeds which surrounded the city. She memorized the locations of other safe places: churches, known friends of their cause, and other aid societies who would help.

Life in the rescue home wasn't all work. Sundays were for church and, for Victoria, family; she spent many of them with her mother and sisters. They would attend services with the Armenian community in Aleppo, and then either go back to the basement apartment or join other families to share food, laughter, and songs.

Those Sundays were bittersweet for Victoria. Since Yegsabet left, both *Mayrig* and Mariam seemed a little withdrawn. Victoria realized her spirited sister had played an important role in their small household.

Victoria understood as well as anyone how important keeping up morale was.

Though it wasn't something anyone at the rescue home spoke of, Victoria learned not to form close attachments there. The goal of the home was, after all, to rescue women from servitude and help them to establish productive, independent lives.

Eventually, Victoria mastered the car. She had, in the months while she was learning to drive and learning the rescue plans, regained her confidence on horseback. Her deeper understanding of the geography surrounding Aleppo gave her a burst of pride each time she successfully navigated a new part of the city or its surroundings.

Marta was the one to tell Victoria she would be joining her first rescue mission.

Her hands were shaking when she joined the small team in Miss Jeppe's office. Misak waited behind Miss Jeppe's desk. The others were a priest from the Church and an American doctor who often visited the home to examine the rescued girls and treat the occasional illness or injury. It was known that Miss Jeppe trusted all three men completely.

Victoria's nerves were all for herself. She was determined not to let them down.

Miss Jeppe often negotiated with the tribes who lived in the desert surrounding Aleppo, offering payment in exchange for young women they had acquired. Miss Jeppe asked no questions about how the women came to be with the tribe and only offered what was fair to get them out. That way, she said, she became, if not an ally to the tribes, at least not an enemy, and her movements through the desert were less restricted because of her connections.

Their mission was to travel to a tribal leader with whom Miss Jeppe had communicated. Misak would drive to the meeting place. The doctor and the priest would accompany Misak to the meeting, while Victoria stayed with the car. She would have to be prepared to get away quickly if things went wrong.

If everything went according to plan, she would simply drive them all back to the rescue home together. Even so simple a plan required they talk it through as a group, understand any potential pitfalls, and be as prepared as possible for any surprises.

Their party made their way out of the city limits, navigating what Victoria was told was a road, though, to her untrained eye, it felt as though they were simply wandering into the desert. She made mental notes as they drove, creating a map of landmarks she could use to avoid becoming lost.

She was glad to be swathed in loose robes and a headscarf. The sun overhead was relentless, and the vastness of the desert unnerved her. The terrain around Aleppo was heartbreakingly familiar, seared into her memory, though it had been five years since she and her mother and sisters had walked into the city underneath the same unrelenting sky.

Five years before, she'd huddled under this sky in rags, starving and terrified. She shuddered and turned her thoughts to the young women they were rescuing.

Had anyone told them they would be exchanged for food, supplies, or whatever it was Miss Jeppe had negotiated for their release? She had seen girls like them when she visited the river. They were often afraid to look up from the work of gathering water even to speak to the other women. Punishments could be swift and severe if the men watching them suspected they were plotting or getting overly familiar with the free women at the river.

Despite this, Victoria was told, some of these girls might resist the exchange and rescue efforts. They would choose captivity because it was predictable. The unknown, after all they'd been through, was simply too much to contemplate.

Victoria understood that all too well. She gave thanks every day she'd had the strength to run when Sidika gave her the chance.

Though she did not ever speak of her lost daughter, Victoria prayed for her every evening. In her dreams, she watched her little girl grow up, grow tall and strong, clever and kind. Often while she worked, she would sing under her breath the old songs she'd sung to her daughter. She imagined the music flying out across the miles to reach her daughter's ears, wherever she was.

While she waited in the car for Misak and the others to return, her thoughts wandered to Nevart.

Though Victoria had memorized Ayşe's family's address after seeing it so often, Constantinople might have been the moon for all that she knew how to get there. Her fantasy self would drive into the Turkish capital, right up to Ayşe's door, and demand her daughter be returned. They would see her determination and give Nevart up to her, and her little girl would remember her right away.

The call of a desert lark popped the bubble of her reverie. Misak's signal of a successful mission. They would be back at the car in moments, and it was time to return to Aleppo.

After that, Victoria joined at least a mission a week. She learned to relish the heat of the dry desert air, and the car engine's roar underneath her. The first time she fled pursuers on one of the ponies, she tumbled off the horse's back in the yard of the rescue home and vomited in the dust.

Marta brought her water and helped her into a bath. "I'd never have the stomach for it," she said.

Victoria was determined to find the stomach for it and rode out again the very next week.

Still, sometimes, she would wake in the darkest hours of the night, her heart pounding with rage and fear. She would wait, wakeful and breathing, until the worst of the fear passed, and she could examine the anger which remained.

Sometimes the anger was directed at the Turkish soldiers who stole her life from her. Sometimes the anger was for the woman who'd taken her best friend under the desert sky. Sometimes it was for Ibrahim Yavuz, who'd violated her body and kept her powerless for years. Sometimes it was for Ayşe, who'd stolen her daughter.

Always she lay still in her bed examining her anger like stones in her pocket, polishing them smooth so she could carry them with her without doing herself any further harm. Those polished stones grounded her when she felt hopeless or overwhelmed.

Often, Victoria wondered if, like her, any of the rescued women were forced to leave a child behind. She made a note to speak to Marta when they returned to the reception house. Here was another way she might help. If she knew that a woman had lost– or been forced to leave behind–a child, she might at least offer some comfort.

As she rode alongside the car one night, as they made their way back through Aleppo to the rescue house, Victoria wondered if, behind the robes and scarves, these girls might have some connection to the world she lost. The long, terrible walk from Gürin to Aleppo had no room for idle chatter, but Victoria had come to know other families from other villages as they went. Their names were lost but she might still know their faces if she saw them.

She thought of Hasmik and said a prayer for her friend.

From time to time, a girl would arrive at the reception house whose situation was similar to Hasmik's.

Despite the likelihood that she would ever see her friend again, Victoria refused to give up hope. The woman who took Hasmik to the village so many years ago might have been good to her as they promised. Victoria couldn't bring herself to believe that every Muslim Turk had approved of the death marches.

More often than not, however, Victoria knew endings like that were few and far between.

There was always a flurry of activity at the rescue home after one of these desert negotiations. In preparation for the new arrivals, extra food was made, and places to sleep secured. To spare the newcomers unwanted attention until they were ready, Victoria was tasked with shepherding the residents away from Marta's efforts to welcome the newly rescued.

There would be time enough the next day for introductions.

When things quieted down, she went to find Marta alone.

"Marta," Victoria interrupted softly, not wanting to frighten the newcomers. "May I sit with you when you do the intake interviews with these girls?"

"Of course, you may," Marta said. "If you like, you may take notes, while I speak with the girls. I shall introduce you to them as an example of what they may expect here." Marta smiled. "I think it would be good for them to see someone like themselves, rebuilding her life."

Was that what she was doing? Victoria rarely thought of it that way. She was simply doing what she knew must be done. Some paths were closed to her now, and until her mother and sisters were safely in America with Yegsabet, she wanted to stay in Aleppo.

After that, she had an appointment in Constantinople.

"Thank you, Marta."

There were three girls to interview.

The first, they judged to be approximately fourteen years old. One girl had no recollection of her birthdate or her family name at first.

She seemed reluctant to speak about the circumstances of how she came to be with the tribe.

It was only when Marta asked if she had any sisters or brothers, that the girl began to cry.

She had been the only girl, she remembered. Her mother had died when she was small, and her father remarried shortly thereafter. The girl's story poured out of her, borne on hard, angry tears. Her older brother was shot in front of her before she and her stepmother were forced out of their home with nothing but the clothes on their backs.

The girl had no idea how long they walked, only that one evening, while they huddled together for warmth, the gendarmes swooped through the small group taking what girls her age remained and handing them over to robed men on horseback who slung them on the backs of their horses and rode off into the night.

Her captors had given her a new name and married her to the man whose horse she rode into their encampment. She was the youngest of wives, she'd whispered, and not treated *as a wife* until her courses came.

She had lived with the tribe for five years and came to look upon the other wives as sisters. She had no other family; survival had depended upon forgetting her old life.

Victoria took notes diligently, but her thoughts raced. Many young women had come through the reception house since she arrived, but she had not heard firsthand accounts of many of their stories, not like this. It dawned on her that despite the hardships, despite the pain and brutality she'd endured, she was fortunate in so many ways. She had not lost her mother and sisters, not in the end. And they would survive together.

The other two girls bore tattooed markings over their faces, necks, and shoulders.

Victoria had heard the stories at the river of the tattooed women, even seen some of them from afar, but facing these girls and hearing their stories once again reminded her that so many were worse off than she had ever been. These women would, for the rest of their lives, bear the scars of their experiences for all to see. It was a cruel thought, but she knew these girls would be harder to find husbands for. The men who wrote for picture brides wanted good Armenian wives–pretty, respectable young women who would give them children and keep their homes, women who knew their traditions. Young women whose reflections in the mirror weren't a constant reminder that they were damaged goods.

The rescues weren't always the heroic endeavors Victoria had imagined them to be. Often, in addition to the negotiations, they simply went out into the marketplace or down to the river and did what they could to convince women in involuntary positions of servitude to walk away from their lives.

Specifically, because of her own history, Victoria was often chosen for this work. There were so many others, like her, whose children now resided in the household in which they worked. Some had been so young when they were placed in those households that servitude was the only safe place they could imagine. The world beyond was uncertain and frightening.

She tried hard not to imagine her daughter, lost to her so young, being frightened of rescue like those girls. Surely her Nevart would know her? Want to be with her?

With her mother and sisters safely away, she and her daughter would build a new life, if not in Aleppo, then in Beirut, or somewhere in France.

Anywhere, so long as they were together.

15

Aleppo, Syria
1921-1922

The rescues weren't always successful. After a time, the nomads stopped allowing the women to go without a guard. Some women would simply disappear from the market or stop coming to the river altogether. On one occasion when Victoria was driving the car, gendarmes were called and a young woman they were trying to rescue was shot.

Victoria didn't sleep that entire night, shaking and sick. There was nothing she could have done; they had followed the protocols of the rescue to the letter. The plan simply failed. And yet, the crack of the rifle, the red bloom of death through the girl's clothing, had left Victoria paralyzed with fear, unable to react. It was only by the grace of the other volunteers, mainly European women who hadn't been through the desert on the death march, that Victoria herself escaped.

For every failure, however, they succeeded in greater numbers. Most women stayed no longer than half a year at the rescue home. Through an ever-growing web of connection, the volunteers and missionaries were able to successfully place the rescue girls with families, or find them marriages.

Her work gave her strength. Her strength protected her from her grief and the shame she carried like a water jug. As time passed, she grew confident in her skills. The volunteers wove a community from their shattered residents, and in that community, Victoria knew moments of genuine contentment.

Her longing for Nevart, never far from the surface, sometimes receded long enough for entire days to pass without the shadow of terror and misery.

She had been at the rescue home for almost eighteen months when Marta once again brought her to Miss Jeppe's office.

"Hello again, Victoria," Miss Jeppe said.

While everyone saw their seemingly indestructible matriarch daily, few of them actually spent time with Miss Jeppe. She spent much of her time corresponding, asking for funds, and working with other similar groups to increase the reach of their efforts.

"Marta tells me you've been with us almost a year and a half. That's a very long time here. She also tells me your help has been invaluable these last months. We are all grateful for every moment of your time, but I think it's time for you to go."

Victoria started to object but Miss Jeppe hushed her with a look.

"This is not a punishment, my child. You are young. You have your whole life ahead of you, and our goal is always to give back as much of the lives that were stolen from our girls as possible. A Near East Relief volunteer brought a letter today from your sister in America. She writes by way of an introduction to a friend of her good husband. This man is looking for a wife, and your sister thinks you would suit. You would travel with a group of the other girls and take a ship from Constantinople in a month's time. I have a letter here from Mr. Reupen Parnagian in addition to the letter from your sister." Miss Jeppe smiled. "I strongly urge you to take this chance, Victoria."

Victoria was still reeling when she took her leave five minutes later. Marta was the first person she saw.

"Will you go?" Marta asked.

Victoria burst into tears. She'd always known her time at the rescue was temporary, but the idea of leaving terrified and saddened her. For all her pride, she was no stronger than the maids in the bazaar, afraid to break away from the safety she knew.

Marta embraced her and kissed both her cheeks.

"We will all miss you, but you deserve a chance to be happy." Marta patted her cheek. "Go read your letters. We will pray for you."

Victoria took the letters outside to read. The other girls would have questions, but the goats and chickens didn't offer more opinions than the occasional cluck or bleat while they foraged in the dusty yard.

Ruepen Parnagian was a doctor in the fabled city of Worcester, Massachusetts. So much aid–and so many husbands–had come from Worcester that it almost symbolized America for many of them in Aleppo. Mr. Parnagian wrote that he had a small house and gave money to the church, as well as several prominent charities. He would send a friend to escort her and another picture bride to Boston, where he would meet her, and they would travel second class as a sign of his regard for her.

Victoria wondered how far that regard would stretch on their wedding nights when he discovered his bride was not what he'd paid for.

The letter from Yegsabet was short and to the point. Married life was different, but she was busy and useful to Levon. Mr. Parnagian was some kind of cousin to Levon, and Victoria was a fool if she turned down the chance to be a rich doctor's wife. Yegsabet asked after *Mayrig* and the girls and told Victoria that she and Levon had plans to buy a home of their own, perhaps several years from now, and *Mayrig* would have a place there.

On her next visit to the basement apartment, Victoria showed the letter from Mr. Parnagian to her mother.

"Of course, you should go. Worcester is an important place. I hear so much about the Armenians there, and it's also in..." Vartouhy stumbled over *Massachusetts*. "It might be near your sister, yes?"

"But what about you and Mariam and Lucine?"

"Mariam wants to find a husband, too, but I think not quite yet. She's still young, and Lucine is still in school. We will be fine here now that the war is over. When it's time, we will come to America as well."

"But, *Mayrig*–" Victoria felt doors closing around her. She didn't dare say why she wanted to stay in Syria. Not the true reason and Yegsabet had gone to the trouble of arranging everything. Her heart longed for her sister.

Mayrig was certain she should take the offer. Marta thought she should go. Yegsabet would call her a fool for her uncertainty. Miss Jeppe herself thought she should go, but what of her work here at the rescue home? What of all the women she might help to save?

What of her beloved daughter?

Even from her ever-growing network of rescuers, aid workers, and volunteers, she'd heard nothing from Constantinople, nothing of Ayşe Yavuz's flight from Aleppo. It was as if they'd vanished into thin air. With all her new skills and resources, she still had no means to travel into the Turkish capital, and no real plan to take back her precious girl.

The weight of it threatened to crush her shoulders. Perhaps she was not so strong after all.

16

The S.S. Braga, North Atlantic Ocean
March and April 1922

Three days out from Marseilles, Victoria was finally able to keep down a little water and stale bread. She'd survived starvation, a forced march through the desert, rape, childbirth, and perilous rescue work, but the ocean was too much. The roll of the ship on the waves twisted her insides up, leaving her dizzy, breathless, and too nauseated to eat.

By the fifth day, she had her feet under her again, even if the wide expanse of rolling ocean still took her breath away.

It had happened when they left Constantinople as well, but she'd thought once it was finished, there would be no more illness.

Kachadoor Minassian was a solicitous young man, serious and tidy, with intelligent eyes and a quick smile. She thought he might be as many as ten years older than she was, but he'd said very little about himself during the passage across the Mediterranean to southern France.

Victoria knew he was preoccupied with the fate of another picture bride he was meant to be escorting to America. The girl hadn't arrived, and no one knew what became of the missionaries she'd been traveling with. Mr. Minassian delayed their departure as long as he could, but it was dangerous for them to linger.

More dangerous than he would ever know. Victoria almost bolted twice after seeing dark-haired little girls on the sidewalks.

His longest speech during that first ten days was to apologize for only having a single stateroom for them to share. He'd blushed scarlet at the indecency of it, but he'd been pickpocketed in

Constantinople searching for the lost bride and only had enough remaining funds for the one room.

It had taken them a few days to work out how to share the space and maintain decorum once her illness passed, but Kachadoor had come up with a solution that preserved both her dignity and his honor. He obtained a spare bed sheet from a steward and created a dividing wall between the two berths, bisecting the small space.

Her mother, if she still lived, would shudder to see it. Yegsabet would have insisted on a wedding at sea, regardless of the promise Victoria made to Reupen Parnagian. Victoria, accustomed to sharing sleeping space, and having survived worse indignities, bore the situation without complaint.

Kachadoor–she couldn't think of him as Mr. Minassian when she'd stolen a peek through the curtain at him in his shirtsleeves washing before bed–would stand guard outside while she changed and washed and climbed into her berth with the bedsheet curtain drawn, then he would have his turn.

He was tall and broad-shouldered with thick dark hair, dwarfing Victoria, but she never felt threatened by his size. There was nothing threatening about him. Even when she was irritable and difficult from the seasickness, he never lost his temper or treated her with anything but politeness and care.

While on the Mediterranean Sea, he'd told her he worked at a bakery, making sweets and candy. He liked the work, he said. It was better than a factory job.

Victoria wondered if he was already engaged to be married. He hadn't collected a picture bride of his own, but he neither wore a ring nor did he speak of anyone at home.

Now she was sick again, and each morning, he'd bring her tea and toasted bread from the dining room. He was too gentle–too handsome, though she blushed to think it–to be wasted as a bachelor.

By the time she was ready to walk on the promenade deck again, the great ship was far from any land, and the air was fresh with salt, and cool on her face.

"You need to eat more," Kachadoor said, glancing at her as they stood at the railing. "I'm afraid you'll blow overboard."

Victoria grinned. "Then what will you say? 'Reupen, I hope you like mermaids?'"

He shook his head sadly. "I have already failed Peter. I'd never live it down if I lost both girls."

"Peter?" The name felt foreign on her tongue but familiar in her memory.

"My friend Bedros, whose bride I lost. In America, he's called Peter."

Victoria refused to accept Kachadoor's version of events. He hadn't lost the other bride. Young women went missing. Terrible things happened. It wasn't something he could control.

Her heart broke again at the thought of the missing picture bride. Kachadoor called her Hasmik, and the name lit a hopeful flame in Victoria's chest when she heard it. A flame extinguished on the road to Constantinople, like the hope of finding her daughter again.

She hid her pain in a poor attempt at humor. "Maybe he'll think you stole me away to keep for yourself?"

Kachadoor looked sharply at her, and she bit her lip. It had been a joke, but her chest felt suddenly as though it were filled with too much air, her ribs stretched too far around all that lightness.

She wished she would blow overboard right then and there.

Kachadoor backed away abruptly. "I'll go see if I can find something else for you to eat."

Shame heated Victoria's cheeks. She squeezed the railing, willing her heart to slow. She wished he was still there; his absence left her prey to her own swirling thoughts.

In America, he's called Peter. In her letters, she remembered Yegsabet had called Kachadoor's friend Mr. Poladian.

As clear as day, Victoria saw the young woman she'd met on the street the first day in Hamidieh Camp.

Eva Poladian.

I have a brother called Peter, in America. Peter will find a way to help us.

Had Peter Poladian gotten his family out of Syria? She didn't find Kachadoor to ask until much later when hunger and loneliness drove her in the direction of the dining saloon.

Where he'd been since he left her, she wasn't sure. He'd mentioned food, but that was hours before. The ship wasn't new, but it was sturdy. It wasn't so large a man could vanish, but there were decks to walk on and places a man might hide if he preferred solitude.

The men sometimes gathered in the lower decks for cards and games away from their women and families. There were many Armenians on the ship, some in second class like them, but far more in steerage, and families from all over, crowded into the lower levels of the ship. If he'd wanted to avoid her, that's where Kachadoor had likely gone.

He was waiting for her outside the dining room, his expression somber.

"I'm sorry," she said as they made their way into the saloon. "I spoke out of turn before. I've been living amongst women for too long. I've forgotten how to be proper."

She thought she saw the corner of his mouth twitch like a smile. "It's nothing. Your barb found its mark. I'm embarrassed by my failure to bring home Peter's bride."

"My sister called him Mr. Poladian. Is that his name?" Victoria asked.

"It is. He lives in Lawrence, where your sister lives, with a house full of women relatives, including a very modern sister who works in the belt factory. Peter is afraid all those women will frighten off his new wife. How do I tell him she was too frightened to even get on the ship?"

Kachadoor's assumption trumped the news that Eva Poladian had actually escaped Aleppo and made it to her brother in America.

"Is that what you think?" Victoria narrowed her eyes at him. "That she was afraid?"

"I don't know. Maybe?" He didn't sound angry, only curious.

Victoria sighed. "Before I agreed to marry, I worked helping other Armenian women get out of bad situations. I organized safe houses and carts out of the city to smuggle out girls who were kept no better than slaves. These girls survived horrors. Safety, even in the hands of a strange man in a strange country, matters more than fear. It was time for me to leave Aleppo, but Constantinople was just as dangerous for women like us. If she could have, she'd have been there."

This was the longest speech she'd made to Kachadoor. He looked taken aback, but there was no way to stop the words now, uncorked as they were.

"More likely, something happened to her or the missionaries she was traveling with. She wouldn't have anyone to protect her from abduction, rape, or death." Victoria was breathing hard. Sweating under her hair. "She was trying to escape exactly those things."

Her hand rested, looped over his arm while they walked, as a courtesy. It was the only time he ever touched her. He was a respectful man that way. Now, he laid his hand over hers where she was clutching the wool of his suit.

"I'm sorry. I was thoughtless. I came to America for a better life and to escape persecution." He took a deep breath to gather himself.

Victoria's mouth watered at the scent of food. Kachadoor pulled out her chair for her. When she didn't sit, or even reply, he turned her slightly, steering her so their gazes met.

"Truly, Victoria. I am sorry. Forgive me?"

His eyes were solemn, but they twinkled with kindness. With a sinking feeling in her belly, Victoria realized she'd forgive him for just about anything.

"Did you truly do those things? Rescue missions?"

Suddenly, she wanted to tell him all of it. How it felt to fly across the dunes on horseback, hoofs pounding along with her heart. How the growl of the car's engine drowned out the cries of armed Bedouins as she drove rescued girls to safety. About the nightmares when it went wrong, and death followed them back to Mrs. Jeppe's Rescue Home.

About the beautiful little girl stolen from her.

One truth would lead to more truths with this man, if she weren't careful, and her secrets would shatter the illusion of a new life she was creating around herself. So, she made light of it.

"A little. Most days I taught needle lace and fine sewing."

Kachadoor's lips curved in a teasing grin. "It's a good thing you didn't have to sail to anyone's rescue, you'd have been too sick."

Victoria couldn't help but laugh, then Kachadoor was laughing too, and they were drawing attention.

She suddenly recalled the original reason for their conversation. "I'll forgive you because there was good news in all of that."

"Oh? And what was that?"

"I knew someone called Eva Poladian in the refugee camp when we arrived in Aleppo. She told me she had an older brother in America who would rescue her, and I can easily see her being very modern and working in a belt factory. I'm glad she was right about her brother."

Kachadoor gave her fingers a light squeeze. Victoria felt that touch to her toes.

17

The S.S. Braga, North Atlantic Ocean
March and April 1922

By the end of the first week out from Marseilles, it was too cold to linger overlong on the promenade, but Vicky couldn't bear to part from Kachadoor so early in the evening. Their walks on the promenade were the only time they had to speak with any privacy. Victoria was determined to stretch their time as long as she could stand the shivering.

They didn't speak in the stateroom. The intimacy of conversation in that small, dark space was too much to bear.

Most nights, he went to the smoking room after dinner while Victoria spent time with the other women in the drawing room.

Several of the women played the piano. There were cards and all manner of fortune-telling. Talk centered around marriage, childbirth, the making of babies, and housekeeping. Most of the Armenian women were going to be married, and too many of them had lost the years and mothers from whom they would have learned such things, but none of it interested her as much as Kachadoor's company.

"Tell me more about Reupen," Victoria said to him as they walked. "We only exchanged a few letters and spare ones at that."

"Is he kind?" She hadn't meant to ask. It wasn't her place to ask him that. Those kinds of hopes were shared among the women in the drawing room.

Kachadoor's mouth tightened. "He's a good man. A good provider."

He didn't answer the question.

So, what if he wasn't kind? Victoria knew she wasn't in a

position to demand kindness. Safety, food, shelter–these were the things she was trading herself for. She burned with the shame of her secrets. She was damaged goods. If she'd told the truth to Ruepen Parnagian, he would have chosen another girl, not a used, tarnished creature like her.

"You are quite fortunate, you know," he said in the playfully serious way that sent tiny wings fluttering in her belly, to her great shame. "He's a doctor. You'll have a nice house in Worcester, where we live. I share an apartment in a building in the city, not nearly so nice, but clean enough and with room for a wife and a child or two if one of us is fortunate enough."

He blushed at the mention of future children, and Victoria's chest squeezed with longing for her baby girl.

This was the moment to ask him about his fiancée, if he had one, but Victoria found she couldn't. She didn't want to know. Here, on the ship, with the endless sea around them and the sky dark and soft like velvet, they were both more and less than they were. Not Soon-to-be-Mrs.-Parnagian or surely-someone's-man, not two single people courting, simply Victoria and Kachadoor. That was all they would ever be, so knowing about the girl who waited for him at home would make it all the more painful.

"So, I'll be a doctor's wife." She hadn't meant to say it aloud, but Kachadoor closed his eyes briefly.

"So you will."

I think I might prefer to be your wife. That thought was whispered in her secret heart. Yet another shame to add to her growing collection.

***

At the end of the second week, there was a terrible storm, which confined Victoria to her berth with another bout of violent seasickness. It was well that she had no appetite; hours of swells meant no meals until the seas calmed.

Kachadoor, along with many able-bodied men aboard, volunteered to help the crew set the ship to right in the aftermath of the storm. After a long, sleepless night, he appeared in the stateroom doorway, filthy and disheveled. Victoria felt much as she feared she looked, pale and clammy, with deep shadows under her eyes.

"Give me a moment," she said, wrapping her shawl around herself for modesty. "You will want to wash and rest."

In her rush to give Kachadoor some comfort and privacy, she'd forgotten how unsteady she would be after a day and a half abed, more than half of that retching over a chamber pot while the ship was tossed about. She wobbled and nearly fell, but Kachadoor was there to take her arm and tuck her against his body to keep her from tumbling.

She spread her palm out on his chest to catch herself up, only to become acutely aware that he was in his shirtsleeves–his damp, dirty shirtsleeves. Her fingertips brushed the warm skin just below his collarbone, where his shirt was unbuttoned, and they both inhaled audibly at the contact.

Victoria snatched her hand away, but Kachadoor still held her lightly. The fluttering in her belly intensified, fueled by the way he was looking down at her, as though he was sorry she had broken the intimacy of her touch.

He cleared his throat and gently released her to the room. She tightened her shawl against the sudden chill left in his absence.

"How are you feeling?" His voice was rough with weariness.

"Better." She couldn't manage more than a whisper; he was so close. "Is the ship all right?"

"There was no real damage," he said. "Just a lot of mess to clean up and things to put right. I heard that the midday meal will be served in the dining room today. Nothing fancy, but food." He surveyed her, looking for signs of recovery. "Will you be able to eat?"

She felt able to eat, but she wanted to accompany him to the dining room again. She was hungry for more of this heady connection with him, so unlike any feelings she'd ever had for a man. Her long-ago girlish crush on Davit Choulijian paled in comparison.

"You wash and dress for luncheon, then," he said, stepping back. He plucked at his dirty shirt. "I can wait. I'll have my turn when you're ready." He ducked his chin, and a small smile lit his features. "Perhaps we can walk the promenade after the meal?"

Victoria felt suddenly shy. They'd walked the promenade almost every day for two weeks. Why should this time feel any different?

"I'd like that."

He excused himself and left the stateroom, and Victoria let a breath out on a long whoosh of air. She ought to slap some sense into herself. She was not a woman for soft looks and gentle touches. She was promised to Ruepen Parnagian, and that was that.

Kachadoor Minassian was not for her.

But she'd seen it in his eyes. She might be inexperienced in matters of the heart, but she could tell he liked her, too.

With anxious hands, she shook out her nicer dress and combed her hair. She would go to the dining room with him, looking like a respectable young woman. They would take an afternoon constitutional together as they had since leaving Constantinople, and she would ask him more about her future husband.

***

Her resolutions lasted another two days.

With their long journey approaching its end, the second-class passengers developed a giddy energy that flavored every part of the day. The talk was cheerful, and spirits were high. There was laughter; conversations turned to what they would do when they arrived. Instead of nervous speculation, even Victoria succumbed to the relentless optimism among them.

That evening in the lounge, a woman who played the piano was joined by a man who revealed a *duduk*–an Armenia flute carved from apricot wood–he'd smuggled across the Ottoman Empire. Someone else had a violin, and a drum was improvised from a bucket.

Someone called out a folk song Victoria remembered, and to her great surprise, Kachadoor took up the tune in a strong, clear baritone.

He sang simply, without embellishments, but the words and the familiar melody took her breath away.

He finished the song to joyous applause, and the impromptu band struck up a dancing song. Without missing a beat, Kachadoor reached for her hand. She didn't have time to think better of it, she simply took his hand and let him lead her into the dance.

From old Armenian songs, the musicians picked up a waltz, then a folk song from Provence which brought more couples to the dance floor the men had created by pushing the furniture to the walls. One of the young American men knew some popular music well enough to lead the band, and before Victoria had time to stop for breath, they'd all danced for hours, many of those hours she'd spent hand in hand with Kachadoor.

Even closer than hand in hand when they'd waltzed–awkwardly, laughing all the while, for she hadn't known the steps–and he'd held her close among the twirling crowd. She ought to have been scandalized. At home, the dancing was mostly divided into lines for men and women–ceremonial folk dances and stories told through the steps, not in close couples.

Waltzing was intoxicating.

Kachadoor walked her back to their stateroom under a dark sky studded with stars and dotted with moon-dusted clouds. He paused when she unlocked the door.

"I think I will sleep in the smoking room." His eyes were sad and guarded.

Victoria missed the playful sparkle she'd grown used to. "Why?"

"I like you, Victoria. Too much. It's not right that I should sleep in the same room as my friends intended, but to do so when my feelings are so much stronger than is appropriate…" His words had tumbled out too fast at first, but now they drifted away.

The fluttering wings in Vicky's belly took flight all at once. He did feel the same way she did. Just as quickly, they turned to ash in her mouth. This was an unqualified disaster.

"I don't know what to say," she confessed.

"Don't say anything." He only looked at her, holding her gaze with his own, as though he were memorizing her eyes. "I'll sleep in the smoking room until we arrive in Boston. It's only three more nights, I heard one of the crewmen confirm it."

She nodded, transfixed by his gaze, until he dropped her hand, which had been resting on his arm, and turned to go.

"Kachadoor, wait." Her heart was pounding, her breath half-stuck in her throat. In three days she would belong to someone else. In three days, they would be surrounded by people who knew them. But now, here, under this infinite sky, cutting through the vast expanse of the sea, there was no one to stop her from being reckless, foolish, and utterly in love with a man she couldn't have.

She took his arm and stretched herself up on her toes to kiss his cheek. "I like you, too. Too much."

Her voice was breathless and impossibly young in her ears.

He caught her cheek in his cupped palm and twined their free hands together. He closed his eyes and leaned his forehead against hers. Their breath mingled, floating out over the sea in little puffs. They stayed there so long that Victoria's feet grew numb, but she would have flown if he'd asked her to.

Kachadoor sighed, a gentle, wistful sigh that coasted along Victoria's skin; then he touched his lips to hers. It was a sweet kiss, full of longing and the special kind of regret that comes with unfulfilled wishes, and Victoria knew she would never forget it, not as long as she lived.

***

They saw very little of one another for the remainder of the journey, save for meals and their daily promenade.

If Kachadoor looked increasingly unkempt from staying in the smoking room, it didn't lessen his appeal for Victoria, who missed the heavy rise and fall of his breathing across the stateroom, missed the scent of his soap in the wash basin. Missed the way his easy laughter offset his quiet, serious nature.

Without his steady presence, she began to fret about her

impending marriage. She expected Reupen to want to finalize their marriage very soon after they arrived. She'd been prepared to meet a priest almost as soon as they were off the ship. Courtships were a luxury, and as she reminded herself, she did not deserve such luxuries.

When disembarking began, Kachadoor sought her out. He did not take her hand or touch her at all. As he had been in Constantinople, he was all politeness and solicitousness.

"I expect Reupen will be with your sister Yegsapet and her husband to meet you. Please give him my regards. I must go and find Peter to give him the bad news about his bride, so I will take my leave and wish you every happiness, Victoria. The Armenian community is not so big here. Perhaps we will see one another again someday."

"Kachadoor–" She didn't want to say goodbye like this, so formal, but his eyes begged her to let him go. She understood, much as the pain of losing him was clawing at her heart. "Thank you."

He offered her a little bow, then turned and disappeared into the crowd making their way off the ship.

***

Victoria was caught up almost immediately in a tide of disembarking emigrés. Hours passed while she waited in an endless line to be formally admitted to her new country. She watched as, just as they had been warned, some of the girls were collected by men who already had a priest by their side.

For her part, she craned her neck, cursing her diminutive height. Yegsabet could be three people away, and she'd never have known it.

Her sister found her, though, and crushed her into a hug. The sisters wept, and Victoria felt, for the first time in years, that she might be safe. Her heart was broken–twice, truly–but she was with her sister again. She had a family again, and soon she would have a respectable doctor for a husband.

Instead of living only for the next stretch of days, she might actually consider the future.

Yegsabet introduced her to her husband Levon, who picked up her carpet bag with a guarded expression. He looked to his wife to prompt them to leave. "Shall we go, Yessa?"

Victoria looked behind her brother-in-law, hoping to see her intended, but no one around them was paying them any attention. She turned to her sister, the question of her future husband's whereabouts on her lips and in her eyes.

Her sister assumed her confusion was over the new nickname. "The Americans like short, simple names. I go by Yessa most of the time." Yessa grinned at her husband. "The Americans will probably call her something like Vicky."

"I like it…Yessa." Victoria tried the short name again. "But… where is Mr. Parnagian? Was he not able to come today because of a patient?"

The idea that he was comforting a sick patient eased some of her worries.

"Did you not get our telegram? We tried to reach Mr. Minassian in Constantinople." Yessa gripped her hands hard. "I'm so sorry, Victoria. He died. Of tuberculosis."

Tears welled in Victoria's eyes. "We never heard."

Yessa squeezed her tighter. "Don't worry. You'll come home with us and live there until we find another husband for you. Don't worry."

Victoria thought of Kachadoor, somewhere in the vast and noisy harbor city, delivering bad news to his friend. She thought of their stunted love affair, blossoming on the ocean only to die on dry land. She'd never asked him about a girl at home, assuming it didn't matter, and now it was far too late.

When she could no longer hold back the tears, Yessa only held her. "We will find you a new husband, *kooyr*. I promise."

18

Lawrence and Worcester, Massachusetts
1922-1923

Yessa and Levon lived in Lawrence, where Levon worked in a textile mill. Whatever he did, it involved hard work and long hours. He came home tired, ate his dinner, and slept early. While her husband was at work, Yessa kept house.

The city was cramped, noisy, and dirty with industry, but Victoria was able to find her way after a few weeks.

Within a few weeks, her sister's prediction came true. Everyone, even the Armenians, called her *Vicky*. She embraced the new name and tried hard to be a new woman to fit it.

She helped Yessa with the shopping, cleaning, and sewing, even learning to cook at her sister's side. For her sister, those cooking lessons were part of her campaign to make Vicky as marriageable as possible. Vicky saw it as another skill she could put toward supporting herself in some fashion.

Her sister's daily life took some getting used to, from the routine set by the working men who supported them to the church they attended. For Vicky, it felt strange not to worship at a Catholic church, but Levon, his wife, and all his friends and family attended the Apostolic church, so that's what she did too.

Each Sunday, they put on their best things–no flour sack house dresses on the holy day–and attended services. They didn't have much in the way of pocket money, but Yessa always made sure they had pins to dress their hair, and fine soap and cold cream for their faces. After so long without little luxuries, Vicky was happy to have them.

She began to suspect that, like her cooking lessons, attending services meant more to her sister than religious observation or social time, at least where Vicky was concerned. For Yessa, the future and Vicky's married status were the most important things to think about.

Yessa invited a parade of eligible Armenian men to dine with them in their apartment. When introductions were made, Yessa made no secret of Vicky's status as a single woman, no matter how frequently Vicky demurred. The tragic circumstances of her intended husband's untimely demise made for a juicy story, and Yessa was on a mission.

The way her sister exaggerated her domestic skills, Vicky suspected her sister would find it unseemly that Vicky could drive or had ridden horses into nomadic villages to barter for stolen girls.

The men who orbited her family were mostly Levon's friends, older men–even more so than Kachadoor–who'd come to America nearly a generation before to make a life for themselves and send money back home. Vicky made conversation, but she refused to encourage their attention.

Levon made a good living and was well-liked among the men. If he and Yessa only muddled along as a couple, that was to be expected. She had come to marry him for security and tradition. He had brought her to Lawrence to help him keep a good home and give him a family. Maintaining their way of life mattered more than anyone's individual feelings on the matter.

Vicky couldn't bring herself to tell her sister she had no plans to marry. She simply quietly turned down any man who asked her to walk with him or asked if he could call again another time.

She often thought of Kachadoor. Somewhere in Worcester, he was going about his business. Did he think of her? Was he looking for her?

Instead of the men her sister hoped to match her with, Vicky gravitated toward young mothers. In every baby, she saw her sweet Nevart's face. She heard her daughter in the laughter of the little girls who played together after the service while the adults drank strong Turkish coffee and gossiped.

Vicky sought out glimpses of the life she'd left behind in Aleppo, torn between gratitude for her current safety and the desire to reverse time and go back to that place where she'd made a difference.

Her sister was grateful for her help, but Vicky knew money was scarce. Yessa and Levon were hoping for a child before too long. She would be a burden to them if she stayed too long after a baby came.

Without a husband, she didn't know what she would do, but she would have to find a solution. Her skills wouldn't earn her enough to have rooms of her own, but if her mother and remaining sisters were here, perhaps they could pool resources and share?

"How soon will we be able to bring Mariam, Lucine, and *Mayrig* here to live with us?" Vicky asked Yessa while chopping the last of the vegetables for a stew.

"I had a thought about that." Picking lentils across the table, Yessa looked like a clever cat with a fat mouse in its paws. "Mr. Poladian never got his wife when you came over. For a while, we thought maybe you two would do fine for each other, but Peter's got that house full of women. Levon says he's still looking. I think Mariam would be better for him. She's used to living with *Mayrig* and the girls already."

Among Peter's house full of women was plain-spoken Eva Poladian, whom Kachadoor had described as *very modern.* Eva often talked about getting a job as a clerk or a teacher and moving into a boarding house for women, but never in front of her brother or the married ladies. Maybe she and Eva could share rooms somewhere?

"We'll see Peter and Eva at Levon's cousin's wedding next month." Yessa was still contemplating matchmaking. "The church in Worcester is well-established. There's bound to be a few young men to catch your choosy eye."

It wasn't her eye so much as her heart that was choosy. She wondered if Kachadoor attended church with Levon's cousin and whether he might be at the wedding.

Her sister went into detail about the Church of Our Saviour on Laurel Street in Worcester. The fabled city was still a mystery to Vicky, and her thoughts drifted to memories of Kachadoor until Yessa nudged her arm.

"So? What do you think about Mariam and Peter?"

"I think you know both of them better than I do, when it comes to marriage."

Yessa dusted her hands on her apron. “I’ll speak to Levon about it.”

***

Vicky quickly learned that Worcester, which had been praised so highly among the refugees in Syria and on the ship almost as though it were the entirety of America, was simply another small city, but with a large Armenian population.

It did boast the oldest Armenian church in America, and Yessa was partially right. The wedding was crowded with young men.

The few weddings she’d attended at the church in Lawrence were barebone affairs with a small luncheon hosted by the parish.

Levon’s cousin was marrying a girl from a well-to-do Worcester family, with a large feast hosted by the bride’s father to follow.

In the weeks before the wedding, Vicky scoured the shops for fabric and made new dresses for herself and Yessa. They wore their best shoes, and Yessa had dressed their hair into fashionable flat chignons with fuller waves that gave the illusion of a bob under their hats. Vicky had recently started taking in mending, particularly lacework that required repair. With her extra pin money, she splurged on a tube of lipstick to share with Yessa.

They giggled like the girls they hadn’t had the chance to be as they checked each other’s faces before pinning on their hats.

It was a pleasure to dress up, even with their modest means, and feel pretty for a party. Vicky boarded the train to Worcester feeling more carefree than she had since Gürin.

They walked the few blocks from the train station to the church, and Vicky was grateful for a gentle breeze that cooled her neck without pulling apart their hairstyles.

Vicky sat with Yessa and Levon behind the groom’s closest family, but still close enough to see the bride’s anxious expression. She was a lovely girl, and her dress was fashionable and well-tailored. The groom was a little round in the belly, like Levon, but his eyes were kind. Vicky said a quick prayer that they would find contentment together.

Perhaps her heart should have been fixed upon the service, but she couldn't help looking around at the sea of faces, drinking in the welcome features of so many Armenian strangers.

She often wondered if she would see a familiar face, a woman from Miss Jeppe's home, or one of the water women from the river.

She and Yessa didn't talk much about the time before they came to Lawrence. No one did.

There were stories about the villages where they'd grown up to be told, traditions to bicker over, and songs from the old country to sing. Perhaps brief inquiries into the welfare of mutual acquaintances, but no one really talked about the worst years or the losses which touched them all. This was their new life, and that was that. There was nothing to say about it to one another, but Vicky remembered, and her heart ached.

She found it difficult not to search the face of every man in the church looking for Kachadoor's familiar and beloved features.

Yessa caught her looking at one point and whispered. "Who are you looking for?"

Vicky turned her eyes back towards the altar and murmured that she hoped to see a friend she'd made on the ship.

It wasn't a lie, but less of the truth than Yessa deserved. Her sister loved her and wanted the best for her, didn't she?

After the service, they walked several blocks to the celebratory luncheon.

While Levon boasted to the men who walked with them about his cousin's new bride–her family owned a single-family home on prominent Belmont Street, not far from the hospital, a home her grandfather had built a generation before, Vicky walked arm in arm with her sister and offered a little of the truth.

"Back in the church, I was looking for Mr. Minassian."

Yessa could sense a scandal a mile away. "The man who escorted you on this ship?"

"Do you know him?" Vicky asked.

"Not myself. Levon has met him. He trusted Mr. Minassian to

bring you to his friend. Tell me he didn't– "

Vicky cut off her sister's questioning. "He was a gentleman. We became friends on the crossing. I wished for more, but it wasn't possible."

Yessa nodded, mollified for the moment.

Vicky continued. "He was easy to talk to."

"Talk to about what?"

"A lot of things, mostly things we never talk about, like before we came to America."

"It was a terrible time. Why talk about it?"

Vicky drew a long breath. "When I lived in Mrs. Jeppe's home, I didn't only learn needlework."

"You certainly didn't learn to cook," Yessa said tartly.

The truth, held back for so long, rushed out. "No. I learned to drive. To read maps. To negotiate with Bedouin traders."

Her sister's mouth dropped open.

"Do you remember our riding lessons, back in Gürin? I learned to ride across the dunes, how to ride along the cobbled roads of Aleppo. How to ride astride with another woman behind me. How to lean in low to the horse's neck to avoid bullets."

Yessa stopped, tugging Vicky's arm as she did. "You mustn't say a word of this to anyone. I'll never get you married."

"That's what I'm trying to tell you," Vicky insisted. "I never told him all of it, but I told him some, and he wasn't angry. He didn't think me improper or unnatural. He *liked* me."

"I'll just bet he did." Yessa's lips were pursed.

"What's the hold-up?" Levon had noticed they'd stopped.

"Nothing, husband," Yessa called brightly. "A stone in Vicky's shoe. We'll be along." To Vicky, she said, "Maybe we will find him. Maybe we won't, but you can't go around telling people you did things like that."

Her hard work, her pride…reduced to yet another shame she would have to carry. For a glorious moment, she'd considered telling Yessa all of it, but now she knew what before she'd only assumed. The very existence of the baby would brand her as tarnished even before anyone knew she'd been raped, and that would count against her too.

"Come along, then. We don't want to be the last ones to congratulate my cousin," Levon called.

"Heaven forbid," Yessa muttered, tucking her hand back over Vicky's arm and propelling them both toward the luncheon.

The party was lavish by their current standards. The fragrant scent of ground lamb and rice teased Vicky's belly. She eyed the platters of *kheema* and *pilaf,* golden loaves of *cheoreg,* and dishes piled high with vegetables and strands of cheese. A feast like this was a rare treat; it would be a shame to let her belly–still churning from her conversation with Yessa–ruin it.

Their hosts offered them Turkish coffee and celebratory glasses of *oghi*. The sting of strong spirits hid the shine of tears when Vicky tasted it; her parents had distilled their own from apricots picked on their property. She was too young to try it, and then, like everything else about home, it was gone.

Vicky smiled patiently as they made their way through the gathering, allowing Yessa to make introductions as she would. Vicky's confessions seemed to fuel Yessa to put more men in Vicky's path, old, young, handsome, and ugly, a sandstorm of male faces passed before her eyes.

The main rooms of the house were packed with well-wishers, and the bride's brothers and uncles were making music on the porch. After they'd eaten, Vicky took a piece of the American-style wedding cake, ringed with sugared violets, and slipped outside for some air.

The voice at her shoulder was so soft, she thought she'd imagined it.

"Victoria, I thought that was you."

Vicky's breath caught in her throat. Kachadoor spoke again, giving her a chance to gather herself before replying.

"Mrs. Parnagian," he said formally, his smile faltering. "I suppose I should have offered condolences, but I was far too pleased to see you again, and forgot my manners."

"Condolences?" Vicky blinked. Her mouth dropped open. "No. I'm not Mrs. Parnagian. Not a widow."

It was Kachadoor's turn to blink, to be open-mouthed with shock. He recovered quickly. "What do you mean?"

The cheerful cacophony of the wedding party faded away, leaving them the only two people in the world.

Vicky blushed. "You're hopelessly behind the times. Your friend Mr. Parnagian passed away before we arrived in Boston. How could you not know?"

Kachadoor gazed down at his shoes. "I confess, I didn't seek him out right away. I was jealous. I didn't want to see him happy with you. He was a friend from my time in Lawrence, a friend of Peter's. No one in Worcester knew to tell me. I heard the news from a customer months after you'd arrived." He looked up at her. "I took the trolley to his neighborhood to call on you and offer condolences, but the house was sold and the new owners didn't know anything about it. I assumed you were in mourning and had returned to your sister."

A laugh bubbled up through Vicky's lips before she could stop it, but this was Kachadoor. She couldn't shock him. She hadn't yet, anyway.

He answered her unguarded laughter with a smile of his own, then released her hands.

"Mourn him?" Vicky said. "I didn't know him. He left no family, nothing for me to remember him by. I have been with my sister this whole time." She shook her head, to clear her thoughts as much as anything. "Why didn't I see you at the church?"

"I was unable to come to the wedding service." He looked down at her plate, where she'd already taken a bite of the delicate sponge cake and sugary frosting. "The bride wanted an American wedding cake, and I work for the bakery that made it. I was busy all morning working on it, and in no shape to come directly here after work. I only just got here. I can't believe I might have missed you."

"But you didn't miss me," Vicky said. She steeled herself to ask the question that had haunted her for months. "What about you? Are you here with a fiancée…or a wife?"

When he spoke, all the formality was gone from his voice.

"I am…unattached," he said slowly. His eyes searched hers for a moment before he spoke again. "I met a girl once." He took a deep breath. "But she was intended for another. I wonder, if she were free, should I tell her how I feel about her?"

Time stopped. Vicky's heart stopped. She could barely meet his eyes, lest the longing in her own pour out of her to fill the room and drown them both.

Her answer came out as a whisper. "I think you should call on this girl, if that's how you feel."

He smiled and nodded, but before they could say more, someone approached; he was swept into the bride's family to offer his congratulations, and Levon and Yessa were on their way back to her.

19

Lawrence and Worcester, Massachusetts
1922-1923

Kachadoor did not call right away. Without amateur detective work, it would've been difficult, since in the excitement of seeing each other again, neither had remembered to exchange any of the pertinent details involved in finding one another.

Vicky didn't have a detective. She had Yessa, who had seen enough at the wedding to put the details together. "Now, this Kachadoor. What does he do?"

It was a valid question. As Vicky's only family here in America, the responsibility of seeing Vicky settled fell to her and Levon. It was a duty Yessa took seriously, and her curiosity was piqued.

"He works at a bakery in downtown Worcester."

"A baker?" Yessa frowned. "That's a bit of a downgrade. Ruepen was a doctor."

"And Levon works in a textile mill," Vicky countered. "So what? It's not glamorous, he says, but steady work. He shares an apartment with two friends for now."

"Well, I suppose he makes a living," Yessa said. "He should speak to Levon if he wishes to court."

"We haven't seen one another for months," Vicky was a little shocked. Until she'd seen Kachadoor again, she'd given up on marriage entirely. The thought of courtship did strange things to her insides.

That Levon was the man to whom Kachadoor should speak chafed. He wasn't her father; he was her *younger* sister's husband, at that. Regardless, she was walking an emotional tightrope. Her feelings for Kachadoor and the once-hopeless dreams she'd carried onboard the S.S. Braga on the one hand, and the dark truths she carried in her heart.

"Never mind that," Vicky said, to cover her embarrassment. "We only spoke for a moment. I don't even know where he lives. He doesn't know how to find me either."

Yessa waved off Vicky's concerns as though they were nothing to worry about. "Oh, that's nothing. There aren't so many of us. I'll ask Levon to find out about him."

There was no help for it. Vicky desperately wanted to see him again.

***

Yessa's husband didn't end up having to look for Kachadoor. Kachadoor came looking for Vicky.

There was nothing special about that Sunday, save that a late arrival at Sunday services caught Vicky's eye and put a blush on her cheeks. Kachadoor Minassian's tall frame and handsome face there, in Lawrence, in their church. He removed his hat and sat in a back pew so as not to disturb the congregation.

Kachadoor approached their small family group at the end of the service. He offered Vicky a warm smile but approached her brother-in-law first.

"Levon. It's good to see you again," Kachadoor said. "I wished to speak to you about Victoria."

Vicky could see the twinkle of humor in Kachadoor's eyes, at odds with his formal speech. He was observing the niceties for her.

"I found her to be a very pleasant travel companion," he continued. "And I was certain when I left her in Boston that she would make my friend a wonderful wife. By the time word of his death reached me, I assumed they were married. Now that a suitable amount of time has passed, I had hoped to call on Miss Karadelian in the hopes she might eventually accept my suit. That is, of course, if she is not otherwise engaged."

Vicky fought the smile attempting to form on her face. He knew full well she wasn't attached. These rituals were performed entirely to stroke Levon's ego, to smooth his path to her, and she knew it.

Levon assessed Kachadoor for a long minute. Yessa clutched her purse, watching her husband with anxious eyes.

Levon stuck out of hand. "You have my permission to call on my sister-in-law."

Yessa sighed audibly in relief.

Again, Vicky tamped down the urge to laugh. It wouldn't do any good to chip away at her brother-in-law's self-importance. After all, she very much wanted Kachadoor to come calling.

It was a brief, but proper courtship. In truth, it was longer than any courtship she might have had with her original intended.

On a soft morning with a hint of spring in the air, Kachadoor formally proposed marriage.

At first, he gave no sign that his visit was anything but a weekly call. "It was a lovely day," he said. "Certainly, warm enough for a walk around the neighborhood."

She saw it in the way his eyes shone, and his hands fidgeted with his hat as they walked. This was not an ordinary call.

Vicky waved in passing to those she knew as they walked, but her attention was on Kachadoor. Their intentions toward one another had always been clear, but she found herself nervous; the butterflies in her stomach threatened to fly loose.

In part, this was because she had decided to tell him the truth, and she knew full well what that might mean. He might decide she was a poor choice. He might return her to her sister's home, and never see her again.

Before he could speak the question that would alter the course of everything, she stopped him.

"Kachadoor, I know I told you some of what happened to me in Aleppo," she began. "But —"

"There's no need," Kachadoor said. "Nothing you could tell me will change my feelings for you, Victoria,"

"I'm not sure that's true," Vicky said.

Kachadoor turned to her, eyes serious. "Nothing. There's nothing you could say that would change my feelings. What's passed is in the past. This is our future. You and me."

Vicky would never be sure, but she thought perhaps he had some inkling of what she might have been about to say. There was something about his seriousness. Something about his insistence on looking forward, instead of behind.

Almost as if he truly didn't care.

She looked at this man, tall and handsome, offering her a future. Perhaps more of a future than she really deserved.

As though he read her thoughts, Kachadoor turned to her. "We can be happy together, Victoria. And I think you deserve to be happy just as much as anyone."

Who was she to argue with that?

Before giving him her answer, Vicky closed her eyes and said goodbye to her daughter. Nevart would always live in her heart, but it was time to give up the last lingering hope that they would ever be together again.

When her eyes filled with tears, Kachadoor took her hand. His palm was warm, and seemed to offer not only the security of marriage and the love she knew would grow between them but understanding and care.

"Victoria," Kachadoor said, her name like music from his lips. "Will you do me the honor of becoming my wife?"

***

Victoria and Kachadoor were married at the Church of our Savior in Worcester, where they'd reunited, and near where he lived and worked. Her sister and Levon were there, along with Kachadoor's roommates, his employer and his family, and most of the regular congregation.

As the wedding approached, Vicky traveled with Yessa to Worcester at least once a week to plan for the wedding with the Danielians, the family who cared for the church. It gave her a chance to see Kachadoor as well. With each visit, she found herself anxious to get to the wedding day, so they would never be separated again.

Sitrek and Azniv Danielian had offered to host the wedding luncheon at their home next door to the church since she had no parents or close family in Worcester to host it for her.

They had two small children–a boy and a baby daughter named Pauline, who captured Vicky's heart from the moment Azniv set the child in Vicky's arms so she could serve coffee.

The tiny girl with her dark hair and wide baby eyes reminded her of Nevart at the same age. While Azniv and Yessa planned the wedding feast and the music for dancing, Vicky rocked Pauline and drank in her sweet, milky baby scent.

For the first time since the awful spring morning in 1915 when she followed her mother out of their village, Vicky felt a village around her again and it made her miss her daughter all the more. She cuddled the baby closer, much to the amusement of Yessa and Azniv.

"Already dreaming of babies, *kyoor*?" Yessa teased.

"You have a way with her," Azniv said. "Anytime you want to, you can come over and rock her. I've got my hands full with John."

"Don't tempt me," Vicky said wistfully.

"Will you and Mr. Minassian look for a home of your own right away?" Azniv asked. Vicky heard the unspoken question: *Will you try for children right away?*

With the prospect of a wife to support and the close quarters they shared on Belmont Street, Kachadoor left his job at the confectioner's and took work at the Washburn & Moen wire factory.

The pay was better, he told her, but the hours would be long and the work demanding. They'd promised one another that it would be worth it when they'd saved enough for a place of their own.

Though she never said so, Vicky missed the way his hands smelled like sugar at the end of his workday. The hours while they walked hand-in-hand from the Danielians' home to the train station, while Yessa pretended not to notice, were nothing short of magic. It was a brief courtship, but a true one, one that left her feeling giddy and girlish in a way she'd never hoped to.

Yessa and Levon came with Vicky to Worcester for the week of the wedding. Levon stayed with Kachadoor and his roommates, while Yessa and Vicky stayed with the Danielians. On Friday night, Yessa and Azniv joined *Yeretzgin*–the priest's wife–and some of the women from the congregation to apply bridal *henna* to Vicky's hands, the way women had gathered for generations in the old country.

With her hands stained and wrapped, Vicky watched her sister and Azniv apply small crescent moons to some of the young women's hands.

Once upon a time, in the months before their lives were thrown into chaos and horror, she, Yessa, and Hasmik had worn tiny crescent moons on their hands at a village girl's wedding. Her eyes prickled with tears for the girls they had been, and she offered a prayer that Hasmik survived and went on to find happiness of her own.

Vicky and Kachadoor married on a mild, overcast day in the early summer of 1922. Vicky thought her heart might burst with affection for everyone who'd gathered to celebrate them. She'd never felt more beautiful, or more loved.

The Ladies Guild of the church presented fine cloth to make their wedding clothes, and, true to her word, Azniv produced a groaning table no less sumptuous than Levon's cousin's party. Vicky felt like the queen she was named for in those dreamlike hours, in her lace-trimmed dress and veil, with her handsome husband at her side.

Only a moment of sadness marred the day. After begging for a moment of rest from the dancing, she'd tucked herself into the long sofa to snuggle Pauline while she slept through the party. Kachadoor, in the midst of accepting congratulations from his friends and co-workers, looked over and smiled tenderly.

Like Yessa and Asniv, he surely assumed she was dreaming of future children. Vicky knew how he hoped for a family of his own, and the weight of her deception struck her like a fist. The memories she kept secreted away often felt like another woman's life. What good would it do now, to tell him the truth and face his censure? None, not when he'd offered her a new life on the night he'd proposed.

And so, she kissed Pauline's sleeping cheek and buried her past more deeply than any treasure under an olive tree.

Levon hushed the room for a toast.

"We are very fortunate to be together today to celebrate my sister-in-law and her new husband. To Mr. And Mrs. Danielian, we are all grateful for your gracious hospitality. I am glad Victoria will have a family here in Worcester." He turned to Vicky and Kachadoor and offered an ancient Armenian blessing. "*Mek bardzi vray tseranak.* May you grow old on one pillow. To Vicky and her Pesa!"

When Levon used the word for bridegroom instead of his name, Vicky knew Kachadoor had a new nickname, whether he liked it or not.

She stretched up on her toes to whisper in his ear. "That's what they'll all call you from now on."

His reply tickled her earlobe, sending pleasant shivers along her skin. "I don't care what they call me, as long as you call me your husband."

They sang, danced, and ate until the stars came out and the musicians were out of breath. Levon and Yessa, who were staying the night as guests of the Danielians, stayed awake to see Vicky and Kachadoor home to his apartment. Levon and Sitrek sang blessings out as they walked, earning a few grumpy shouts from the neighbors, but Vicky was too elated to fret over it.

Kachadoor's apartment was barely a half mile from the church, in an impressive double triple-decker on Belmont Street. It was a large building, with two apartments on each floor, stacked three high. For tonight, anyway, his apartment was theirs alone. His roommates were staying the night with a cousin to give the newlyweds a short honeymoon, one that would end on Monday when Kachadoor went to work.

Kachadoor seemed uncertain as he unlocked the empty apartment, as though she might object to her new living arrangement, but after staying with Yessa and Levon, Vicky was used to living with extra working men.

"There are two married couples sharing an apartment on the floor below," he said, all in a rush. "They came in yesterday to clean everything, and Mrs. Dean, she owns the building and lives on the first floor, left food for a cold supper…I wanted you to feel welcome."

Kachadoor delivered this last bit with the same tortured shyness she remembered from the boat, just before telling her that he liked her…too much.

It meant a lot to him then, that she felt welcome and cared for.

Vicky looked around the small apartment. There were only three rooms–two bedrooms and a common area with a meager kitchen. It was sparsely furnished but tidy and recently scrubbed. She wasn't the homemaker her sister was, but she would do her best, and work to get his roommates married off to nice girls with extra living space. As soon as possible.

They shared a bathroom with another apartment on the same floor, just as Yessa and Levon did. Kachadoor escorted her down the hall to show it to her and returned to the apartment while she used it.

Vicky stepped inside the apartment tentatively. Her hands were clammy, and her pulse skipped wildly. While she was weary from the long day of celebrating, the wedding was not wholly completed.

She understood the mechanics of how it was done all too well. What she couldn't predict was how she would feel when the time came. On the one hand, the very thought of it turned her stomach sick and made her head swim with memories she preferred to keep buried. But then there was the reality of Kachadoor, with his kind eyes and gentle manners, his serious way of speaking tempered by the humor in his eyes, and the undeniable flutter she felt deep in her belly when they were together.

"It's probably good there's food," she said, stifling a laugh. "Once you find out how poor my cooking is, you'll send me back to my sister."

Kachadoor smoothed one of the fashionable curls that lay against her cheek. "I am never sending you back to your sister."

The words were sincere, his tone serious, but Vicky could see her favorite playful twinkle in his eyes. She resisted the urge to pinch herself in the arm. Every day since Levon's cousin's wedding months before, she'd woken certain that this would be the day when it was all taken away from her, but here she was, married to this good man she loved.

She bit her lip thinking of the awkward conversation she had with Yessa the day before. Her younger sister had been married a few years and was expecting their first child. She sat Vicky down and gave her a very blunt explanation of the marital act; their talk concluded with Yessa patting Vicky on the knee and saying, “You get used to it."

Vicky had stared into her lap to hide the shame she knew her sister would see in her face.

Kachadoor was still gently stroking that one curl against her cheek, his fingers work-roughened but delicate against her cheek. His other hand rested against her waist like a question.

“Are you hungry?" His voice was husky.

In the beat it took for him to clear his throat, Vicky made up her mind.

"No,” she said, placing her hands on his broad shoulders. "I think it's time we went to bed."

20

Worcester, Massachusetts
1922-1923

That first night alone together in the apartment with bread, cheese, and cold chicken to share, was better than any wedding night she could have dreamed up.

They stretched what food was left for the entire next day, entranced with one another, and Vicky thought she might more than get used to the sweet intimacy of her marriage bed.

Pesa, for he decided he liked Levon's nickname, left for the factory Monday morning. Vicky hummed to herself as she watched his tall form striding down Belmont Street. She'd saved the last of their wedding supper for his lunch today, and the novelty of sending her husband off to work with his sack lunch left her feeling light and easy.

She could just make out the red brick of the wire factory's roofline from their third-story window. Today while Pesa worked, she would take a long walk to get used to her new neighborhood, then perhaps pay a visit to Mrs. Dean to thank her for the supper, and to the couples on the second floor who'd been so kind. She knew the housework would be significant, with three working men living there. Starting from a fresh, tidy space was a more generous wedding gift than she'd expected.

She didn't have to seek out Mrs. Dean. Their landlady was returning to the building as Vicky let herself out of the front door. Vicky felt a little starstruck to see her. Here was a woman who owned not only her home but the entire building. Mrs. Dean looked to be at least Vicky's mother's age, and she was chatting animatedly with a trio of nurses crossing the street from the Washburn Dispensary.

The older woman caught sight of Vicky and waved. Vicky caught her farewell to the nurses, who continued on toward the trolley stop at the bottom of the hill.

"Good morning, Mrs. Dean," Vicky said, blushing at the stilted sound of her English.

"*Pahree looys*, Mrs. Minassian." Mrs. Dean laughed when Vicky's mouth opened in an O of surprise. She had not expected her landlady to greet her in Armenian as halting as her own English. "Regretfully, I can only say a few phrases, but I have had many tenants from among your people, dear. Congratulations on your wedding. Kachadoor is a steady young man."

"Thank you, also, for the supper. You are very kind."

"It's my pleasure. Where are you off to this fine morning?"

It was a fine morning, and despite the butterflies that beat tiny wings in her belly at the thought of being on her own, Vicky was excited to explore her new city. She sought out the words to reply in English. "I go to look at the city. Find my way."

"Very good, dear. Enjoy your walk, and anything you need, please come to me."

For the first time in her life, she was truly free to go where she liked. As the trolleys sped down the main streets, Vicky smiled.

Perhaps one day soon she and Pesa would ride one.

***

That first day established what would become Vicky's routine over the next few months. She'd see Pesa off to work six mornings a week. On Saturdays, he only worked in the morning, and those afternoons were often spent exploring the city.

What they lacked in money, they made up for in imagination and friendship. Vicky loved to ride the streetcars with Pesa at her side, or they would take long walks on sunny days.

While Vicky wasn't a natural homemaker, she knew how to stretch her pennies. Their Saturday afternoons were filled with simple picnics by the pond near the factory, or in the shade of the trees in Elm Park.

Vicky had never seen such a place, public land designed solely for leisure. In Gürin and Aleppo, she'd seen markets and squares that took her breath away. Her family's estate had gardens, a lawn, and even a nearby wilderness, but nothing like this lovely park with its man-made pond and picturesque paths. Mrs. Dean told her the park was designed by the same great man who designed Central Park in New York City, then showed her a picture postcard of the vast, beautiful park in New York.

She visited her landlady several times a week, at first with simple questions about the best butcher shop or where to buy fabric and thread. Those halting conversations quickly turned into informal English lessons.

Mrs. Dean learned of her skill with needle and thread and began spreading the word around the neighborhood. Under Mrs. Dean's tutelage, Vicky picked up more than enough English to do her errands and talk to her customers confidently. That confidence awakened the sense of purpose she'd left behind with Miss Jeppe and the rescuers, and she turned to Azniv for advice.

Asniv was more than happy to put Vicky to work. The need was overwhelming, as a constant flood of displaced Armenians arrived in Massachusetts. Young women newly arrived who needed work and places to stay, picture brides who needed to learn English as Vicky was doing, and orphanages overseas which needed funds and supplies.

Before long, Vicky was not only volunteering with Azniv, but she was also bringing in a little money from mending and lace work. Both roommates had their eyes on young women from the church, and as much as she enjoyed their company, Vicky encouraged their attachments. If their roommates left, she was certain she and Pesa could cover the rent, and they would have a home all their own.

Her work with Asniv left Vicky brimming with satisfaction and weighed down with the knowledge she could only do so much. To her surprise, she welcomed the contrasting emotions; they reminded her of her time at the rescue home.

It was strange to feel homesick for such a difficult and dangerous time in her life, but those years in Aleppo were not so far in her past.

Some days, Miss Jeppe and the rescue home were more real to her than Mrs. Dean and the house on Belmont Street. Some days she floated through, daydreaming about her future with Pesa.

Regardless of how homesick or buoyed she felt, Vicky went home every evening to prepare supper for Pesa and their roommates, who made her laugh with their stories. Their boyish charm was infectious. The apartment was full of joy and affection, unlike anything Vicky had known before.

They were a different kind of family, but a family nonetheless, and Vicky loved them. Sometimes Vicky lay awake long after Pesa had gone to sleep, with terror clutching at her chest. Her secrets, her shame, would flood through her body, beating like the blood in her veins. If they knew the truth about her, her beautiful world would come crashing down around her.

When things were quiet, Vicky sometimes spent time at the Danielians, cuddling and singing to Pauline, who grew more bright-eyed and plumper with each passing month. Every smile Vicky earned from Pauline was both a balm and a penance, for she still kept her secrets from Pesa, whose tenderness never wavered.

She promised herself, rocking Pauline as she slept, that she would confess everything before their first child was born.

Six months later, Vicky's monthlies stopped.

When they didn't happen for the next month either, Vicky went to see Azniv.

Her friend immediately settled Vicky on the sofa and gave her tea. "How far along are you?"

"Maybe two months? I don't know for certain."

"Too soon to show, then, but not too soon to share the happy news with Pesa. What does he say?"

"He doesn't know yet," Vicky confessed.

"He'll be so happy. You must tell me as soon as he knows. I'm terrible at keeping secrets!"

Azniv tucked herself on the sofa with Pauline between them and began to tell Vicky how the pregnancy would go. Little did her friend know, Vicky was altogether too familiar with her pregnant body.

"I'm glad you're so calm. But again, you want this baby." Azniv scooted Pauline into Vicky's lap. "Some of the refugees I see, they–"Azniv paused and dropped her voice, as if Pauline could understand, "They were raped, and their pregnancies mean they will never find a good husband. It's terrible to see."

Pauline took her hands. "Your fingers are like ice. Let's get you some more tea."

Another three weeks passed before Vicky was willing to consider telling Kachadoor. She struggled with the nausea, but it typically held off until after the men left at dawn for work. If she was weary at the end of the day, the men didn't notice or chalked it up to her hard work keeping them fed and in clean clothes and linens.

She would have to tell Pesa soon, and her sister would be hurt if she wasn't the next to know.

The trouble was, Nevart was more real to her than this new life that fluttered within her, delicate like a moth's wings. Nevart was alive somewhere in the world, living a life Vicky would never know. The stranger growing inside her was literally taking her daughter's place in her body.

The fear that she would somehow slip up and reveal that this was not her first pregnancy, her first expected child, dogged her steps and haunted her sleep.

One morning, she woke from a dream of the Syrian desert and the echoes of a baby's cry. She found she couldn't go back to sleep; the desert's dry breath lingered on the back of her neck. Slipping out of bed as quietly as she could, she pushed back the curtain and let the moonlight cool her. A dream like that was no mystery, and her daughter's face stayed with her as she watched the sleeping city outside her window.

"*Eench eh, hokis*?" Pesa rolled over and spoke softly. *What is it, my love?* "Why are you awake so early?"

Vicky sent a silent prayer of love to her daughter and turned to her husband. Her dearest love, her sweetest friend. He deserved to know, and he would be so very happy. Perhaps his joy would wash her clean of her sin and shame.

She crawled back under the covers and turned so they were facing each other.

"We are going to have a baby," she whispered.

"Why so solemn? This is wonderful news." He caressed her cheek and brought out her smile. "How far along are you?"

"A little more than two months," she replied, avoiding his first question. "I'm not so sure."

"Are you feeling well?" He pulled her close and tucked her against his body.

She released a breath she hadn't meant to hold. His solid warmth dismissed the last of the dream. "A little sick in the mornings, and tired, but nothing unusual…or so I've heard." She hoped he wouldn't notice the way her heart jumped at the lie.

That morning Vicky sat down to write a letter to Yessa after cleaning the breakfast dishes.

A week later, she received a reply. Her sister wrote to say that she and Levon planned to take the train the following Sunday to attend church with the Minassians and stay for dinner. Vicky took the opportunity to invite the Danielians as well.

She didn't remember being so tired when she carried Nevart, but perhaps it was all relative. The Yavuz's had worked her very hard before she was pregnant, but their desperate desire for a child drove them to pamper her once they knew she was expecting.

Now she found herself doing the cooking and washing for three grown men who'd grown up with–if their stories were to be believed–saintly mothers who could serve the soup with one hand while delivering a baby with the other, then get up to wash the dishes after.

What Vicky saw now was that even in her own privileged childhood, her mother had had other women around her to share the burden. Despite the extra cooking and cleaning necessitated by her sister's upcoming visit, Vicky looked forward to having her sister nearby, if only for an afternoon.

On her way home from doing the shopping, she ran into the new woman who lived downstairs. She had a sister a mother, and a brand-new husband to look after, and they were planning to move west as soon as they could, just like their predecessors.

The two married couples who shared the apartment downstairs had done the same shortly after Vicky found out she was expecting. There was factory and railroad work for those willing to relocate and established families like Pesa's sisters who were willing to sponsor Armenian workers.

With their heads close together on the pillows and her hands resting on her only slightly rounded tummy, Vicky asked him if it was something they should consider, not because she wanted to leave but because of the opportunity. Pesa confessed that he didn't want to go. He didn't want to take her away from the only family she had.

"You and this baby will be my family wherever we are," she whispered, but she was glad just the same.

The moment Vicky confessed her condition over Sunday dinner, Azniv deposited baby Pauline in Vicky's lap and joined Yessa in helping to serve the meal. Grateful for a break, Vicky cuddled Pauline, humming and singing to the cheerful little girl in her lap.

Her eyes met Pesa's over Pauline's downy crown of dark hair; his expression was tender.

By Easter, the morning sickness had subsided, but Vicky's energy hadn't returned. Not the way it had when she carried Nevart. As they had at Vicky and Pesa's wedding, the Danielians hosted an Easter dinner for the church community with everyone who could contribute a dish.

Yessa and Levon decided to travel to Worcester for the celebration and Vicky was overjoyed to have her sister's help in the kitchen.

Her sister, typically forthright, was hiding something. It was clear from the way she and Levon shared silent conversations across the room. Vicky wondered if they were also expecting. They'd waited a long time already without a baby, and Vicky knew they wanted children.

While she and Yessa mixed the meat, rice, and onion filling and wrapped it in grape leaves for *dolma*, Yessa finally revealed the secret she'd been keeping from their letters.

Levon and Peter would be taking jobs at a mill in Providence, Rhode Island, and buying a triple-decker house together with what they'd saved over the years.

Providence wasn't much closer on a map than Lawrence, but factory connections between Worcester and Providence meant direct rail lines. They could visit one another much more easily.

Not only that, Yessa said with a grin, but she was expecting as well.

"I knew it," Vicky said, hugging her sister. "This is wonderful. Cousins the same age to play together! Have you written to *Mayrig*? What about your matchmaking? What does Peter say?"

Yessa gave her a smug grin. "He's definitely considering it. Maybe we'll have *Mayrig* here when our babies are born!"

Azniv took a particular interest in Vicky's pregnancy. She would walk over almost every day with sweet tea, or toast and some fruit. Azniv would fold towels or dry dishes while catching Vicky up on their charitable projects and refugee work, without making it seem as though Vicky was neglecting her chores or being lazy.

"You shouldn't wear yourself out taking care of me," she protested.

"This is restful for me, too. I promise," Azniv said, as Pauline slept in Vicky's lap and John played with his favorite toy, a miniature painted cast-iron replica of a tractor that rolled over Vicky's floors with a metallic clatter. How the baby slept through the clatter was a mystery. "She's a little sister. She's never known anything else," Azniv laughed.

Moments like that punched the air from Vicky's lungs. Her baby would be a little sister or brother, but they would never know the noise and clutter of their older sister.

As the months progressed, Vicky's fatigue and anxiety only

increased. When she told Azniv she was worried, Azniv brushed it off with her usual good cheer.

"Every pregnancy is different," Azniv reassured her. "You'll see. The next one will be easy. You'll be cooking and sewing and birthing all at once like the mothers in the old country."

Her friend winked and Vicky laughed, but when she was alone, it was hard not to fret. This pregnancy was unlike her previous one in every way, but she didn't dare let on.

The secret of her daughter was too dangerous. Too precious.

When she didn't gain weight and grow rosy and plump everywhere like the other girls, Pesa worried.

"Every pregnancy is different. Maybe I'll get fat next time," she chided. "That's what Azniv says." Still, she did her best to stay cheerful when he and their roommates were at home to keep her husband from worrying.

Despite Azniv's reassuring presence, Vicky missed her sister. Yessa could be a bit overbearing, but she was family. Vicky wrote daily, sending a long letter every week, and looked forward to her sister's replies, which were increasingly full of plans to bring Mariam to Providence to marry Peter Poladian.

Vicky wondered if Eva and the rest of the Poladian women were moving to Providence as well. Yessa wrote back that Eva Poladian had qualified as a teacher. She'd perfected her English and gone out to get herself a job when it became apparent there were more than enough women in the household to take care of housekeeping. She intended to stay in Lawrence with two of her cousins, but the elder Mrs. Poladian was going to Providence to keep house until Mariam arrived.

Mariam had always been the most maternal of them and a natural peacekeeper. Vicky thought she would be well-suited for the situation.

In her next letter, though, Yessa was already working on marrying Peter's mother to the widower down the block from the new place–Frank Street, she called it–so Mariam could have a home of her own.

Vicky had to laugh. Yessa, who had learned the art of coffee cup reading from *Mayrig* in Aleppo, said there were weddings and babies in the grounds, but Vicky couldn't help but wonder which came first, her sister's prophecies or the machinations that brought them to life.

Yessa and Levon moved to Providence. Peter and his mother followed. Vicky's belly continued to swell. Some days she struggled to get out of bed, and supper was the only meal she ate, mostly because Pesa and the boys watched her to make sure she was eating.

21

Worcester, Massachusetts
1923-1924

The cramps woke Vicky from a sound sleep like a vise closing around her abdomen. She bit her lip to avoid crying out, but the pain was too much. She drew her knees up and squeezed her eyes shut tight, but it receded only to rise up again like the waves that had once nearly swamped the deck of the S.S. Braga. This time there was nothing she could do to hold back her cries.

Pesa rolled over, awakened by her distress. "Vicky? What is it?"

Another spasm rocked her belly and a warm sticky flood gushed between her legs, soaking the bed linen and leaving her breathless.

Pesa sat up and gathered her in his arms, his face a mask of horror at the site of all the blood. "What do I do?"

She screamed as another cramp tore through her.

When the pressure eased, she was able to gasp out the only instruction she knew to give. "Go downstairs and ask one of the ladies to come back with you."

"I can't leave you here like this…"

Vicky panted with the strain. Her heart was pounding. "You have to. I need help."

With shaking fingers, Pesa pulled on the pair of trousers he'd put out for work in the morning and pushed his arms to the sleeves of a shirt, not bothering to slow down to button it up properly. He dashed out of the apartment and Vicky could hear his feet pounding on the stairwell, followed by his fist against the door of 2B. After that, she was lost in another swamping contraction.

By the time it passed, her husband returned with Mrs. Dean herself. The commotion woke their roommates, who were shuffling around the kitchen, unsure of how to handle women's troubles, but clearly anxious for Vicky's well-being.

"Get some towels, and you two–" Mrs. Dean was regimentally brisk, and she accompanied her English with pantomime to make sure the men understood. "Boil some water."

To Vicky, Mrs. Dean murmured gently, directing Pesa to hold a cool cloth to Vicky's forehead. "Do you want me to send for your friend at the church?"

Vicky shook her head. Azniv had two children and a husband to look after, she needed to be sleeping.

"She needs a doctor," Mrs. Dean said, gesturing out the window at the hospital across the street. "A hospital. The bleeding won't stop. Can you carry her downstairs? I'll go ahead to the Dispensary to tell them you're coming." To the boys, she pointed out the mess. "Cold water for the blood. Make yourselves useful."

Pesa nodded mutely, helping Mrs. Dean wrap her in the blanket from the bed. When he picked her up as though she were a doll, Vicky surrendered to the pain.

Between the wracking tides, Vicky observed the crowd in the apartment with a weird detachment, as though she were watching this tragedy unfold in a stranger's home. It didn't matter whose apartment this was.

Her baby was gone.

Azniv came to see her in the hospital two days later, but her children weren't with her.

She pulled a chair over to Vicky's bedside and took Vicky's hand. "Do you know what happened?"

Vicky had been awake all morning, but the medication made her feel fuzzy, and she ached all over. Tears welled up and spilled over; she was too weak to wipe them away.

Azniv was gentle, using a nearby washcloth to dry Vicky's tears. "The doctor said he explained it, but I want to make sure you understood what he said."

"The baby is gone."

Azniv nodded mutely, still holding tight to Vicky's hand.

"Was it a daughter or a son?"

"A little girl." Azniv's voice caught. "Tiny and perfect, just like she was sleeping."

"Where is my husband?"

"He stayed all day yesterday, but he had to go back to the factory today. You know how they are over there. No excuses, no pity. It broke his heart to leave you. He's such a good man. It's a shame..." Azniv stopped suddenly.

Through the haze of grief and medicine, Vicky heard the hesitation in her friend's voice. She knew the sound of bad news.

"What is it?"

"There was too much bleeding. They couldn't stop it."

Azniv's face blurred behind Vicky's tears. The terrible pain in her belly, muted by the medicines they were giving her, burned low and menacing.

"The doctor had to remove your uterus. To save your life." Azniv's voice trembled. "I'm so sorry, Vicky. But you won't be able to have any more children."

Vicky hardly recognized the keening wail that escaped her own lips. Azniv squeezed her hand, but nothing could hold her. Once more she was standing in the Yavuz house in Aleppo, paralyzed by terror.

Her baby was gone.

Azniv was speaking. Vicky needed to listen, but the air around her seemed to darken, growing thick and sour.

"Sitrek and I will have you come stay with us when you are sent home. At least until your sister can come up and stay for a few days to help you get back on your feet."

Azniv's face swam in and out of focus as the darkness closed in, and Vicky's heart cried out for her lost babies as she sank under again.

***

When her husband and sister brought Vicky home to the apartment, her roommates were nowhere to be found. Yessa told her the two men were staying with friends while Vicky recovered. Azniv had come by to help with the chores, and Mrs. Dean regularly left food.

As soon as she was able, Vicky dutifully followed Yessa's instructions to get up, to wash, to sit in the kitchen, and keep her company, but she felt like a sleepwalker.

Her husband slept beside her every night, careful not to jostle her. He carried his grief in his eyes, so Vicky stopped looking at him unless they were speaking. She simply couldn't bear it.

It was hard to ignore her sister's rosy glow and burgeoning middle. Yessa was the old-world matriarch, waddling competently around the apartment, hanging out the washing and peeling potatoes while she sang the lullabies *Mayrig* sang to them as children.

The lullabies Vicky had sung to Nevart what felt like a lifetime ago.

Vicky slept for hours during the afternoons, much to her sister's dismay, and one afternoon when she woke, she heard Yessa and Azniv speaking to Mrs. Dean in the hallway outside the apartment.

"She isn't recovering as quickly as I hoped she would," Mrs. Dean was saying.

"I hear her whisper a name: Nevart, in her sleep. She must have chosen a name. My heart breaks for her." This was from Azniv.

Vicky's heart raced. *What else might she have said?* But the women moved on to strategize Vicky's recovery.

"I can't abandon Levon much longer," Yessa said. "I should have gone back to Providence a week ago."

"We'll look out for her." Mrs. Dean was reassuring as always, and Vicky's cheeks burned. Shame upon shame. She was soiled, ruined, and not able to be a mother to any child, ever again, and now she was causing her loved ones trouble.

That evening, she forced herself to take up the potato peeler and make an effort to prepare supper. Yessa seemed pleased. After dinner, Yessa told her what Vicky had already overheard. Her sister would be returning home to her husband. To prepare for her own baby.

Eventually, their roommates returned, and while they tried to be helpful, they were young men accustomed to bachelor living or having a woman to care for them. Vicky shuffled around the apartment listlessly, putting what food she could manage on an increasingly sad table, no matter how many dishes Azniv brought by, or how many women from the church came to help with the housekeeping.

Weeks passed and Vicky's body slowly regained some strength, but she couldn't find her smile. Couldn't find the steely resolve that once carried her. She felt like a melon, scooped clean of sweetness and vitality. She was a husk of a woman in every way.

As time passed, the sadness in Peso's gaze turned warm with concern. Even so, they stumbled through conversations, both in mourning, with Vicky's burdens between them like a citadel wall.

She didn't know how to knock it down, or even if she could.

At the end of a workday, Pesa sat down across from her at a table laid with food she hadn't prepared and said, "I've had a letter from Levon."

Vicky looked up from picking at her plate.

"Yessa had her baby." He took a deep breath and glanced at Vicky, who forced herself to look at him. "All is well, and you have a niece. Levon also writes that your sister Mariam will arrive from Constantinople in a few months. It's all settled."

Vicky mustered the echo of a smile. A niece. Another sister on her way.

"Levon described the building they bought. It's like this–well, like half of this. Like next door." He took a deep breath. "He offered us the third-floor apartment, and I think we should accept. You need your sister, and Levon says there are factory jobs in Providence."

Vicky thought of Azniv and Sitrek, boisterous Johnny and sweet little Pauline, and kind Mrs. Dean. Lovely Elm Park, and this neighborhood she'd only just begun to love, but Pesa was right.

She wasn't able to manage on her own, and this apartment was full of memories she would be better off leaving behind.

Their marriage was suffering, and Pesa deserved happiness. Perhaps in a new place, she could find a way back to herself, and maybe even make him happy again.

Pesa took her hand across the table. "It doesn't matter where we live, so long as we're together."

Vicky couldn't stop the bitter thoughts. They would be together. Just the two of them. Forever. But Pesa wouldn't understand just how deeply the knowledge cut her. "How soon does my brother-in-law say we can come?"

"As soon as we're able." Pesa's shoulders dropped in relief, and Vicky realized how much worry he'd been carrying since her miscarriage. "He'll speak to the hiring manager at the factory for me in the meantime."

22

Providence, Rhode Island
1924

The move to Providence was embarrassingly simple. They owned very little. Most of the furniture and pots and pans were left with their roommates, who'd already arranged for two more young men from the wire factory to take the empty bedroom.

The move may have been Levon's idea on paper, but it was Yessa who made it happen. Vicky missed Azniv's humor as she watched her sister direct the men as they carted Vicky and Peso's possessions up the stairs. With her new baby in her arms and the welcoming scent of food rifting from her kitchen, her sister was the picture of the ideal Armenian wife and mother, and yet her sister never lost her blunt nature and sharp tongue.

They left Worcester behind, but Vicky's grief and sadness followed her south. Everyone made her feel welcome, and without the burden of work, her body was able to rest and recover, but her spirits sank lower.

The third floor was smaller than the lower two floors, but with just the two of them living; there was enough space. Her sister's kitchen was much larger and her dining room more suited to gathering, so Vicky and Pesa took to eating with everyone for weeknight suppers and family dinners. They were often joined by Peter and his mother, who always had something to say about their preparations for Mariam's arrival and their wedding.

Levon was promoted to floor manager and used his new influence to get Pesa a better position, and Peter took a job clerking for a law office, which suited him far better than millwork. Pesa made friends at his new job, and Yessa introduced Vicky to the women in the neighborhood. On the surface, everything looked better.

Vicky learned to mimic contentment to keep her family from worrying. Her only true pleasure came from watching her niece give Yessa a break from the baby's constant demands, and even that came at a cost.

No one spoke of what she'd been through. After a few months, the physical pain was mostly gone, though she was often weak and tired easily. It was easier for her family to show support than to speak of it.

With the advantage of distance and time, Vicky saw that their silence was a legacy of the march through the desert and the horrors around that time. She couldn't blame them. Mayrig set the tone all the way back in Hamidieh Camp; there was nothing to go back to, so why speak of it?

So, she rocked her niece and mourned in silence.

When Nevart was taken from her, survival forced grief deep into her heart. One more sharp stone in a collection that included *Hayrig* and her brothers, their home, and her childhood. Staying alive outweighed pausing to examine the terrible sadness.

In Yessa's rocking chair with the soothing bundle of her niece in her arms, there was nothing but time and her thoughts. No soldiers with guns, no men who would claim her as property. No adversaries to outmaneuver.

No womb. No hope of ever carrying another child. No son or daughter for her Pesa.

In her darkest moments, she begged God for an explanation. Was this a punishment for deceiving her husband? For not being clever or strong enough to hold on to Nevart?

Pesa too felt the loss of their child, but the wide chasm of her shame divided them. Vicky didn't know how to reach for him without the whole sordid tale gushing out of her like pus from an infected wound.

Every day when they were first married, he'd come through the door whistling at the end of the day, holding her and kissing her hello. Now their greetings were awkward and formal. They conversed with the others, but barely spoke when they were alone.

Yessa watched her when she thought Vicky wouldn't notice. Vicky pretended not to feel her sister's worried gaze. Like everyone else, Yessa clucked when she heard about refugees who had babies but no husbands, or were pregnant when they arrived, without a marriage to legitimize them. Even Azniv expressed dismay in her letter, when a newly arrived bride was rejected for being soiled in some way.

If her beloved sister and her truest friend felt that way, how could she ever tell anyone about Nevart and her time with the Yavuz's?

23

Providence, Rhode Island
1924-1925

Half a year passed in that dull gray fog of grief and pain.

Vicky should have expected Yessa wouldn't be content to let her drift like a ghost. What she didn't expect was that her sister would awaken her resilience and renew her soul.

Early that morning, Yessa barged into Vicky's bedroom, opened the shades to let in the light, and insisted that she sit up. "I can't begin to understand what you've been through, but neither can I watch you go through this anymore. We are all worried about you, especially Pesa. It's as if your light has gone out, but I don't believe that. Find it again."

Her throat was ragged with emotion. "I don't know if I can."

"I do," she said gently. "Pesa does. We all do. We love you and we need you. Now, get up and listen to me." Yessa steered them toward the sofa and sat close to Vicky. "More and more refugees are coming every day, women and girls like us. They may not need rescuing, but they still need help. The church sewing circle can't keep up with demand, and I can't keep up my share of it, not with the baby and the house. I need you to help with my workload."

"I don't know if I'm up for all that."

"*Babam*. In Worcester, you did all that mending and lacework. We have the nicest linens of anyone on the block because of your skill, and you told me you taught others when you lived in the rescue home. What if you did that for the ones who wanted to learn?

Vicky shook her head. "Pesa might think I am being foolish to relive my youthful adventures".

Yessa took her hand and brought her to the mirror. "Pesa will be happy to have his lovely bride back without limp hair, ashy skin, and sad face. Do it for your marriage. And do it for yourself. You deserve to be happy."

While Vicky wasn't convinced that she deserved happiness, she knew that the sullen face looking back at her in the mirror was not the wife that Pesa deserved.

"I'll do it." Her sudden confidence surprised them both into laughter.

She greeted Pesa at the door freshly bathed and dressed, with a warm kiss when he came home from work. She told him the news and her plan and waited for his response.

He touched her cheek. "You could be like your Miss Jeppe, but here in Providence."

That he remembered her beloved mentor's name warmed Vicky's heart. Pesa tucked a stray lock of her hair behind her ear. She leaned her cheek into his palm, breathing in the familiar scent of him–pomade, machine oil, and the starch Yessa used on his shirts.

He leaned down and pressed a questioning kiss to her mouth. "You'll be marvelous."

Later that night, while Kachadoor slept beside her, Vicky imagined a room full of women eager to learn. She grasped tight to the sliver of hope and her old confidence.

When Kachadoor turned to her in his sleep, Vicky met his warm embrace and gently reminded him of the love and desire between them. Afterward, in the faint glow of streetlight that bled through the window shades, she held him close while he slept and was grateful.

Vicky wasted no time and asked Yessa how to get started the next day.

Yessa bustled into the apartment with a basket of fine cotton thread and a beautiful set of needlework tools.

"Do you remember the cloth importer I told you about? The one who brought not only his wife but her sister and the sister's three orphan daughters?" Yessa paused long enough for Vicky to nod. "The sisters and the daughters were rescued by your Miss Jeppe. They were learning needlework. The kind you're so good at, but there's no one here to finish teaching it." Yessa pushed open the curtains and dismissed the dimness in which Vicky hid. "The eldest daughter was pregnant when they took her out of the household where she was a maid. It's shameful, the way she was treated, but the truth of it is, the girl has no prospects. Her parents will probably end up supporting her, so it would be good if she had a skill to contribute to the household."

Amot. Shameful. Yessa had no idea. For the first time since her miscarriage, the shame burned hot like anger. This poor girl would have a skill, and a valuable one if Vicky had anything to say about it.

Yessa beamed. "You'll come with me to the sewing circle. We're already using the church hall. You can offer lessons in needlelace and sewing. The girl's uncle will send her. Leave that part to me, and the others will follow."

Once more, Vicky wondered if her sister was gifted at predictions, or the architect of their outcomes. Events progressed just as Yessa envisioned.

The girl's uncle did send her. She was heavily pregnant, which gave Vicky a pang of sorrow, but worse were the dark circles under her eyes, and her haunted expression. She barely spoke, only took up the needles and thread and started a lovely pattern suited for fine table linens.

"Your work is beautiful," Vicky said, keeping her voice low so as not to startle the young woman.

"Thank you, Mrs. Minassian. I'm very grateful to continue learning from you."

"Did you meet Miss Jeppe when you were staying at the rescue home," Vicky asked.

"No. I was only there for a month. They located my mother and sisters very quickly, and my uncle was already arranging for them to travel here. Miss Jeppe is a formidable woman."

Formidable. It was a good word for Karen Jeppe, but it didn't tell the whole story. "I'm sorry you didn't. She is also very kind."

"You know Miss Jeppe?"

"We spoke twice." Vicky chuckled softly. The young woman's regard made her feel older than her years. "I was there myself only a few years ago. I lived in the rescue home for a year and a half after I was rescued, mainly as a volunteer and teacher."

For a few moments, the young woman worked silently on her lace. When she spoke, she reminded Vicky of a child who'd been naughty and expected a smack. "May I ask where you were rescued from?"

Knowing something of the young woman's background, Vicky laid a gentle hand on her arm. "I was a maid in a Turkish household in Aleppo."

The girl glanced down at her advanced pregnancy, then back at Vicky.

A sea of silent secrets coursed between them before Vicky drew in a fortifying breath. "Before you know it, you'll be making fine linens and lace for gowns, and fetching good money for your work."

There was a light in the young woman's eyes when she left that afternoon that hadn't been there when she arrived. Such a small thing, but Vicky carried that triumph with her all the rest of that week.

So smoothly Vicky hardly noticed that transition, Yessa took on less and less of the organizing, and Vicky found herself guiding the sewing circle as they made clothes and raised funds for newly arrived refugees and orphans overseas. She wrote to Azniv about it, and her friend sent back letters brimming with ideas.

Don't be afraid, Azniv wrote, *to keep an eye out for eligible bachelors and empty bedrooms. Much can be accomplished there, as well.*

Vicky kept Azniv's advice, and when Pesa told her about a friend from work who'd had a terrible accident on the factory line that resulted in not only a lost leg but a lost fiancee, Vicky knew just the girl to send his way with a basket of food and cleaning supplies while he recovered.

By the time Mariam arrived six months later, Vicky was teaching two dozen women and girls the needlework she learned as a girl and perfected during her time in Aleppo. Between the sewing circle's efforts and Vicky's own work, she and Yessa were able to give Mariam not only a lovely new dress for the wedding, but a treasure of fine linens, shawls, afghans, and decorative pieces for her new home.

Mayrig sent word with Mariam that she and Lucine would stay until Lucine completed her schooling. Aleppo was the only home Lucine remembered, and now that it was safe enough to be there, *Mayrig* didn't want to tear her away.

Three or four years was a long time to wait, but in the meantime, there was work to do and, in her own way, women to rescue.

24

Istanbul, Turkey
Late Spring, 1963

"Where is it that you and father are going again?" Gül's daughter Leyla watched her mother packing. Her daughter was newly married and still visited often while her husband was working.

"Gürin," Gül said, using the Turkish name for the village Victoria described in her letters. She didn't look up from her folding. "There are dolls from the Sivas region I'm interested in."

It wasn't entirely a lie. Gül hoped to learn more about Armenian dolls if there was anyone there who knew about them, but this trip was to prove to herself, one way or the other if Victoria's story was true.

If her own story was a lie.

Her daughter's eyes narrowed in suspicion. "Father is taking time away from work to look at dolls with you?"

Gül tamped down her irritation. Ahmet had surprised her. It took weeks for Gül to work up the courage to tell him about the letters. When she finally confessed, hands shaking, her husband held her.

You are my wife, Gülüm, and that is what matters. The war changed so many lives. You know my father was a soldier. He always said it was a job, not an ideology for him. He saw terrible things, though he rarely spoke of them. If what this woman writes to you is true, you were given a great gift. Your mother's family gave you love and safety, an education. They gave your soul to Allah for keeping. They gave you to me.

If you wish to humor this old woman in America, it changes nothing for me.

He'd supported her decision to write to Rose, and he'd read every letter from Victoria that arrived in a fat bundle one day. A lifetime of heartache on mimeograph paper.

He continued to view Gül's upbringing as a gift. He saw the potential truth of her birth as an unfortunate accident rectified by Allah. Nothing to bother him. Like her dolls, the letters and the American women were a hobby in his eyes.

Their friends, Ahmet's coworkers, and even Leyla and her husband might not be so understanding. Even Gül herself wrestled with the likelihood of her birth mother. Her daughter was a patriot, a child of the capital, and so young. For her, there were few gray areas.

"Yes, darling, he is." Gül finished folding a light sweater and set it down on the bed. "We'll only be gone a few days."

Leyla caught the hint of rebuke in her mother's words–Gül could see it on her daughter's face.

"Of course, Mother," Leyla said. "I didn't mean to be nosy."

"You're forgiven." Gül laughed. Leyla's contrition was childlike. "But you *did* mean to be nosy."

Gül took a moment to memorize the young woman her daughter had become. All throughout Leyla's childhood she had done this–almost as though she were taking a photograph of them in her memory.

She saw so much of Ahmet in Leyla. The twinkle in her daughter's eye, the set of her jaw when she was frustrated. Now she wondered what traits her daughter carried that might have belonged to Victoria.

Somewhere in America, in a place called Providence–which was, according to the atlas, not far from New York City, not really–her daughter had cousins who were just as tied to her by blood as the cousins she still celebrated holy days alongside.

She feared Leyla would reject the idea outright.

The only other person Gül shared any of this journey with was her close friend and neighbor, Selma. Selma was adopted from an orphanage in Ankara by a Turkish Muslim family. She was left there as an infant, with no papers or identifying items.

Her friend had struggled with her identity over the years and offered sympathy for Gül's situation.

It was a day and a half from Istanbul to Kayseri via Ankara by train, then they would travel on to Gürin. As Constantinople slipped into the distance, the trip began to feel like a vacation. She and Ahmet rarely traveled farther than their families' homes.

Ahmet wanted to explore the foothills around the town while Gül went to explore the town. She decided to begin at the town offices to inquire whether there was a record of the families who had lived in the area before the relocations.

Despite the decades, Gürin still bore the scars of conflict. The village seemed to retain the memory of suffering. She felt that remembered pain as she looked around the town center. She passed a small market in the shadow of the ruins of a church and was told it had once been called Holy Mother of God by the infidels.

Had the Karadelians worshiped at that church?

At the *Gürin Belediye İş Hanı*, a helpful clerk asked why she was inquiring, Gül told him as much of the truth as she dared.

"I heard a family story about two Armenian girls burying a child's treasure in this area before they were relocated."

That was putting a gloss on the situation, but it was as much as Gül felt comfortable sharing.

The clerk didn't have much in the way of helpful information, but an older woman–perhaps in her late fifties–approached.

She offered Gül her arm and leaned in close. "You'll have a parade of treasure hunters behind you if you keep that up."

The woman glanced back to the clerk's window. "The village knows the Armenians buried valuables before they were relocated. They'll follow you and hope you're a treasure map in city clothes."

Gül took in the woman's conspirators' expression and stiffened. She hadn't expected any of this.

"I have lived in this town my whole life. I knew those girls. The ground around the house was dug up years ago. There's nothing there, but that won't stop my neighbors from trying."

Gül saw the moment the woman slipped into the past, her eyes seeing a faraway time, instead of the government offices around them.

"I was in school with…Mariam," she whispered, the name coming slowly, as though she were drawing it up from a deep well. “She was my age. We played together. She had older sisters. Victoria and Yegsabet. Us younger girls thought they were very sophisticated, but that was a lifetime ago.”

The name Victoria caused Gül’s pulse to thump against her breastbone. "Would you tell me about them?"

"Tell you about them? I can do better than that. Walk with me.” The woman coughed to cover the emotion that crept into her voice. “I will show you where they lived.”

While they walked, the old woman told stories of going to school in the early years of the new century, of celebrating with their neighbors, and of the terrible sadness that followed the relocation. “Those families were our friends, our neighbors, but the soldiers–and then the politicians–were very convincing.”

Eventually, they came to the ruins of an Arabic-style house near the edge of the village. The terrain stepped away from the road, held back by retaining walls which now held back only a wild tangle of flowering plants and desert foliage with no rhyme or reason.

A cemetery slept peacefully across the road.

It was very beautiful, but also very sad.

“There were beautiful gardens here once,” she said softly. "This was where they lived. Mr. and Mrs. Karadelian and the children. There were two older brothers, as I recall. Yenov was the eldest. He was very handsome. And kind to the younger girls.”

Gül saw the echo of the young girl the woman had once been in the wistful curve of her smile. It reminded her of falling in love with her husband so many years ago.

"Not that my father would have allowed me to marry whomever I liked. Our marriages were carefully arranged,” she said with a wry laugh. "But we are all entitled to our girlish infatuations, are we not?”

Gül had to agree. She’d daydreamed about her fair share of young men before being introduced to Ahmet.

The old woman's expression fell. “The men left to help with a project for the government. The women had to leave for their own safety, but I remember the gunshots.”

“Some of the Karadelians survived. I know a little of what befell

Victoria and her sisters in the aftermath." Gül tried to stay calm but her pulse was racing. Everything this woman remembered matched Victoria's letters. "I'll tell you what I know."

Her new friend offered a soft smile. "I'd like that very much, but we mustn't linger here long. The treasure hunters will be along soon if we do."

Gül gave the old woman a moment with her memories before pressing on. "Do you remember a very old olive tree near here?"

Her new friend's smile widened. "I do. In the cemetery. You can see its canopy from here."

The next day Gül and Ahmet walked to the cemetery. With the warning of being followed around with spades in her ears, they stopped at several graves to study the names and dates as though they were searching for information, not a treasure site.

"Remind me again the significance of this olive tree?" Ahmet asked as they drew closer to the tree itself.

"In the letters, there was a story about Victoria and her sister burying a treasure under an ancient olive tree near their home. The woman I met at the town offices told me this is that tree. I wanted to see it."

"I remember now," Ahmet said. "But why do you care? The letters describe the treasure of a child. Dolls, coins, hair combs. Nothing of value to you."

Ahmet didn't mind her search for the truth, but neither was his patience infinite. "Victoria grew up believing the tree to have been planted by the prophet Nüh after the Deluge. I thought it might be interesting."

"Treasure *and* a prophet's tree?" Ahmet laughter. "What an adventure."

Alone among the headstones in this section, the tree was ringed by a low stone wall amid a circular terrace paved with worn stone. It was massive–as wide as a small car; Gül couldn't see around the trunk when she was standing in front of it. Its knobby, ancient roots rose and dove again into the soil, giving rise to almost otherworldly branches and a canopy nearly too perfect to be real.

Even Ahmet was impressed.

"If there was ever a tree to bury treasure under, this is it." He peered closer at the tree and began to walk its perimeter, treading carefully where the roots were most prominent. Gül tried to imagine the youthful courage it would have taken to sneak out, to bury their most precious possessions in the face of so much fear.

“Nothing on this side,” Ahmet called out.

Gül quashed a pang of disappointment. A small, secret part of her wanted to find evidence of two Armenian Nuri dolls buried underneath the ancient olive tree, despite the very real wish that this was all a terrible mistake, and she could go back to being who she’d always known she was.

"Maybe tomorrow," Ahmet said, "We can ask after any dollmakers in the area."

Gül very much doubted there were any traditional Armenian dollmakers still living in the area, but she loved her husband for thinking of it. "Yes, perhaps."

Later that evening, they shared a meal at a cafe in the center of the town. They finished the meal with coffee and lokum. The sweets always reminded her of her mother. For the rest of the evening, they were simply a couple sharing a meal while traveling.

That night Gül dreamed of the olive tree under a round, full moon, and a beautiful house falling into ruin, swallowed by a bleeding chasm.

She woke up determined to revisit the ruined house. Some of Victoria's letters described it, and she wanted to look around–treasure hunters or not.

Despite her dark dream, the ruins of the house were still where she left them. There was another house nearby, this one well-maintained and obviously lived in. It was not as large as the footprint of the ruins, but also built in the Arabic style.

After pacing the perimeter of the ruins, leaning down to touch the crumbling blocks of marble that had once lined the courtyard, she decided to call on the neighbors.

A woman answered the door, but she didn’t want to talk about the ruins. All she would say was that her grandparents moved in in nineteen-seventeen and the house had been in the family since then. Before Victoria's letters, she'd have thought nothing of it, but now the provenance of the house seemed sinister.

Had this house too belonged to an Armenian family whose men died on the road, whose women walked with death in the Syrian deserts?

"I am a dollmaker," Gül said, feeling awkward about her suspicions. "I am in the area researching folk traditions that include dolls. Can you tell me anything?"

The woman's gaze danced across the cemetery's rolling topography before falling on the blue glass eye that hung sparkling in the sun.

It wasn't lost on Gül that the eye watched the ruins of Victoria's childhood home.

Later that week, once she and Ahmet were settled back into their comfortable routine, she visited Selma. Her friend was willing to share the burden of her concerns, and Gül needed advice.

"I can't deny any longer that Victoria is who Rose says she is. Her letters and Rose's descriptions match everything I discovered in Gürin," Gül said. "I almost wish this could be your story."

"If Allah wishes to reveal my past, he will," Selma said. "Instead, he wills you to travel this path. What does Ahmet say?"

"He thinks he is indulging in a pet project. He is not bothered by the possibility of my ancestry. So long as it doesn't disrupt his life."

Selma chuckled. "Men are predictable. Even the one you married."

"I think he will be predictable when I tell him I want to travel to the United States to meet this woman."

Selma's gaze snapped to hers. "Surely not?"

"The niece who writes to me says her aunt's health is fading. If she is dying, I might miss the opportunity to speak to her. Selma, this woman is very likely my biological mother. If that's true, I have to know what happened."

"But travel to America?"

"I can hardly ask a sick, old woman to fly to Istanbul."

"That's true. What will Leyla say?"

Gül didn't answer. She might be able to sway her husband. He was a curious man, and a trip to America would be hard to resist. They had savings, but their daughter no longer needed them. When would such a chance arise again?

"I'll have to tell her. All of it."

She'd deeply underestimated the depth of her daughter's feelings. Leyla, stubborn and proud, the wife of a young government employee, rejected every word of Gül's story.

"Mother, you can't be serious? Some Armenian comes begging and you want to travel halfway around the world because you actually believe she might be your biological mother. It's nonsense. Imagine what Nene would think."

Leyla knew bringing up her grandmother would hurt. Gül and her Ayşe–had always been close. She mourned her mother still.

"I am not looking for a substitute for my mother," Gül struggled to keep her temper in check. "But I want to know the truth."

"The truth?" Her daughter's fury painted bright spots on her cheeks. "You are my mother. The wife of Ahmet Nacar. The daughter of good, hardworking, faithful people. Turkish people. That is the truth."

Oh, to be young and so sure of everything.

Gül sent her daughter home in tears, too exhausted to argue anymore, but the hard feelings stung. Ahmet took their daughter's side, though he didn't outright forbid the travel. If she was determined to see it though, he would allow it, but he could not in good conscience go with her.

Again, she turned to Selma.

"He will let you go on your own?"

Gül sighed. "He thinks I won't go alone. But neither of them understands how I feel."

Selma took her hand. "I do, my friend. And you'll go. I know it."

Gül wrote again to Rose. This time not only to request more information. She was building a bridge across the wide ocean between them, and when it was ready, she would cross it.

25

Providence, Rhode Island
1929

Vicky loitered in the church hall after the sewing circle, listening to her students' chatter. She thought of them as girls, though some were older than she was. All their talk of husbands and babies left her feeling far older than her twenty-nine years.

As she packed her lace needles into her sewing basket, an older woman approached in the company of the *Yeretzgin*.

The priest's wife made introductions. The woman was newly arrived, along with her picture bride daughter, and in possession of enough money to pay for a proper wedding gown.

"I thought you would be perfect, Vicky," *Yeretzgin* Margaret said. "You make such lovely clothes, and your lacework is the best of all of us."

"Only until my youngest sister arrives tomorrow," Vicky laughed. "Lucine can reproduce any lace she sees, and she's mastered techniques I never had time for."

"And we will gladly put her to work when she's ready," *Yeretzgin* Margaret said. "In the meantime, I'll leave you two to get acquainted."

By the time Vicky arrived home, Pesa was already back from work, and the homey scent of supper drifted down from Yessa's kitchen upstairs.

While Pesa watched from his favorite chair, Vicky wrapped her dress form in a length of cream linen.

"What will that be, my love?"

"A wedding dress for a picture bride," Vicky said, smiling coyly around the form, before making a few folds and pinning them to get an idea of the shape. "*Yeretzgin* Margaret is sponsoring the mother and daughter until the wedding, and they have hired me to sew it."

She wasn't able to keep the pride from her voice, but this was Pesa, who was proud of her for anything she put her hands to.

"She's a lucky girl," he said.

Vicky moved to perch on the arm of his chair. "If her husband is anything like mine, she is."

"Have you and Yessa worked out where your mother and sister will stay?"

"Yessa's spare bedroom has better light, but with her daughter, our spare room is quieter. Mariam and Peter offered to have them both move into their second floor when Peter's sister and her husband move back to Lawrence in the fall…"

Pesa finished her thought for her. "So you want to have your mother stay here for a few months, and Lucine can stay with Yessa until they can have the apartment with Mariam?"

Vicky smiled. "You won't mind very much, will you?"

"My parlor is a dress shop, my spare room will have my mother-in-law." He tugged Vicky into his lap and kissed her. "What do I care? I have you."

They were both laughing when Yessa hollered for supper and the pounding of her children's feet on the stairs called them up to dine with her family.

***

Vicky could hardly sleep that night for excitement. Finally, they would all be together again. Peter and Levon had taken the train to New York that afternoon to meet *Mayrig* and Lucine's ship and they all would be back in the afternoon.

Her mother and sister weren't all that kept her up. Pesa was teasing, but his words tumbled around her wakeful brain like newsprint in a gale. *My parlor is a dress shop...*

She couldn't say exactly when she'd begun to want more than her work teaching sewing and fine lace to newcomers. Since she'd begun, dozens of girls and women had come through her sewing circle; many of them took new skills and a way to contribute to their households when they moved on. Some stayed and helped. Some married and never picked up a needle again, but she'd given them friendship and a community of women to support them.

She'd nudged unmarried girls into the notice of eligible young men, introduced spinsters and widows to older men, matched young men in need of roommates, and helped to place orphans where they would be cared for. It was a good life, far better than she deserved, but even so, she wanted something for herself.

Was a dress shop too ambitious?

Pesa's whisper was soft on her cheek. "*Hokis*, you're thinking so loud Yessa can hear you upstairs."

Vicky turned. His profile, limned in moonlight, was familiar and beloved. "I was daydreaming."

He chuckled softly. "It's the middle of the night."

"Just dreaming, then."

"Tell me."

In the darkness, it was easier to speak the wish aloud. "You said your parlor was a dress shop, and I know you were teasing, but..."

"You would like to have a dress shop in the parlor."

Vicky could detect no irritation or impatience. Pesa knew her too well. "Yes."

"What will you need?"

"Nothing I don't already have or can't get." Drawn from dreams into possibility, she could see it now. The dress form, her basket, a sewing machine once she'd saved a little more, and Pesa could build her a table for it.

A small sign on the mailbox that read *Victoria Minassian, Dressmaker...*

Again, Pesa's gentle laughter rumbled in his chest. "Go to sleep.

There'll be time to plan tomorrow."

***

There wasn't time to plan the next day or the day after. *Mayrig* and Lucine arrived exhausted and desperate for a warm bath and a bed that didn't sway with the tides.

Mayrig was asleep in a chair in Yessa's parlor with her youngest grandchild snoozing in her arms when the food and drink ran out and Mariam and Peter carried their children next door to put them to bed.

Yessa stuffed her own sleepy children to bed while Levon and Pesa stepped outside for a smoke on the porch, leaving Vicky and Lucine alone for a moment.

Vicky looked at her sixteen-year-old sister and saw how she might have looked in another life. They were alike in coloring, with the thick-lashed, deep brown Karadelian eyes, but where Vicky's limbs were wiry and her body small and frail, Lucine was only a little way from her voyage. Her cheeks were plump and rosy, and her figure curved like a healthy young woman's.

Lucine took her hands and chafed them in her palms. "Your fingers are like ice, Victoria. Vicky." Lucine tried out the nickname she'd heard bandied around the room all evening. "I like your American name."

Vicky grinned. "Then you must have one, too…Lucy."

"Lucy," said her sister, eyes twinkling. "I think Ardashes will like that as well as I do."

Vicky clasped her sister's hands. "Who is Ardashes?"

Lucy blushed. "A young man I met on the voyage. Perhaps I'll be like you and marry my true love from the ship."

"You're too young, and you've only just arrived, and we know nothing of this young man."

"I don't want to marry him now," Lucy giggled. "For now, he will write to me. He's to be a goldsmith's apprentice here in Providence, and he'll live with his father. He's not much older than I am, and his father found him where he was living in an orphanage in Greece and paid for his travel. He's ever so kind and handsome, *kooyr.*"

It was hard to douse her sister's affections, especially as Vicky had married her true love from the ship, but Lucy was terribly young, and only newly arrived.

"Time will tell, sweet girl. I'm just glad to have you and *Mayrig* with us at last."

***

Lucy was a bright light in Vicky's days from that evening on. Her sister's skill at lace brought in pocket money and contributed to filling the family coffers, and her sister's youthful energy infused the sewing circle with fresh laughter.

Lucy also helped her to ready the front parlor of the apartment for Vicky's first customers, and her modest home dress shop was born. Word spread quickly of the wedding dress and the fine lace the two sisters made for trimming, and Vicky soon had enough work to keep both of them busy.

Vicky took her sister to Worcester to meet Azniv and little Pauline, who was growing like a weed. Lucy wanted to see the church where she and Pesa married and confessed her young man was writing every week.

"He's begun his apprenticeship, and says that he might be a partner someday, or even have a jewelry shop of his own if he works hard."

Later, while Lucy played with Pauline, Azniv took Vicky aside. "You have been busy, my dear."

Vicky was curious. "I have, but how do you mean?"

"The church held a bazaar to raise funds for orphans, and one of the young married women, newly arrived here with her husband from Providence, sold the most beautiful tablecloths, runners, and doilies. They brought in some of the highest donations, and who do you think taught her to make lace?"

Azniv confessed the woman's name, and a warm rush of pride filled Vicky's heart.

"She also told me you introduced her to her husband." Azniv wrapped an arm around Vicky's shoulders. "I'm glad you took my advice to heart."

Vicky and Lucy rode the train home together that evening with weary feet and full hearts. Lucy watched the countryside roll past with a dreamy, faraway expression Vicky assumed to be for her young man.

A woman her mother's age sat across from them, knitting to the rhythmic clacking of the rails. She nodded in Lucy's direction and leaned across the aisle. "Your daughter is lovely."

Vicky's heart lurched in her chest. She supposed she did look old enough to be a sixteen-year-old's mother. Nevart would be ten this year, only six years younger than Lucy. Her little girl would never ride the train with her to visit friends, and it was unlikely her daydreams would be spent on an ambitious young man in an American city.

"Thank you, but she's my baby sister."

"Oh, pardon me," the stranger said genially. "Forgive an old woman?"

"It's already forgiven," Vicky said, unable to be upset. After all, Lucy was a lovely girl, and Vicky could see how such an assumption would be made.

"What was that about?" Lucy asked, having slipped out of her musings long enough to catch the end of the conversation.

"She thought you were my daughter," Vicky said lightly.

"You don't look that old," Lucy laughed. "Certainly not old enough to have a daughter my age."

When Vicky couldn't find an answering laugh, Lucy's face fell. "Oh, stupid me. I'm so sorry. I sometimes forget about the baby you lost."

Like the child she still was, Lucy wrapped her arms around Vicky and squeezed. "Please forgive me?"

Vicky kissed her sister's forehead. "Nothing to forgive. I promise."

26

Providence, Rhode Island
Spring 1933

Lucy's young man proved steadfast and patient. Vicky proved their champion.

When *Mayrig* worried about their youth, it was Vicky who soothed her fears. When Levon frowned at Ardashes's prospects, Vicky argued the young man's case. When Mariam and Yessa paraded other young men through dinners and church socials, Vicky found other girls for them to court. Ardash brought great energy, a cheerful demeanor, and a sense of humor to their already animated family and was well-liked by all.

Her youngest sister's sunny nature was undimmed by waiting while her sweetheart established himself, and the very same day he was given a full-time position as the shop's manager, he respectfully asked *Mayrig* for Lucy's hand in marriage. He took great pride in presenting Lucy a diamond he'd set himself.

The two women planned Lucy's wedding dress together, and Vicky took special care in sewing it. Her bride's gift to her sister was a length of white silk far more luxurious than any of the other sisters had worn, and the stranger's words on the train stayed with her as she stitched.

Your daughter is lovely.

If Vicky imagined sometimes that Lucy was Nevart, standing still on the small pedestal in the front parlor while Vicky slipped pins in the gown's hem and bodice, she knew both her daughter and her sister would understand and forgive her.

The night before the wedding, Vicky crawled into bed long after midnight, sore and chilled, but the dress and veil were finished and pressed, waiting on a hanger for the bride to arrive before church in the morning.

“You give us all so much, my love,” Pesa whispered into the dark. “I hope your sister knows how fortunate she is in you.”

Vicky kissed her husband’s shoulder and lay still while his breathing slowed, and he slipped back into sleep. Her heart banged against her chest, as though all her secrets might burst from her chest.

I failed everyone who needed me most.

I failed my living child. I lost her forever.

I lied to everyone I loved and hid her from the world.

I failed our baby girl. My body wasn’t strong enough to keep her alive.

I failed you, my love.

Rolling over, Vicky let her silent tears soak into the pillowcase. She would not fail Lucy and that would make up for all the secrets.

***

Providence, Rhode Island
September 1935

The morning of the Exhibition it rained, but only enough to rinse away the grim on the streets, leaving Providence shining under a sky dappled with gilded clouds.

Vicky read the newspaper announcement so many times the English words seemed to drift apart and come back together on the page. The Rhode Island Tercentenary Industrial Exhibit would include an Armenian National Arts display, including a rug woven by a Mrs. James Altoonian from Whitinsville, Massachusetts, and examples of

Aintab-style whitework by Mrs. Ardashes Kasparian.

Mrs. Altoonian would demonstrate her skills at the loom for onlookers, just as Lucy would demonstrate her talent for *Aintab kordz*. Though it was not her strong suit, Vicky had learned the method at Miss Jeppe's home, at least well enough to pass along the tradition. Lucy, who's stayed in Aleppo longer than her sisters, had not only learned it while she was finishing school, but excelled.

Lucy's two exhibit pieces were a bride and groom, each in silhouette, facing one another from their own frames. The pieces were worked on fine linen, their cut-away features outlined in white linen thread by Lucy's immaculately delicate stitches.

Her sister planned to begin a pair of siblings in a similar fashion, based on sketches of Yessa's two children, and complete the work over the three days of the Exhibition.

Vicky was excited for Lucy and Ardash. Not only was her youngest sister being acknowledged for the uniqueness of her skill, but Lucy and Ardash were expecting a child. The news was very recent, so much so that Lucy didn't show at all, but Vicky saw it in the warmth of her sister's gaze when she looked at Ardash.

He'd had as hard a time as any of them, and yet he was a gentle, merry soul, no longer a jeweler's apprentice, but the manager of the shop where he'd learned his trade, and in a good position to take over the business in a few years when the owner retired.

His and Lucy's marriage was, to Vicky's mind, the best of the old world and the new, with traditions of the life they'd left behind, and all the shiny optimism of their new country.

Even after years of courtship and marriage, Ardash looked at Lucy like she hung the moon, and Vicky loved him for it.

Despite the ten-year difference in their ages, Vicky and Ardash were fast friends since he married Lucy. Vicky had liked him since the very first time he sat down at Yessa and Levon's table.

Now, as they walked to catch a streetcar to the Cranston Street armory, a boisterous family group, Vicky allowed her thoughts to wander back in time.

Twenty years had passed since the Turkish soldiers forced them out of Gurin. Twenty years since their father and brothers' brutal deaths. Twenty years since she walked into the desert, unsure that they would survive. But survive they did, and half a world away they traveled together down the streets of Providence, Rhode Island, as a family to celebrate Lucy's talent.

None of them spoke of these things, but Vicky knew she wasn't the only one to feel the significance of the day.

The family party moved slowly. *Mayrig* was hearty for her age, but she was not young, and this trip was far longer a walk than her determined march to the Catholic Church each morning for Mass.

Mayrig was the only one who clung to her Catholicism, even though she didn't understand the Latin Mass. Everyone else assimilated to their husband's preferences and attended services at the Armenian churches in Providence, just as they had done in Lawrence and Worcester.

If the religion was a little different, their language and traditions lived on there.

Vicky walked arm-in-arm with Pesa, enjoying the warmth and joy of the day. The seasons in this part of the world never failed to delight her, though she was always particularly sad to see the summers fade. It was warm for September, and Vicky hoped to convince Pesa to go to the park for a picnic after church the next day, if the weather held.

Yessa walked with *Mayrig*, her mother's gloved hands tucked into the crook of her arm. Mariam herded the children ahead while the rest of the men strolled at the rear looking dignified in their suits.

Lucy had gone ahead with her friend to look around the exhibit hall, since she would be stationed near the display of her work for her demonstration, and unable to view the rest of the exhibition.

Lucy's friend asked Vicky why she hadn't submitted some of her needle lace to the exhibition. Vicky laughed. "Everyone's grandmother can make lace. What Lucy does is special."

Since opening her parlor to paying customers, word of her skill–and her teaching–had traveled. Vicky's needlework instruction to the young ladies at the church had expanded. Her sewing circle at the Armenian church had a reputation not only for helping newly arrived Armenian girls and women to learn or sharpen their sewing and needlework skills, but as part of a network to help them find work, husbands, and help with their children if needed.

Rescue, Vicky discovered, didn't always mean midnight flights on horseback or tense negotiations in the desert. Sometimes rescue was as simple as making sure a family had enough to eat, the means to clothe their children, or someone with better English, to help them navigate the new world.

When they reached the streetcar stop, Pesa brushed a stray leaf where it caught on her sleeve. "You're quiet today."

"Just thinking how fortunate we are."

Her husband squeezed her hand.

27

Providence, Rhode Island
December 1943

Vicky's front door flew open ahead of her sister. Lucy's grin was wide, her eyes sparkling with glee.

"What is it, *kooyrig,* sister?" Vicky dropped the shirt she'd been mending and stood, ignoring the way her vision swam when she stood too quickly.

"He got it! The owner will retire and Ardash will buy the business! He thinks he'll be able to put his own sign up in a few weeks." Lucy grabbed Vicky's hands and bounced on her toes. "He's been working so hard, and it's all coming together. He says he'll need my help to get things going, to ring up sales and keep the shop tidy, but only until he can hire someone to do that."

Vicky pulled Lucy into a hug. "Congratulations! This is wonderful news. And of course, anything I can do to help. You know Rose can spend as much time with me as you need."

Lucy and Ardash's four-year-old daughter Rose delighted Vicky. She was a funny, imaginative little girl, full of songs and laughter.

Vicky's teaching had slowed as fewer immigrant girls streamed into the country. She still led a sewing circle, contributing clothing and blankets to orphanages, but it was the dressmaking and lacework that occupied her time now. Having Rose at the apartment was never a hardship.

Not only did Ardash set out his own sign, but his shop also flourished, and Lucy discovered she liked being a part of it, which meant that once Rose started school, she came home to Vicky's apartment for her lunch and to play after school. As news from

Europe grew darker and the shadow of war stretched over their lives again, Rose was the sunlight in Vicky's days.

When the U.S. joined the war, the wartime effort bustled in Providence as it did all over Rhode Island. Newport and Quonset brought sailors to the region, as well as Naval engineers and scientists testing weapons, and the Army barracks were busy supporting the troops overseas.

Vicky's eldest nieces, Mary and Alice, thrived in the final years of the war, working for the USO in Providence. Each of them had a sweetheart in service, and though none of the older generations spoke their deepest fears aloud, they were all children of war. They worried, even once the fighting was over, until both young men stepped off their ship home.

No one was surprised when engagements followed.

Mary and Alice's beaus, Jack and Eddie, wanted a double wedding. Vicky and her sisters got to planning.

The morning of the wedding, a joyful kind of chaos ruled Frank Street. The air was fragrant with traditional Armenian wedding dishes, and music and laughter rang out from the open windows.

On the third floor of Yessa and Levon's triple-decker, Lucy and Ardash's daughter Rose stood on a chair in Vicky's small kitchen, trying not to squirm while Vicky pinned several yards of handmade lace to the hem of her new dress.

"Are we almost done, Auntie Vicky?" Rose was long tired of standing still, but Vicky was almost finished.

She smiled around a mouthful of pins and nodded yes.

Vicky's pinning–and Rose's squirming–were interrupted by a knock at the door. Mariam let herself in. "Your dress is very pretty, Rose."

"Hello, Auntie Mariam," Rose said. "Auntie Vicky made it for me."

"I know, *yavroom*, my dear," Mariam said, pausing to straighten Rose's hair and praise Vicky's work on the dress. "I found these in my sewing box. There's enough for all the children's outfits."

Vicky held out her hand to receive a palm full of blue glass beads. They were old, their surfaces scuffed with time. They reminded her of the glass beads she'd seen in the markets of Aleppo so many years before.

"Where did you get these?"

Mariam perched on the arm of the divan to tell her a story involving one of her friends in the neighborhood whose mother had passed recently. The beads had been among her sewing things, which had been offered up one afternoon over coffee, pita, cheese, and olives with the ladies, but Vicky's memories rose around her like a cloud, and Mariam's story faded into the background.

These blue beads, roughed up with previous use, were very like the ones sewn into the skirts of the dolls she and Yessa buried under the tree in Gurin.

She hadn't thought of their Nuri dolls in half a lifetime, but now their dark almond eyes and brightly patterned skirts came to mind as vividly as if it were the night that they left the dolls behind.

Vicky squeezed the handful of beads, blinked back tears, and smiled at her sister.

They're perfect, Mariam," she said. "I'll sew this one into Rose's dress now and come down to do the others after."

"Good," Mariam replied. "I'd do it, but Yessa and I have a lot more food to prepare."

Mariam bustled out of the apartment, leaving Vicky with the beads and little Rose still standing on the kitchen chair.

"Why do you look so sad, Auntie Vicky?"

"Oh, it's nothing, *yavroom*." Vicky spilled the beads into her pocket and patted them. "I was just thinking about a doll I had when I was your age. Auntie Yessa had one too. They had *gabut kholums,* blue beads, sewn into their skirts just as I'm going to add to yours."

Rose was the perfect age for dolls; her eyes lit up. "What kind?"

"Just like your Raggedy Ann, we called ours Nuri. We played with ours, but sometimes on festivals and holy days, special Nuri would help the village celebrate. I barely remember, it's been so long." She finished sewing into Rose's skirts and snipped the thread.

"Mama doesn't remember living in the house you grew up in," Rose said.

She wouldn't, Vicky thought. She was so small when they fled. Her childhood memories would be of Aleppo and the basement apartment.

"Does she ever tell you about the time I sang to the snake?" Vicky grinned as Rose's eyes went wide.

"I'll tell you that one, too," Vicky said with a laugh. "But first I'll tell you of the great treasure your Auntie Yessa and I buried under an olive tree back in Gurin."

As Vicky recalled the night she and her sister sneaked out to bury their dolls and jewelry, naïvely believing they would be back before long to reclaim their treasures, she wished her daughter were here, listening to the story with her cousin.

While she spoke, Vicky helped Rose change out of the party dress and back into a skirt and blouse until it was time to get ready to go.

When she finished, Rose said, "Do you think your treasure is still there?"

"I can't imagine," Vicky said. "That was many years ago. Yessa and I were just girls. We didn't know how to protect a treasure in the ground. I think those dolls must have gone to dust a long time ago."

"I wish I had a Nuri," Rose said.

Their dolls had been simple cloth dolls with embroidered faces and fine yarn hair. Their clothes were sewn by a dollmaker from remnants of the cloth woven at her father's factory. Each doll had even had her own shawl in the Gurin style, like the one Vicky still kept, now the only remaining token of the life she once had.

Looking back, Vicky realized how many textiles their village produced. Cloth, fine shawls, dolls, and needlework. Miss Jeppe had understood the value of those textiles and the traditions around them. Vicky let a wave of gratitude swell over her and sent up a prayer to Miss Jeppe's memory.

"Tell you what," Vicky said, brushing off the memories. "I shall make you a *Nuri*, and she will have some of my lacework on her skirts. Just like yours."

She sent Rose downstairs to find her cousins and began to rummage through her scrap fabric. There was a large enough remnant of Lucy's linen to make the doll's body and she was sure she could recreate Nuri's dress and shawl from the bits of wool and cotton in her basket. Setting those aside on the table by the window she used for sewing, Vicky reached into her pocket to roll the blue beads reassuringly against her fingertips.

There was just enough time to sew beads into the older girls' dresses before she would need to change for the wedding.

With one last glance at the pile of fabric, Vicky wondered if the older girls might like Nuri as keepsakes; and if she were to make dolls for all her nieces, would anyone notice if she made one extra and tucked it away for the daughter she would never know.

In the weeks after the wedding, Vicky refined the pattern for the doll and her clothes. With each new one, she remembered a little more about the one she'd left behind.

Watching her niece play with her dark-eyed Nuri was a window into the life Nevart might have had with her. The ache in her heart was sharpened and eased all at once, imagining her daughter playing on Frank Street, leading the pack of cousins as the oldest.

Rose carried her new doll everywhere. The novelty of the old-world Nuri dolls meant that all of Rose's friends wanted Nuri of their own as well, and Vicky took orders from all around Providence.

To her delight, some of the dolls she sewed were for the babies and children of women she'd taught, women she'd helped.

Some girls still came as brides into arranged marriages when they had no family to sponsor them, but those were less frequent and more furtive as immigration laws changed to stem the tide of newcomers to the country. More often than not, the women who arrived now were young women who'd grown up in orphanages and rescue homes seeking a future in America.

It made no difference to Vicky whether or not these girls knew the same trials and horrors she'd lived through. What mattered was that they had every chance for a good life.

Vicky promised them all as she sewed, that she would give them what she had not given Nevart.

Providence, Rhode Island,
October 26, 1947

To Miss Nevart Karadelian
Providence, Rhode Island

Sireli aghcheegus,

Today you are twenty-eight. It has been a hard few months. My mother, my Mayrig, passed away. I miss her terribly. Even when we were separated, I knew her love was with me. She survived so much and knew such loss, but she never wavered in her love for her daughters.

Even in my grief, that thought gives me hope that somewhere in your deepest memories, you know I love you and that my love is always with you.

I always thought I had to hide your existence from my mother, lest the shame of how you were conceived tarnish her love for me. Now that she's gone, I'm not so sure. I wonder if I will regret never telling her the truth about what happened in Aleppo.

The one thing I cannot regret is you, my precious daughter. I wish with all my heart I'd been able to take you with me, that I'd seen what was about to happen and somehow gotten away with you as I'd planned. But even though I lost you, I can never regret that you were born, that I was able to love you when you were small, and that you are in the world.

When the priest gave his homily at the funeral mass, he spoke of the mystery of God's plan, and the strength required for my mother to travel the path she did and stay rooted in her faith. He rejoiced in her reunion with her husband and the children who went to Heaven before her.

I pray for you to have a long and beautiful life, and to know that I am waiting in Heaven to know you when you arrive and that in the time I have left, I can be brave and strong like my mother before me.

Always,
Your loving Mayrig

28

Warwick, Rhode Island
August 1948

Rocky Point Park reopened that summer. Vicky, Pesa, her sisters, and their families took the bus together.

After years of wartime austerity, it was a relief to spend a day on something so indulgent as an amusement park. Ten years before, a hurricane flattened the old amusement park and destroyed the dining hall. When the park reopened in June, to much fanfare, it seemed all of Rhode Island was desperate to see it.

By August, the children were clamoring to visit.

Temperatures had hovered over ninety degrees for days. The sea air off Narragansett Bay struggled to make its way into the city, leaving the neighborhoods to labor under a heavy, wet heat. On Saturday, Yessa declared they were going to the park, and a picnic lunch was packed and divided among the households.

Vicky and Pesa loitered at the back of the family pack, their share of the food in a basket over his arm. Nine-year-old Rose skipped in circles ahead of sixteen-year-old Grayce, while Mary and Alice and their husbands walked with Yessa, Levon, Mariam, Peter, Lucy, and Ardash.

Vicky knew Yessa and Mariam in particular were delighted to have their daughters and sons-in-law join the party. Mariam was trying to be subtle about watching her daughter Alice's midsection for signs of pregnancy.

To Vicky's eye, she was failing, but it was sweet to watch.

The music from the Midway calliope floated in the warm air, and the bay sparkled in the sun. The scent of chowder and clam fritters mingled with the salty breeze and the oiled steel scent of the thrill rides. Vicky hummed to herself, thinking fondly of the picnics she and Pesa shared in Worcester's Elm Park when they were newlyweds.

Rose ran up and tossed herself into Vicky's lap. "Auntie Vicky, I want to see the boats!"

Vicky smoothed her skirts and shifted her niece out of her lap to stand. "Then we will see the boats."

Pesa rose and followed them, leaving Lucy and Ardash to enjoy a quiet moment without their daughter.

Rose kept up a stream of chatter as they walked the path to the dock and back, taking first Vicky's, then Pesa's hands as they walked. To passersby, they might have been a family of three themselves. The ghosts of her lost children walked with them, and Vicky wondered if Pesa could feel their daughter's spirit between them as she could.

"Mama says you and Uncle Pesa met on a boat, just like she and Papa. A very long time ago," Rose said, watching a sailboat coast across Narragansett Bay.

"Not so long ago," Pesa laughed. "Your Auntie Vicky was the prettiest girl on the ship. And the kindest." He ruffled their niece's hair and Vicky smiled at him.

Rose dropped their hands and skipped ahead.

"Our daughter might be married by now, had she lived." Vicky spoke softly to keep Rose from hearing.

My living daughter might be married. She might have children. You might be married to a grandmother.

The words flooded her throat. If she told Pesa of them now, as though the girl she'd been in Aleppo was someone else entirely, would he take them on? Would he hold them for her and keep her strong so she might share them with her sisters?

"You know I never wanted anyone but you, love," Pesa said gently, watching Rose as she danced along the path. "I would trade a dozen children with someone else for the years I've had with you."

Rose chose that moment to barrel back to them, pointing at a three-masted yacht, sails billowing in the wind. "Auntie Vicky, is that ship like the one you sailed on?"

Pesa swung the little girl up to rest in the crook of his arm. "We sailed on a great steamship, like a floating town."

Vicky's secrets, like the frail clouds overhead, broke apart and drifted away on the breeze. She knew, like the clouds, they would return someday.

They rejoined the family party. Vicky settled near her sisters and let the warmth of the sun and conversation wash over her. So often in recent years, her body tired long before her thoughts quieted. Dancing wore her out, but she could play cards with her sisters for hours.

A small voice in the back of her mind reminded her that she'd never felt the same since she'd lost the baby, no matter how many girls she taught to sew, or how many laughing hours she spent with her husband or her sisters. Pesa crouched by her side with a thermos cup of thick, strong coffee and one of Mariam's signature *bourma.* Her sister was the undisputed queen of desserts.

Vicky pretended to push the plate away. "I'll get fat."

Pesa laughed. "If anything, you're too thin. Enjoy, *hokees*."

Mariam's laugh floated past them as she yelled to stop the older children from teasing the younger girls.

By the time they all crowded back into the bus, the children sunburned and sticky, the adults flushed with sweat and full of *choereg* and cheese, *lamahjun*, and a few American treats, Vicky was exhausted. She fell asleep on the bus with her head on Pesa's shoulder.

He woke her just before their stop and held her hand as they walked home.

Her secrets could wait. For now, she had her sisters, darling Rose, and the love of her life by her side.

29

Providence, Rhode Island
1955

Pesa walked home from work every evening with a group of men from the neighborhood, all of whom worked at the wool mill, including her brother-in-law, Peter.

He'd made friends there, and those friends made their neighborhood feel ever more like their own little village, where the food and the Turkish coffee flowed, and you were never alone–even if you wanted to be.

This particular night, Vicky was sitting on the porch with Mariam and Lucy. Dinner was in Mariam's oven, and the night was soft. The three sisters were waiting for Yessa to come home from the market. They were hoping for time to play a few hands of *skambel*, their favorite card game, before the men got home and expected to be fed.

Vicky heard the shouting first, and her blood ran cold. She knew the sound of fear deep in her bones.

"Somebody, call an ambulance! Mariam! Vicky!"

The cluster of men rounded the corner onto Frank Street holding Pesa up between them. Vicky could see from the hall a block away that his chest was heaving and his skin gray and slick with sweat.

Mariam dashed into the house. Her kitchen had a telephone, as did Yessa's, but theirs was the only one between the two buildings. Vicky heard her sister's frantic instructions to the operator as if she were underwater, and she was running down the street.

He was stooped over, leaning heavily on Peter's shoulder. Vicky reached up to cup his cheeks in her palms. "What happened?

Mariam's calling the ambulance." She trailed behind the men as they sat Pesa down on the front steps.

Peter was panting with the effort of holding his taller brother-in-law upright. "He said he felt weak, that he couldn't breathe. His face went the color of bad milk, and he nearly fell over."

Vicky sat next to her husband, taking his weight against her slight frame. His heart was racing, banging against his chest.

"You're going to be fine. They'll take you to the hospital and you'll be fine. You'll be fine." She was repeating herself, but the words became a prayer, whispered in her native tongue. A plea to God to spare her husband.

Pesa whispered in her ear, then his weight went slack and heavy against her, and Vicky cried out. Peter lifted Pesa's weight, and the assembled family went silent.

"*Serem kezi, hokis." You are my soul. I love you.*

Her husband's last loving words echoed in her ears days later when she laid him to rest in the family plot at North Burial Ground.

"Give me a moment?" Vicky asked Yessa, who lingered while the others took their leave. There would be a long stream of mourners visiting the apartment, and a huge amount of food to serve.

When she was sure her sister was out of earshot, she took a deep breath.

"I know you will meet our little girl in Heaven, my love. There were times I wanted so badly to tell you she was not my only child, that I have a daughter who, God willing, is alive somewhere in the world, but I was a coward. I thought we would have more time. I thought I could wait to find the right moment for such a secret. Now, it's–"Her voice faltered and she couldn't hold in her sobbing. "Now you're gone and there's no more time. I'm sorry. I am so sorry. *Amot eenzee*, shame on me". Vicky couldn't hold in her sobbing. Tears for her shame, tears for her daughters, tears for a family she couldn't give him, tears for her brothers, baby sister, and father, and tears for losing her soulmate.

Vicky took a deep breath and sat for as long as she could. "If she's with you in Heaven, please love her for my sake, and know I wished all my life that she was truly your daughter and we could have raised her together."

The confession and shame left her hollowed and sore, like a lanced wound. She turned and waved to Yessa, who waited with Levon to take her home.

Slowly Vicky began to weave herself a new kind of existence. After Pesa's death, Vicky took to sitting on the front porch of the triple-decker when the weather was fine. In the evenings, her sisters and their husbands would join her, and she had company for her lonely heart.

The dressmaking kept her busy during the days, but she missed Rose's presence. At nearly fifteen, her niece no longer needed an aunt to keep track of her after school. The neighborhood children all knew that Mrs. Minassian always had sweets in her pockets, and their visits almost made up for Rose's absence.

Rose grew into a pretty, sweet girl with a quick smile and a sharp sense of humor, the very kind of young woman Vicky imagined Nevart had been. Rose resembled Vicky enough that people still sometimes mistook them for mother and daughter, though Vicky's hair was fully ivory now.

It was all in the eyes, eyes Vicky was certain Nevart had inherited as well.

All her life, Vicky watched the men play *tavloo*.

In Gurin, it was a game for men. For no better reason than habit and tradition, only the men played in their circles as well.

One evening, Ardash sat out on the front porch with her. Her other brothers-in-law were around the corner at the store, likely picking up cigarettes. Ardash's backgammon board on the low table between the chairs where he and Peter had a game going before supper.

He caught Vicky eyeing the board. "Have you ever played?"

She shuffled seats, shaking her head no. Pesa played regularly. She knew her brother-in-law missed him as well.

"I don't see why you can't," he said. "If you want to."

She took to it quickly; where her body grew increasingly frail, her mind was sharp and quick. Over the board, pitting strategy against luck as the pieces moved toward their homes, a new kind of friendship popped up between them like the dandelions that persisted in the sidewalk cracks.

Before the *tavloo* board unfolded between them, Vicky hadn't known about the Armenian wife of a Turk who hid young Ardash in her barn and helped him escape into Greece when he was a boy. Hadn't known that he still woke up with the scent of hay, goat manure, and his own fear in his nose.

Even Lucy didn't know that.

There was plenty her sisters didn't know; Vicky wondered if Ardash would hate her for the secrets she kept. She thought not, but there was no way to be certain without confessing it all.

Peter and Levon returned from their errand. Peter was the first to notice Vicky leaning over the board. "What's this? You needed someone to beat since you've taken a thrashing tonight?"

Peter and Levon laughed good-naturedly, inspecting the board.

"Oh," Levon said, grinning. "She's beating you, too."

"Maybe this is why you never invite the women to play?" Vicky laughed. "Afraid we'll never let you win."

Ardash rolled and moved his pieces with a satisfied click. "Not so fast. I might beat her this time."

Weeks passed and Vicky spent her evenings playing *tavloo* with her brothers-in-law. That was how her healing started.

Providence, Rhode Island
October 26, 1957

Sireli aghcheegus,

Today is the 10-year anniversary of when my mother died. In a little while, the whole family will pile in cars to attend a service and visit her grave at Saint Ann Catholic Church and Cemetery. She insisted on being buried among fellow Catholics rather than beside her daughters and their husbands at the cemetery where most Armenians are buried. We can only guess at her insistence on a way to honor the Catholic missionaries who kept us alive in those dark days in the refugee camp in Aleppo.

We will never know so much of our mother's soul because she wouldn't allow us to ask questions or to talk about "the old country". Can you believe that she hung a picture in the kitchen of two boys but forbade anyone to talk about it? As if it weren't there. Of course, we knew it was of our brothers but we couldn't utter their names.

It makes me wonder what other secrets my mother brought to her grave. Did she bring guilt and shame with her? If so, is that why she lived a pious life? Was she fearful of shamefully facing her husband? I wonder how life could have been different if we were encouraged to talk about our past and face our secrets, however horrific. We will never know. What I do know is that she would have loved you and cherished a girl who was named in her honor.

I miss both my Roses every day - you and her.

Your Mayrig

30

Providence, Rhode Island
Spring 1963

Yessa read the coffee cups that afternoon when the sisters and their daughters met for coffee.

They lingered over the coffee; Yessa said you got better readings that way. When everyone was nearly finished, they swirled their last sips before drinking them to distribute the grounds, then flipped the cups over on their saucers.

Yessa always said if you wanted to know something specific you had to put something related to your wish or question on top of the cup while it rested upside down in the saucer. Rose reached into her purse and took out a lace doll stocking to place on her cup.

Vicky remembered teaching Rose to turn her heels.

Yessa raised a questioning eye. “Something to tell us, Rose?”

“Auntie.” Rose’s cheeks went hot. “Just hopeful.”

Yessa read her own first and declared that the several dark flecks of coffee grounds represented good fortune, which obviously meant Levon would be able to retire soon, with his full pension from the mill.

Rose wanted to go next. Yessa asked Rose to remove the shoe from the cup, then turned it over and peered inside.

Though Vicky always let her sister do a reading for her, she never cared much for the results. Not since the long-ago afternoon half a century before, when Hasmik overheard the older ladies reading coffee grounds and deduced that Vicky's father was hiding a second family in their house. She glanced into Rose’s cup now, but as usual, saw nothing but splotches and swirls of damp ground coffee.

Yessa squinted into the cup, lips pursed, for a moment before setting the cup and saucer down. “I see two distinct markings. Maybe you will have two children in your lifetime.”

Rose glowed so brightly it almost hurt to look at her.

Vicky wasn’t interested in specifics, so there was nothing to remove from her cup. Yessa turned it over and gasped. Both Rose and Vicky looked at her in alarm.

"What is it, Auntie Yessa?” Rose asked.

Whatever had shocked her, Yessa recovered quickly. "Oh, nothing. It’s only I thought I saw a new beau for Vicky."

Vicky laughed out loud. “I’ve had my share of that foolishness for a lifetime.”

That’s a lie, she thought. *I miss my Pesa every day.*

Rose took her to leave and Yessa shut the door firmly behind her.

“Are you feeling okay?” she asked Vicky.

Vicky didn’t like the way her sister’s brow wrinkled. “Tired, but I’ve had a lot of sewing work lately.”

“Go see the doctor,” Yessa said ominously.

“Oh for heaven’s sake,” Vicky said. “Why?”

Yessa’s voice shook, which scared Vicky far more than her next words. “There was sickness in your coffee grounds, *Kooyr.*”

***

How could this coffee cup know? What else did it know? She knew she was dying. They all knew she was dying. They didn’t need a doctor to confirm it, though they’d had the doctor come. Ardash came to talk with her almost every evening. Lucy would bring her supper upstairs and sit with them, but she always went downstairs first.

Vicky sometimes thought her sister was too sad to stay.

Ardash brought up the *tavloo* board, but he was equally willing to talk or keep her company in easy silence.

There was nothing to do, except finish the pair of Christening gowns–one for a boy, once for a girl, since she might not live to meet Rose's child…or any others who followed.

Ardash answered a knock on her door and called out. "Rose is here to see you."

Rose's visits always lifted her spirits. "Send her in."

Her niece looked well–cheeks pink and plump, eyes sparkling. "Hi, Auntie Vicky."

Rose pulled a chair close to her bed and took her hand. The young woman radiated health and strength. It warmed Vicky's heart to see it.

"How are you, *achchigus*? All done with morning sickness?"

Rose laughed. "Yes, thank goodness. Today I was up at sunrise and desperate to be busy."

"Nesting." Vicky winked. "You're already on your way to being a wonderful mother."

Rose sat gingerly by Vicky's side on the sofa. "I have a letter from Istanbul."

31

Providence, Rhode Island
1963

Vicky's heart throbbed hard against her breastbone.

"Mrs. Nacar wants to come here. She wants to meet you." Rose hesitated. "If you want. She says I should write to her to agree on arrangements."

Vicky closed her eyes as the room swam and spun. Her daughter. Found. And wanting to travel halfway around the world to see her. It was everything she'd always dreamed of.

Almost too late.

Vicky summoned her strength and opened her eyes. "Read it to me, please."

Dear Rose,

After reading your letters, I have given much thought to your aunt's story, and to my own history. After much deliberation, I have decided to accept your invitation and travel to Providence so I can meet Victoria. Our daughter is having a more difficult time accepting that this may be true. She has chosen to remain here in Istanbul with my husband.

She is still young, and strong in her belief in what is true and right. I find I am not that young anymore, and can't ignore what is possible, though it is uncomfortable, to say the least.

I will write with our travel plans when they are finalized.

Yours,
Gül Nacar

Rose was watching her, eyes sparkling with concern. "What should I say to her?"

"Tell her to come," Vicky said, her voice breaking over the words. "As soon as she can."

She would simply stay to see her daughter, to meet Rose's little one, no matter how tired she got, or how Pesa's voice sometimes greeted her on the edge of sleep.

Rose stood and gathered her handbag. "I'll write to her tomorrow. Perhaps she should send me her travel plans by telegram?"

"Whatever you think best." Vicky squeezed the arm of the sofa to stop her hands shaking.

"Auntie, there's something else."

"Yes, *aghchig*?"

Rose perched on the arm of the sofa. "It's time to tell the family the truth."

For a heartbeat, the enormity of it threatened to choke her. But no. She was strong. She'd survived the desert, servitude, danger, and an Atlantic crossing. She'd lived through heartbreak. She could do hard things.

"I'll do it."

After Rose left, it was Yessa who came up. "I ran into Rose on her way down."

Vicky patted the side of her bed to invite her sister to sit. "I want to make a *Nuri* doll for the baby, along with the gowns."

Yessa sat. She didn't mention that Vicky could barely stay up for a few hours at a time to work on the Christening gowns, and Vicky was grateful for it. "Any help you need, Mariam and Lucy and I, we will do it."

"Lucy embroiders the best eyes," Vicky said.

"All she has to do is look in a mirror. She has our mother's eyes," Vicky said wistfully.

"Just like yours. I always envied those lashes," Yessa rolled her eyes. "Of all the things."

"A lot of good they did me," Vicky said, but they both knew she'd always paid special attention to her eyeliner and mascara.

Yessa riffled through Vicky's sewing basket, taking stock. "If you're up to it, Mariam's girls are coming for Sunday dinner with the kids."

Sunday, then. Everyone would be gathered already.

"I'll come down. I don't want to miss them."

Before she left, Yessa adjusted the drapes and plumped the pillows behind Vicky's head.

Vicky took the needles and thread from her basket and tied the first knots to start a simple pattern. It would be good to keep her hands busy, and the practice pieces would be for Nuri's dress.

After so long alone with her secrets, she would speak them aloud to the family, letting the ghosts of her past float into the room. Her father, brothers, Hasmik, Ayşe, Sidika, and even Ibrahim. Her daughter's sweet face, the unborn girl, and Pesa, all ringed around her and ready to play out the tragedies of her past.

If her secrets were freed, perhaps the future would see her family whole.

That was the future she and her sisters had fought for. Survival and connection, their children, their heritage, and traditions.

She would give that to Nevart, and Nevart–Gül would be her gift to the family's future.

32

Providence, Rhode Island
One Week Later

Vicky entered her sister's parlor to greet her family feeling heavy and burdened with the secrets of her past weighing her down. When everyone was gathered, she started speaking, almost as if this message had been prepared for years. The words simply rolled off her tongue.

"Pesa was my true love. my soul. My sisters, Yessa, Mariam, Lucy, you are my blood. No matter what happens, our blood is thick, and we are woven from the same fabric. And now this fabric has grown to include our beautiful nieces, Mary, Alice, Grayce, and Rose. Our *Mayrig* was the strongest woman I have known and was my guidepost. My brothers-in-law, Levon, Peter, and Ardash, you are my brothers, my friends. The respect and kindness you showed me after Pesa died helped me to heal. We played hundreds of *tavloo* games where I let you win."

Everyone smiled. Yessa jumped in to move along the conversation so they could eat. "Vicky, We know all this. We have had hard lives, it's true. And for the most part, we've been able to keep the memories away by creating a new life here in America. What more is there to say? Let's eat."

Vicky's confidence grew. "You know how important it was to *Mayrig* that we didn't talk about the past. As if our brothers and baby sister didn't live. It's time I tell you a story you haven't heard. A story of another life, a very precious life to me."

The room became very still. Rose encouraged her with a smile, gave her hand a squeeze, and said, "Go on. We're all listening."

She took a deep breath and said "Do you remember me talking about helping the women at the Rescue Home with needlelace? It wasn't only needlelace I taught. I used my childhood horseback riding experience to rescue other women, maids in Turkish homes, and desert tribes who weren't treated well. It was very rewarding, and I am very proud of the work I did with Karen Jeppe to help keep away the horrors."

"You spoke of your time there fondly," Yessa said. "It must have been an adventure, volunteering like that."

Vicky took a moment to respond; her sister didn't understand, but that wasn't her fault. "I didn't choose to volunteer. I was one of the girls that was rescued. I fled the house where I was kept as a maid when the master died, and his wife stole my child."

Yessa looked away, shocked. Lucy's eyes filled with tears. Mariam put her face in her hands as if to shield what she knew Vicky was going to say next.

"Ibrahim Yavuz forced himself on me again and again. I was ruined. I became a mother." She smiled at the memory of her infant daughter, despite the painful memories. "I gave birth to a sweet little girl. They named her Gül, a Turkish word for Rose. I secretly called her Nevart in honor of our *Mayrig*, Vartouhy. I was kept on as the nursemaid and dreamed of how we would escape together."

She stopped to gather herself. Her throat hurt with the effort of speaking, but the worst of it was done.

"It's okay, Aunt Vicky," Rose whispered.

Vicky inhaled slowly before continuing. "I had a plan. It took me months to arrange it, but the night before Nevart and I were to be rescued by Karen Jeppe, Ibrahim died suddenly, and his wife took my baby and fled."

There was a collective gasp from her sisters. Yessa, Mariam, and Lucy settled close to her. Yessa took her hand and held it.

"If I'd stayed, I would have risked being blamed for killing Ibrahim. Leaving meant I would never see Nevart again. What kind of choice was that? If I did have a choice, it would have been death."

She let the awful terror of that time alone in the Old City before the meeting at the fountain flow through her. She'd lived through it;

she could tell it "I went with the rescuers as I'd planned, but without my daughter, and drowned in sorrow. Like angels, they pulled me up and gave me hope. They renewed my spirit by letting me help others, often from even worse conditions. They loved me even though I was soiled and "lost" my baby." She paused and looked at Yessa. " Then you were able to arrange with the missionaries for me to come here as a picture bride. I listened to *Mayrig* and put the past behind me to start a new life." They all nodded knowing what she was saying was true. "When I lost my second baby, I wondered if it was God's way of punishing me for not protecting my first baby. I have carried this shame for all these years."

It was Lucy who broke the tension. "Do you know what happened to her, where she is?"

Vicky smiled and let Rose take the story from there, more grateful than she could say for the love and understanding her niece had offered at every turn.

33

Providence, Rhode Island
1963

Vicky woke early on the day of Gül's arrival. She still practiced her daughter's name to herself. Over the years, she'd thought of her solely as Nevart. She was an old dog, she told Ardash, but this was an important trick, and she would learn it, as the American phrase went.

That Sunday dinner, with the younger children sent outside to play and with everyone gathered around, Ardash had been stalwart in his support. When Yessa and Mariam were shocked into silence, when Levon and Peter were outraged at a man long dead, and when Lucy cried for the sadness of it all, Ardash sat by her side and held her hand. She hoped Pesa was listening; it was easy to imagine his strong hands on her shoulders as she talked until her throat was raw with emotion.

When Vicky was finished with her story, Rose filled in the details Nevart–Gül–had shared in her letters and informed the family that she'd written again to make arrangements for Gül to visit.

It all came together shockingly quickly after that. Rose and Gül exchanged telegrams. Travel agents were engaged, and the reunion was scheduled for six weeks later.

The prospect of the visit left Vicky alternatively terrified and overjoyed, but either way, it was a distraction from her body's wasting away. Every day, a little more of her energy washed away like sand on a beach, but she refused to acknowledge Death's quiet stalking.

That could wait. She wasn't finished living just yet.

Rose planned to drive up with her father to meet Gül's flight in Boston, but she came over early to help Vicky wash and set her hair.

"You must think I'm silly, wanting to fix my hair for this."

"I think no such thing," Rose said, crouching down to apply shadow and liner to Vicky's eyelids. Rose's belly was more solidly rounded these days, but she still moved with ease. "I can't imagine what you're going through."

Vicky wasn't sure she could describe it herself.

She'd looked at the photograph from the newspaper enough times she'd rubbed away the newsprint on the edges of the paper, memorizing the grainy features of her daughter's face.

No amount of staring at a printed picture could prepare her for the woman who stepped tentatively over the threshold several hours later.

The hush which fell over the room was a living thing, pulsing around them as Vicky locked eyes with the little girl she'd lost forty years before. No longer a girl, but a woman grown, with threads of ivory in her hair.

The tender smile of a toddler, imprinted on Vicky's heart for so long, was still there in the gentle curve of Gül's mouth.

"I look just like you," Gul said, then clapped a hand to her mouth, looking around the room at the expectant faces of the other three sisters and their husbands.

Ardash broke the tension with his cheery laugh. He moved to help Vicky up from her chair, but Gül was already there, dropping to her knees at Vicky's side and taking her hand.

"I hardly know what to say."

Vicky's hand trembled as she touched her daughter's hair. "Hello is enough for now, *sireli aghcheegus*, my dear daughter"

Hours later, Gül sat by Vicky's bedside, voice hoarse from speaking, telling Vicky about her daughter, Leyla.

She was a grandmother, after all. *We are grandparents, Pesa, my love.* She could almost see him, waiting on the edge of the room, tall and handsome in his wedding suit, patient as ever.

"I visited Gürin," Gül said. "I found the tree from your letters, and I met a woman who'd gone to school with your sister Mariam."

"It still stands." Vicky tried to smile, but the effort of staying away took all her energy. "Our Nuri dolls are long gone, I think."

"I think so," Gül said softly.

"We lived across the lane from that cemetery. It was a beautiful house."

"There's not much of it left." Gül shook her head. "Just some walls and the foundations, really. I tried to ask at the neighbor's house, but I couldn't learn much."

"Hasmik and Davit lived there." Vicky mustered the energy to wink. "I wanted to marry Davit when I was a girl."

Gül chuckled knowingly. A young girl's crush was a common language, no matter how it ended, and decades had softened Vicky's grief into memories.

An inevitable awkwardness stole over them the next day when Gül returned. Yessa came down to help Vicky wash and dress before Gül arrived. Yessa set out coffee and sweet bread and stayed until Gül arrived.

Vicky let the silence stretch, but Gül seemed far away, her gaze floating over Vicky's front parlor. She fought back against her bone-deep weariness. "Can you forgive me, Nevart - I mean Gül?"

"There is nothing to forgive," her daughter replied softly. "I had a good childhood, I have a wonderful life. Now I have a new family if they will have me. Like anything new, the fit feels strange, but I think we'll grow comfortable with one another in time."

"I like the sound of that," Vicky said. "Will you tell me about your childhood? I imagined it so many times, but I only saw Constantinople once, when I took a ship for America with Pesa all those years ago."

Gül smiled. "I still think of the part of the city where I grew up as Constantinople. I was maybe ten when the name changed. Where I live now, I think of it as Istanbul. Is that strange?"

"I think I can understand how a place might have two names in your heart."

"I was told my mother's family lived in a house very like the one where I was born." Gül stopped, realizing she was touching Vicky's story now.

"Go on," Vicky said. "I want to hear about your life."

The awkwardness faded as Gül spoke, recounting mischief with her cousins, her wedding to Ahmet, her aunts, and uncles, and her grandparent's stern but generous natures.

"I've exhausted you," Gül said, noting Vicky's heavy eyelids.

Vicky reached for her daughter. "You'll come again tomorrow? I have something for you."

Vicky was asleep before Gül's answer reached her ears.

Gül returned the next day with Rose, who bundled Vicky into the car and drove them to the cemetery. Vicky told Gül about *Mayrig*, and all the sacrifices she made to see the family safe through their ordeals.

Rose listened wide-eyed. The sisters rarely spoke of the march across the desert, never summoning the ghosts of the father, brothers, and baby sister they'd lost. This was more of the secret history Aunt Vicky shared with the family. More of her own legacy.

Gül noticed Pesa's grave nearby. "Is this your husband's stone?"

"Mine, soon, I think," Vicky said. Seven years since he'd left her, and she still missed him every day.

"Not so soon," Gül said. "I'm going to come back in the fall. I want Ahmet and Leyla to meet you."

"The fall, then," Vicky said, but her touch lingered on Pesa's stone as she passed on the way back to the car.

When they returned to the house on Frank Street, Vicky left Gül in the sitting room for a moment.

Vicky remembered exactly where she put aside the extra *Nuri* doll. She'd made an extra when she'd made a batch for her nieces so many years ago. While it was intended for Gül, Vicky never dreamed she'd be able to give it to her daughter. The doll was more of a talisman for Vicky to treasure and imagine how her daughter might have played with and loved such a doll and treasure. Now, the dream was true, and Vicky could give a *Nuri* doll made with her own hands to her daughter who'd grown up to become a doll-maker.

Gül wept over the doll, cradling it to her chest. "I know her name. She's called *Nuri*. I heard about these dolls from the Armenians I met in Istanbul and Gürin." She knelt by Vicky's chair. "And you made her? What a beautiful gift. I'll treasure it forever. Perhaps," Gül said wistfully, "my daughter will see its beauty and be willing to hear more about all of you."

***

At the end of the week, Gül boarded her plane bound for Istanbul, and Vicky slept for nearly a day straight. Her body was so frail now it could barely contain her joy. She dreamed of the little girl she'd raised in the courtyard of the house in Aleppo. She dreamed of Davit Choulijian and Pesa.

When she woke, Rose was tidying up her apartment, stopping to stare into the distance. Vicky watched her, remembering her own pregnancies and that feeling of gazing into both nothing and everything simultaneously.

Vicky's gaze fell on two framed photographs: one of Gül and Vicky outside the Frank Street house, the other of all four sisters and their daughters.

"Good morning, sweetheart." Vicky's voice was creaky with sleep. She touched the frame closest to her. "Thank you for this."

"It's nothing," Rose said. "I took the film to the express developer yesterday on the way home from the airport." She reached into Vicky's sewing basket, where the two Christening gowns were early finished. When she straightened, her eyes were full of tears. "Why two?"

"For a boy or a girl," Vicky said. "Just in case I–"

"None of that, now." Rose brought Vicky a fresh glass of water. "Can I bring you some breakfast?"

Vicky caught Rose's arm, stilling her next to the photo of Gül. "I have everything I need right here. My heart is full. I am at peace."

EPILOGUE

Rose's Home, Warwick, Rhode Island
September 1991

Tory found her mother in the kitchen. Jim carried the dolls and their scarf in a spare paper bag.

"Well, hello. What a nice surprise."

Rose noticed the bag; her gaze flipped between Tory and Jim. "What's all this?"

"Mom," Tory said gently, pulling out a chair at the table for her mother, "We found something at Aunt Vicky's grave today."

Jim set the paper bag on the table in front of Rose, who sat slowly, wiping her hands on a kitchen towel as she did.

"Open it." Tory couldn't hide the tremor in her voice. They'd waited and hoped for so long.

Rose pulled the bundle from the paper bag and unwrapped the dolls with misty eyes. "How lovely…"

Her voice trailed off as she discovered the envelope, and her fingers shook as she unsealed it.

"You read it. I can't bear to," Rose said, handing the folded, cream stationery sheet to Tory.

"Are you sure?" Tory said.

Her mother nodded, so Tory unfolded the letter. With a glance to her husband for reassurance, she began to read:

Dear Rose,

Please forgive the informality. My name is Yasmin Rıza, and I am a student at Brown University, here in Providence, but I was born and raised in Istanbul, Turkey.

I am Gul Nacar's granddaughter.

I'm certain over the years, you've wondered why your family never heard from my grandmother again. It is my sad duty to tell you that my grandparents were killed in a tragic accident shortly after my grandmother visited Providence to meet Victoria.

I never knew them. They died before I was born, but her friend Selma was like a grandmother to me and my older siblings.

Selma recently told me as much of Nene's story as she knew. No matter how my grandmother–and her friend Selma after Nene's death–tried, they were unable to convince my mother to accept the truth about her biological grandmother. My mother refused to believe she was of mixed Armenian heritage and destroyed your letters along with Victoria's.

Selma recalls your first name, but her English is very limited. She urged me to seek out your family, especially since I am so close to where you once lived and may still be. My research brought me to the North Burial Ground. It may sound foolish, but I believe that by the grace of Allah and my grandmother's spirit, I was able to find Victoria's gravestone.

My mother carried on Nene's doll-making legacy and has passed the tradition to me. I am presenting you with a doll dressed in traditional Turkish clothing and a doll in traditional Armenian clothing to honor my grandmother's skills and heritage.

Selma told me that Nene believed truth is healing, that it can begin between a woman and family she didn't know she had.

It is my sincere hope this letter reaches you and your family, and that you are willing to meet me while I am in Providence.

Your cousin,

Yasmin

Tory's voice hitched as she read the last line. Tears flowed down Rose's cheeks. Jim gave Tory an encouraging grin and slipped out of the kitchen to give the two women some privacy.

"She's not so much younger than you, Tory," Rose said, reaching for the pages. "You should be the one to contact her. I think we would all very much like to meet her."

THE END

GLOSSARY

Word	*Definition*
Aghchigus	Term of endearment in Armenian meaning “my girl”.
Adhan	Islamic call to public prayers.
Al-Jdayde	Historically predominantly Christian neighborhood of Aleppo.
Allah	The common Islamic word for God.
Aintab kordz	An Armenian traditional handmade needlework style.
Aman	An interjection used to express grief or anguish.
Amot eenzee	Translates to “shame on me” from Armenian.
Anoushig	Term of endearment in Armenian meaning “my sweet”.
Apoploxy	The term formerly referred to what is now called a stroke.
Armenian Genocide	The systematic destruction of the Armenian people and identity in the Ottoman Empire beginning in 1915. Over 1.5 million Armenians were massacred.
Asr prayer	The fifth mandatory Islamic prayer of the day.
Babam	Common Armenian slang term that translates to “enough already”.
Bay or Bey	A respectful way to address a man in Turkish. Officers and bureaucrats, for example.
Bayan or Bayam	A respectful way to address a woman in Turkish. Wives of Officers and bureaucrats, for example.
Bedouin	A nomadic Arab of the desert.
Beit	A fine house in Ottoman Empire

Belediye İş Hanı	Municipal Business Center in Turkish.
Buzdig	Translates to "little" in Armenian.
Cheorag	A traditional Armenian sweet bread often served on holidays.
Church of our Saviour	The first Armenian church in the US and the western hemisphere built in 1891 in Worcester, Massachusetts.
Constantinople	What Istanbul was called before 1930.
Der	Armenian prefix for priest.
Der Hayr	Armenian priest.
Digin	An Armenian term of respect for an older woman.
Dolma	Stuffed vegetables or grape leaves with meat, rice, and seasonings.
Duduk	An Armenian flute carved from apricot wood.
Eench eh, hokis?	Translates from Armenian to "What is it, my love?"
Effendi or Efendim	Turkish for master, madam, or sir.
Elm Park	A historic park in Worcester, Massachusetts that was added to the National Register of Historic Places in 1970.
Fajr prayer	The third mandatory Islamic prayer of the day.
Gabut Kholums	Translated as "blue beads" from Armenian, they are widely believed to possess a power to ward off the evil eye.
Gendarmes	Armed Turkish police officers.
Gulum	Translates as honey in Turkish.
Gurin or Gurun	A town and a district of the Sivas Province of Turkey. Gurin and the Sivas province was part of Armenia before the Genocide.

Gurin shawls	Gurin was the center of the shawl weaving industry, famous for its top-quality products. It was said that artisans working on the looms were so ingenious that no competitor outside of Gurin would dare challenge their handicraft.
Hamidieh Camp	Armenian refugee camp in Aleppo where many survivors from Gurin lived.
Hanimefendi	A Turkish term of respect for the wife in the household.
Hanum	A respectful way to address a woman.
Henna Party	The henna party took place at the home of the bride-to-be given by the women of her family and her friends, before the wedding. The honor of mixing and applying the henna to the bride's hand was reserved for the wife of the priest.
Hokis	A common term of endearment often between spouses, meaning mine, the one who I care about the most, my soul.
Hrishdag	Angel.
Kheema	A traditional Armenian dish made with raw meat and savory seasonings.
Kooyr	Sister.
Kooyregus	My sister.
Kuru	A basic monetary unit of Turkey.
Lahmajun	An Armenian meat pizza.
Lira	A basic monetary unit of Turkey.
Lokum	Turkish sweet treat.
Mahgrib prayer	The first mandatory Islamic prayer of the day.
Meg bardzi vray tseranak	Armenian proverb and wedding toast that translates to "may you grow old on one pillow".

Mary Dean Three-Decker	A historic triple-decker house in Worcester, Massachusetts built in 1892 and owned by Mary Dean. Tenants came from Armenia and included workers in the city's wire works, clerks, bakers, and painters.
Muezzin	A man who calls Muslims to prayer from the minaret of a mosque.
Near East Relief	American organization originally dedicated to the aid of Greek, Armenian, and Assyrian victims of the Ottoman Empire.
Noah's Ark and Mount Ararat	Mount Ararat is believed to be the resting place of Noah's Ark. Despite lying outside the borders of modern Armenia, the mountain is the principal national symbol of Armenia and has been considered a sacred mountain by Armenians.
Nuh after the Deluge	Noah, also known as Nuh is recognized in Islam as a prophet and messenger of God leading to building the Ark and the Deluge, the Great Flood.
Nuri doll	The Nuri doll was part of several rituals that Armenians celebrated with dolls associated as a goddess of mother nature. According to the belief, when people and animals suffered from water scarcity, Nuri cried, and her tears soaked the soil and the fields came back to life. Armenian girls named their best dolls as Nuri.
Oghi	An Armenian spirit distilled from fruits or berries. It is widely produced as moonshine from home-grown garden fruits all across Armenia.
Ottoman Empire	Historically and colloquially the Turkish Empire, the Empire controlled much of Southeast Europe, Western Asia, and Northern

	Africa between the 14th and early 20th centuries.
Pahree looys	Good morning.
Pilaf	This traditional rice and noodles Armenian dish is a traditional favorite.
Rhode Island Tercentenary Exhibit	In 1936, an article in the Providence Journal highlighted the Rhode Island Tercentenary Exhibit, which showcased a section of the Armenian National Arts collection, notable for its 300-year-old rug, textiles, and ceramic pieces.
Serem kezi, hokis	You are my soul. I love you.
Skambel or skambill	A card game often played by Armenians.
Sireli	Translated from Armenian to Dear, as in a salutation of a letter.
Sivas	A city in central Turkey and the seat of Sivas Province.
Streets are paved in gold	Used to describe a place where it is easy to become wealthy or live well.
Tavloo	Popular backgammon game.
Vichaki Arus doll	Prior to the feast of Ascension, Armenian girls collected seven handfuls of water from seven springs, seven petals from seven flowers, and seven stones from seven running waters. They put these items in a special flowerpot with the Vichaki Arus doll on top. They were left outside overnight and brought to the fortune-telling square the next morning. During the Ascension ceremony, girls awaited their fortunes and gave out wreaths made from the flowers.
Washburn & Moen Manufacturing Company	Washburn & Moen—the largest wire mill in the world—employed most of Worcester's Armenians.
Yavroom	A term of endearment.

Family / Friends of Victoria / Vicky (Karadelian) Minassian

Word	*Definition*
Alice Poladian	Niece to Victoria, daughter to Mariam (Karadelian) and Peter Poladian, marries Eddie.
Ardashes (Ardash) Kasparian	Brother-in-law to Victoria, married to Lucine (Karadelian), father to Rose, grandfather to Tory.
Bedros (Peter) Poladian	Brother-in-law to Victoria, married to Mariam (Karadelian), father to Alice and Grayce.
Choulijians	Neighbors to the Karadelians in Gurin.
Churmartians	Tory and Jim's surname loosely translated to Armenian to honor the author's surname. Chur (Water) + Mart (man).
Danielians: Sitrik, Azniv, Pauline, and Johnny	The original caretaker family of Church of Our Saviour in Worcester, Massachusetts, who cared for Victoria.
Davit Choulijian	Victoria's childhood love and neighbor in Gurin, brother to her best friend, Hasmik.
Eva Poladian	A girl that Victoria met upon arrival at Hamidieh Camp in Aleppo.
Hasmik Choulijian	Victoria's best friend and neighbor in Gurin.
Jim Churmartian	Married to Victoria's great niece, Tory, who is Rose's daughter, Lucine's granddaughter, and Victoria's namesake.
Hayrig	Victoria's father, Hovsep Karadelian, translates from Armenian to "father".
Kachadoor Minassian	Victoria's (Vicky's) husband and love of her life.
Karen Jeppe	Karen Jeppe was a Danish missionary and social worker, known for her work with Ottoman Armenian refugees and survivors of the Armenian genocide, mainly widows and orphans at her Rescue Home.
Levon Bedrossian	Brother-in-law to Victoria, married to Yessa (Karadelian), father to Mary.
Lucine (Karadelian)	Victoria's sister, married to Ardashes, mother

Kasparian	to Rose, grandmother to Tory.
Mariam (Karadelian) Poladian	Victoria's sister, married to Bedros (Peter), mother of Alice and Grayce.
Marta	Intake worker at Karen Jeppe's Rescue Home in Aleppo.
Mary Bedrosian	Niece to Victoria, daughter to Yessa (Karadelian) and Levon Bedrosian, marries Jack.
Mary Dean	Katchadoor and Victoria's landlady and owner of the now historic triple-decker in Worcester, Massachusetts.
Mayrig	Victoria's mother, Vartouhy Karadelian, translates from Armenian to "mother".
Michael	Victoria's great nephew, twin brother to Tory, son of Rose, grandson to Lucine and Ardashes Kasparian.
Misak	Karen Jeppe's adopted son and worker at her Rescue Home in Aleppo.
Nevart	Pet name for Vartouhy that translates to Rose and what Victoria calls her birth daughter.
Pauline Danielian	Daughter to Sitrig and Azniv, the original church caretakers of the Church of our Saviour in Worcester, Massachusetts.
Reupen Parnagian	Victoria's sponsor to become his wife through the Picture Bride program.
Rose	Niece to Victoria, daughter to Lucine and Ardashes Kasparian, mother to Tory and Michael.
Tory Churmartian	Vicky's niece and namesake, married to Jim, daughter to Rose, granddaughter to Lucine and Ardashes Kasparian.
Victoria / Vicky (Karadelian) Minassian	The main protagonist of the novel, wife to Kachadoor Minassian, and the symbolic dollmaker's mother.
Yeghsabet/Yessa (Karadelian) Bedrosian	Victoria's sister, married to Levon, mother to Mary.

Family of Gul (Nevart) Yavuz Nacar

Word	*Definition*
Ahmet Nacar	Second husband to Gul, father to Leyla.
Anne	What Leyla calls Gul, translates to "mother" from Turkish.
Ayse Yavuz	The woman of the house where Victoria worked as a maid, Leyla's grandmother.
Ibrahim Yavuz	The man of the house where Victoria worked as a maid, Gul's father.
Gul (called Nevart by Victoria) Yavuz Nacar	A central protagonist of the novel, widow to Ibrahim Yavuz, married second to Ahmet Nacar, mother to Leyla, grandmother to Yasmin, symbolic dollmaker's daughter.
Nene	What Leyla calls Ayse and what Yasmin calls Gul, translates to "grandmother" in Turkish.
Selma	Gul's best friend and travel companion.
Sidika	The cook and housekeeper of the Yavuz household.
Yasmin	Gul's granddaughter, daughter to Leyla.

ACKNOWLEDGMENTS

Growing up in an active Armenian church community and in a bilingual, multi-generational home with immigrant survivors of the Armenian Genocide, I embarked on this journey with a strong understanding of my family history, ethnicity, and culture—or so I believed. However, I was humbled to discover just how much I didn't know.

Throughout the years, I delved into reading, researching, journaling, and conducting interviews, drawing inspiration from those who blazed the trail before me. I must express my sincere thanks and recognition to my coach and editor, Cameron Garriepy, whose storytelling talent enhanced the flow of beautiful words and brought characters and stories to life. Aline Ohanesian, who edited the manuscript, provided invaluable guidance on language, poetics, and plausibility. Without the superb expertise of Dee Marley from Historium Press, this book would not have come to fruition. I am deeply grateful to early readers, Diane Giampa, Michael Kasparian, and Kristina Kill, whose candid feedback ensured my passion shone through with authenticity.

My journey was enriched by the knowledge and expertise of globally renowned experts in history and genealogy, including George Aghjayan, Luc Vartan Baronian, Mark Arslan, Taner Akcam, and Khatchig Mouradian. I also received invaluable education from curators Gary and Susan Lind-Sinanian of the Armenian Museum of America, Marina Khachmanukyan of the Yerevan History Museum, and art critic Ani Mkhitaryan, who enlightened me on Armenian dolls, needlelace, and embroidery.

Living and working in a region rich with Armenian history provided me with the opportunity to incorporate local stories into my novel. One of the greatest blessings was meeting Pauline Agazarian in her 100th year, where I learned firsthand about Armenian wedding traditions in Worcester, Massachusetts. I extend special gratitude to Mary Jane Rein of the Strassler Center for Holocaust and Genocide Studies at Clark University, Bill Wallace and the team at the Worcester Historical Museum, Ruth Thomasian & Arto Vaun and the team at Project Save, Jason Sohigian and the team at The Armenian Museum of America, Der Mikael and Yeretzgin Susana Der Kosrofian of St. Asdvadzadzin Armenian Church, the Armenian Church of Our Saviour, the Armenian Historical Association of Rhode Island, and many of my church friends and supporters who cheered me on throughout the entire process.

I am immensely grateful to the leading authors who generously made time in their busy schedules to offer advice and guidance, including Nancy Agabian, Maral Boyadjian, Matthew Karanian, Dawn Anahid MacKeon, Judith Saryan, Roxana Trabulsi, Dana Walrath, and Aida Zilelian.

My gratitude extends globally to the hundreds of active members from several Facebook groups who provided unique insights and helped solve mysteries I never thought possible. Much love goes out to the active members of Arev Hye Book Salon, Armenian Genealogy, Gurintsi Armenians, and We Love Reading Book Club.

Closer to home, I deeply appreciate the conversations with my relatives, reminiscing and remembering our grandparents, the survivors of the Armenian Genocide and main characters in the novel. I will forever cherish the nostalgic and eye-opening moments with my brother and cousins Cheryl, Edrina, Richard, Jim, Joy, Leon, and Marilee.

Sharing this journey with my twin brother, Michael, has been a surreal experience, strengthening the unique and special bond we share. Creating this legacy, to live on through our children and future generations, fills me with immense pride.

To my dear husband Jim, who believed in me from the beginning and stood by my side through years of research expeditions and explorations, I am deeply grateful and blessed by his unwavering love and support. Jim, I love you, and I thank God for bringing us together with our children and grandchildren to create our new tree of life.

VICTORIA ATAMIAN WATERMAN

ABOUT THE AUTHOR

Victoria Atamian Waterman is an Armenian American storyteller and speaker who draws inspiration from the quirky multigenerational, multilingual home in which she was raised with her grandparents, survivors of the Armenian Genocide. Her empowerment of today's women and girls makes her voice ideal for telling the little-known stories of yesterday's women leaders. Her TED Talk, "Today's Girls are Tomorrow's Leaders" has been seen by thousands of viewers. When she is not writing and speaking, she is reading, puzzle-making and volunteering. Victoria lives in Rhode Island and is enjoying this next chapter of life with her husband, children, and grandchildren. "What She Left Behind" is her first novel.

Visit her website to learn more: www.victoriawaterman.net

REVIEWS ARE APPRECIATED

www.historiumpress.com

www.thehistoricalfictioncompany.com/victoria-atamian-waterman

BOOK CLUB QUESTIONS

1) What is the significance of the title? Who do think it refers to?
2) What scenes would you point out as pivotal moment(s)? How did they make you feel?
3) In Tory's letter to Gul, she states, "Truth is the only way to heal, even if it begins between a woman and a family she didn't know she had." Do you agree with this statement? Why or why not?
4) Were you surprised by Gul's reaction to receiving Rose's letter? At what point could you understand the underlying dilemma?
5) What were the main themes of the book? How were those themes brought to life?
6) What are your thoughts on the book's structure of a multi-year timelines and using ethic names and expressions? Did it serve the story well?
7) Is the Armenian Genocide a time period that you knew a lot about before you read this book? If so, did you learn anything new? If not, did you come away with a greater understanding of what this time and place in history was actually like?
8) What do you think the author's goal was in writing this book? What message was she trying to send?
9) If the book were made into a movie, who would play younger Victoria, older Vicky, and Gul?
10) If the author came to your book club discussion, what would you ask her?
11) How did you feel about the ending? How might you change it?
12) What do you think will happen next with Tory and Yasmin?

www.historiumpress.com